SoWest
So
Wild

SoWest
So
Wild

Twenty original Wild West tales from the
Desert Sleuths Chapter of Sisters in Crime

DS Publishing
Scottsdale, Arizona

Original Cover Design by Martin Roselius
Cover Photograph: Copyright © Ted Stratton
    Moving Pictures LLC, Phoenix AZ.

ISBN – 978-0-9828774-1-8

DEDICATION

This book is for all mystery lovers who share our appreciation of the unique blend of critters that inhabit the landscape of the American Southwest. Saddle up and enjoy the ride.

ACKNOWLEDGMENTS

Big thanks to Marty Roselius for your captivating cover design and to Ted Stratton for the generous contribution of the background photograph.

Meg Gardiner, Toni L. P. Kelner, Lesa Holstine and Becky Coffield, we appreciate your very fine endorsements of our efforts.

We are grateful to editors Nancy McCurry, Virginia Nosky and Isabella Maldonado for their dedication and hard work.

And a very special thanks to lead editor, Deborah J Ledford for her tireless efforts to bring this book to life. You ladies rock!

As always, we owe a debt of gratitude to the worldwide network of our Sisters in Crime for their unfailing support.

TABLE OF CONTENTS

TABLE OF CONTENTS

THE GHOST IN THE ROCKS
JOANNE ZETERBERG

A lizard skittered through the heat waves and across the sandy trail in front of Emerson Onesalt's horse. The chestnut gelding barely seemed to notice as the creature cleared the trail and stopped to complete a pair of push-ups before darting under a nearby creosote bush.

"Ah, see that, Kiitsoh?" Emerson asked his horse. "Our brother is a good Navajo lizard. He knows to seek shade when the sun is hot. I'm afraid he is smarter than both of us, old friend." Kiitsoh, whose Navajo name meant Big Boy, huffed in reply without breaking his plodding gait.

Emerson noted the sun's location in the sky above the crimson walls of Canyon de Chelly and guessed it to be shortly after three. He glanced at his watch and smiled. Ten minutes past the hour. He'd played this game with the sun since he was a boy some seventy summers earlier and was pleased that age had not yet impaired his skills.

The trail he and Kiitsoh followed curved gently around the base of Spider Rock, a red sandstone spire with a white top that loomed above the canyon floor like a cloud. Emerson remembered his mother's stories of how Spider Woman taught the first Navajos how to spin the wool from their sheep and use the dyed strands to create woven rugs and blankets rich in color and pattern. But it was his grandmother's tales of how Spider Woman gobbled up naughty boys and girls, eating their flesh and leaving their bones to dry on top of the spire that gave him nightmares as a child.

Emerson tapped Kiitsoh's sides with his heels. The horse snorted and picked up his pace. "Only a few more miles. Then you can rest." *And my work will begin.*

They continued east and entered a narrow side canyon just beyond Spider Rock. Emerson removed a small tin of hand-rolled cigarettes and a lighter from the chest pocket of his shirt. He chose a cigarette, lit it and replaced the tin and lighter in his pocket as he exhaled a gray plume. While he smoked, Emerson considered the note that had been delivered to his hogan the previous afternoon by young Benny Chapo.

Written by Benny's mother Estelle, the note had asked the old *hataalii* to come to the Chapos' hogan because her husband was sick again. Emerson had been called to see Frank Chapo many times over the years for his so-called ailments. Chapo's biggest problem, at least as far as Emerson was concerned, was that he was a lazy man who lived a very un-Navajo life of excess. Too much fast food, too much gambling and too many trips without his family to visit his loud *bilagaana* friends in the city.

Estelle's note said that Frank was suffering from pain in his stomach. She thought he needed a sing to bring him back into *hozro*, the Navajo's revered state of balance and harmony. More likely, Emerson thought, Frank had just eaten too much and drunk too much and gotten himself a bad case of the squirts. Emerson chuckled at the thought of Frank Chapo trying to haul his enormous bulk to the outhouse before his bowels cut loose.

The harsh *kak-kak-kak* of a turkey vulture interrupted Emerson's thoughts. Even Kiitsoh's ears perked up at the sound. He gave the reins a slight tug and the horse came to a stop. It took a moment of scanning the light and shadows of the canyon to locate the source of the squawking. About fifty yards ahead, a pair of vultures perched atop a pile of rocks. The area was near the canyon wall where a mix of boulder-size and smaller rocks littered the ground. A few scraggly mesquite trees provided patches of shade.

Probably a trapped sheep, Emerson thought, and they're waiting for it to die. He stubbed out his half-smoked cigarette on the saddle horn and put the butt in his pocket.

"Let's go see if we can help," the old man said to his horse as he kicked him lightly with his heels. Perhaps it was not too late.

As they came within ten feet of the rock pile, the vultures, which had been watching their approach with glassy black eyes, flew to a nearby mesquite tree. Suddenly, the breeze shifted and the stench of death filled Emerson's nostrils. Kiitsoh snorted and shifted restlessly from side to side.

Emerson covered his nose and mouth with his hand to block out the putrid smell. Too late—the vultures would have their meal after all. He was about to ride on when something caught his eye. He urged Kiitsoh forward.

At the end of the mound closest to him, Emerson could see the tip of a brown boot protruding from between the rocks. He looked more closely. Toward the far end of the pile, where fewer rocks were stacked, tufts of red hair stuck out.

"That's no sheep, Kiitsoh," he said, his voice barely above a whisper.

This dead human was a *bilagaana*. In the heat of the full sun the old medicine man shivered. No doubt this man's *chindi*, its evil spirit, was not far away, waiting to cause sickness in whoever came upon it. In fact, Emerson reasoned, this *chindi* would be particularly angry and vengeful since its human form had been murdered. After all, dead white men don't bury themselves among rocks. Someone ended this *bilagaana's* life before its time.

A female voice came from behind him and was one that Emerson knew well.

"You should've just kept on riding, old man. Now I've got another problem to fix."

Slowly, he turned in his saddle to face Martha Magee, who, along with her husband Buck, owned the Blue House Trading Post. She stood no more than ten paces away, tree-trunk legs spread wide, pointing a handgun directly at Emerson's chest. Tendrils of gray hair stuck to her sweaty face, a leathery road map of life's challenges. From what Emerson had learned over the last two years, few of Martha's life experiences had been good.

"Get off your horse," Martha commanded. "As long as you're here you might as well help me finish what I started."

Emerson hesitated a moment, then leaned forward, swung his right leg over the saddle and lowered himself to stand next to Kiitsoh. He gave the horse a reassuring pat on the rump.

"What happened here, Martha?" Emerson asked, pointing with his chin in the direction of the half-covered body. "Is that your husband?" Emerson was careful not to speak the man's name lest his *chindi* hear the call.

Martha let out a derisive snort. "Who the hell else would it be? You and everybody else in this godforsaken valley know my Buck's the only red-headed man in this part of the rez. But you and me are the only ones who know the bastard's dead." Martha fixed Emerson with a narrow gaze. "Now, you're gonna help me cover him up or I'll shoot you where you stand. Move!"

For the next two hours, as the sun baked his skin and parched his mouth, Emerson hauled stones as large as he could carry from the canyon floor to cover Buck Magee's body. Martha stood a few feet away, chain-smoking and barking orders whenever Emerson's pace slowed. As he piled on the rocks one by one, Emerson used the time to alternately plan his escape and pray that Buck's *chindi* could differentiate between the woman who killed him and an innocent old man who got caught in her web.

Emerson placed the last rock on the burial pile and straightened up, wiping the sweat from his brow with the sleeve of his shirt. His back hurt and his head ached with the effort of carrying the load that now entombed Buck Magee.

After a moment of silence, as much for himself as the dead man, Emerson risked a glance at Martha's face, which was drawn tight. She clutched the gun in her right hand, which hung down at her side. In her left hand was a cigarette, burned nearly to the filter. Her eyes were locked on the rocky mound. He took a step closer to her. When she seemed not to notice, he took another and then another. Suddenly, Martha snapped out of her trance and raised the gun.

"That's close enough, old man."

Emerson stopped. He was only about five feet away—close enough to see the tears in Martha's eyes, but not close enough to reach for the gun. One more step might have done it, but he didn't dare take it now.

"Martha," Emerson said in what he hoped was a calming voice. "I'm sure whatever happened between you and your husband was an accident. Perhaps if you tell me about it, we can figure out what to do next."

Martha dropped her cigarette and ground it out with the heel of her boot.

"Stalling for time, Onesalt?" she asked, her mouth twisting in a wry smile. She waved her free hand toward the canyon wall where the waning sun created a band of shade. "Over there. I need to get out of this damn heat." She motioned for Emerson to lead the way.

As he walked forward, a plan formed in Emerson's mind. Halfway to the canyon wall, he stopped, bent forward and started coughing. He counted to three as he fake-hacked, hoping Martha would advance at least a few steps before stopping. A furtive glance behind him revealed the woman now stood only a few feet away.

With all the speed his age and exhaustion allowed, Emerson straightened and whirled on Martha, intending to knock the gun from her hands. He wasn't fast enough. Martha jerked the gun up above his hands and, as the barrel pointed to the sky, she squeezed off a shot. The report boomed off the canyon wall, scattering the vultures that had been keeping vigil and spooking Kiitsoh, who took off down the canyon at a gallop.

"Damn you, Onesalt!" Martha raged as she retreated a few steps and drew a bead on Emerson. "I needed that horse! Now I'm going to have to walk the five miles back home. First my damn horse spooks at a snake and takes off, and now you've gone and scared off the other one. I should kill you right now!" Her index finger tightened on the trigger.

Emerson held up his hands. "Martha, wait. Kiitsoh will not go far," he said, thinking quickly as his heart hammered in his chest. "He's been my horse for fifteen years and I can call him back. Let him run off his scare and I will get him back for you. If you shoot again, he'll just keep going."

Emerson watched the indecision play out on her face. Twice she drew the gun up and aimed. Twice she lowered it, seeming to weigh the choice between killing Emerson immediately for the satisfaction and having a horse to ride home. Exhaustion prevailed.

"One chance," she growled. "You get *one* chance to call him back. If he doesn't come, you're dead."

Emerson guessed she would probably kill him anyway, but at least this development gave him more time to come up with another escape plan. He allowed himself a relieved breath.

"We need to let him run to calm down and then find his way back to me. Then I'll call to him. Come, sit in the shade."

Without waiting for Martha's approval, Emerson resumed his walk toward the shady canyon wall. With a grunt, he eased down onto the sand and braced his back against a boulder. Then he closed his eyes for a moment and willed his heartbeat to slow. He heard Martha come closer and settle about five feet to his right. As he opened his eyes and watched, she lit a cigarette.

"I believe I'll join you," he said, reaching slowly for the tin in his shirt pocket. He didn't really want a cigarette, but hoped the shared action would calm Martha. They smoked in silence as the sun slipped below the canyon rim and cast milky-gray shadows on the landscape.

After a time, Emerson cleared his throat. "So, tell me what happened between you and your husband."

Martha looked in the direction of Buck's resting place.

"Not much to tell," she said in a voice barely above a whisper. "Stupid bastard got what he had coming to him."

"You must have had a good reason to kill him and risk the wrath of his *chindi*."

"His *ghost*?" Martha spat out the word out as though it left a bad taste in her mouth. "That's Navajo hooey. I don't believe in that crap."

Emerson shrugged. "Seems to me a whole nation of people wouldn't believe in hooey. But it's up to you. We'll know soon enough."

Martha was silent so long that he doubted she'd taken the bait.

"What are you talking about, old man?"

Emerson repressed a smile. Now he had to proceed carefully. As a *bilagaana*, chances were that Martha knew very little of Navajo beliefs. The Magees had only owned the Blue House for two years, which meant they were practically strangers to the community. And *chindis* in particular were not something the Navajo people would talk about with outsiders. Still, Emerson trod lightly between fact and fiction.

"It's almost dark," he said as he glanced up to the sky. "Your husband's *chindi* will wait until then to make itself known to us."

As if to punctuate this thought, an owl hooted in the distance. Once, then twice.

Martha smirked. "Anything you say, Onesalt. Buck can't do anything worse to me in death than he did in life."

Emerson remained quiet and wished she would quit saying her husband's name. He said nothing and the silence carried on for several moments. Like most white people, Martha was uncomfortable with extended silence and eventually started talking to fill it.

"I suppose it's not news that Buck liked his liquor," she said as she stubbed out her cigarette on a rock and flicked the butt into the sand. "The life of the party, that was Buck. When we lived in Phoenix it was fine because I could send him out with his cronies and he could drink and fight and do whatever the hell he wanted." She reached for the pack of cigarettes in her shirt pocket, lit another and took a deep drag. "But when we moved up here after I inherited the trading post from my father, Buck had no friends. He did his drinking at home and the only one there to fight with was me. I was his punching bag."

The owl hooted again, closer this time. Once, then twice.

Seemingly oblivious to the owl, Martha continued. "I just couldn't take it anymore. Three weeks ago he got so drunk and so angry I thought he was going to kill me. He choked me 'til I passed out. The next day, I got his gun, loaded it and waited in the house until he came in from working on his truck. He looked so surprised. Even after I shot him the first time, it was like he didn't believe what was happening. He just kept staring at me. I looked him square in the eye and shot him again. When I was sure he was dead, I put his body in the big freezer in the back room, cleaned up the mess and started telling people he was out of town visiting relatives."

Emerson nodded, as if what she said made perfect sense and was what any normal person would do. "Why bring him out here, now?"

Martha barked out an ironic laugh. "The freezer died last week and he started to stink. Obviously, I couldn't call anyone out to fix it, so I figured I'd bring him out here and bury him." She shook her head and a wry smile crossed her face. "For once, I was glad he was such a scrawny son of a bitch. I was able to use the pulley he'd rigged up out back last year to unload pallets from our truck to get him up on the horse. Any bigger and there's no way I'd have been able to hoist him by myself. I thought I had it made and no one would know." She looked Emerson directly in the eyes. "Then you came along, stuck your nose in where it don't belong and here we are."

Hoot, hoot. The sound was closer still, raising the hairs on Emerson's arms. It wasn't like owls, or any wild animal for that matter, to get *closer* to humans. Suddenly, Martha jumped and swatted at something near her head.

"What the hell?" she exclaimed and swatted again.

"What is it?"

"I don't know. A bug or something in my hair."

"Could be, I suppose. Then again…"

"What? Buck's ghost is messing with my hair? Ha! That's a good one." Martha's attempt at laughter was weak and unconvincing. A moment passed and Emerson watched as Martha flinched and swatted again at her hair. She fussed and picked among the gray strands until she pulled out a small pebble, which she threw to the ground.

"Damn it! That's enough." She stood and walked a few feet away.

The canyon was almost fully engulfed in darkness. A sliver of moon peeked above the high walls and a multitude of stars glittered like thousands of watchful eyes.

A shrill cry rose from the area near Buck Magee's body.

"Who's out there?" Martha yelled, swinging the gun around. The only answer was a distant scratching sound from the rock pile. Low at first, then louder—stone rubbing on stone. "Get out here and show yourself, damn it, or I'll shoot."

The scratching stopped and the silence near the rock pile was complete. Too complete, thought Emerson. No insects, no more hooting. None of the normal night sounds that would exist in the absence of a close human presence. Suddenly, understanding began to dawn on Emerson.

"It's your husband," he said calmly and stood slowly to draw Martha's attention but not to startle her. "He's angry that you murdered him and has come to take you with him."

Martha whipped around to face him. "Shut up, you old fool! I'm sick of your ghost stories and we've waited long enough. Call your damn horse so we can finish our business and I can get the hell out of here."

Emerson puckered and tried to whistle, but no noise came. Martha took aim at his chest.

"Try again," she demanded. "Get that damn horse back here now!"

The old *hataalii* wet his lips and whistled what he hoped was a convincing horse call.

One of the rocks from the far edge of Buck Magee's burial mound tumbled down with a clatter. Martha turned and shot at the pile, scattering shards of rock. Emerson let out an expletive in Navajo and whistled again to draw her attention back to him.

"He's not coming, Onesalt," Martha screamed. "I gotta get out of here." She aimed the gun at Emerson. He tried not to flinch as her finger tightened on the trigger.

Another cry, long and high-pitched, came from the boulders directly behind Martha. As she turned toward the howl, Emerson made his move and tackled her to the ground. The gun came loose and he was able to grab it. After a short struggle, all the fight seemed to leave Martha. She went limp beneath Emerson and started to sob. He stood and backed away several feet.

"It's all right," Emerson called toward the boulder. "You can come out now."

He smiled as Benny Chapo emerged a moment later, leading Kiitsoh and his own horse, a fawn-colored mare.

"I make a pretty good *chindi*, don't I, Grandfather?" The boy asked, using the traditional Navajo term of respect.

Martha's sobbing subsided as she looked up at the boy, her surprise at being so easily fooled clear in her expression. Red sand dusted her hair and face, and ran in small rivulets down her cheeks as it mixed with her tears. She pounded the ground with her fist, a mumbled curse mixing with a new round of sobs.

"Yes, you make an excellent ghost, my young friend," Emerson said as he patted Benny on the head with his free hand. Then he tucked the gun safely in Kiitsoh's saddle bag. After digging briefly in the satchel, he withdrew a ball of thick twine. "How did you come to be out here at night? Your mother will be worried." As he spoke, Emerson went to Martha and, after a brief struggle, used some of the twine to bind her hands behind her back.

Benny waived off the *hataali*'s concern with his hand. "She sent me to look for you when you were late. We thought maybe you'd gotten lost," he said, then smiled sheepishly as if he realized this might be an insult to the old man. "I was almost here when I heard the shot and a couple minutes later your horse came trotting my way. I knew something was wrong. I caught him, rode back here and heard you talking to the *bilagaana* lady about the *chindi*. I figured if we convinced her it was real, she'd get scared and run off."

"That was quick thinking and I'm most grateful to you," Emerson said, genuinely touched by the boy's bravery and resourcefulness. "And the owl hooting, that was you as well?"

"I thought you might recognize it and know that I was here to help you." Benny glanced at the burial mound, a look of concern clouding his face. "Is there really a dead man under there?"

The possibility of a real *chindi* seemed to unsettle the boy. The old man took Benny gently by the shoulders and turned him away from the remains of Buck Magee.

"Unfortunately, there is. But, I believe this man's spirit will know the difference between us and the woman who killed him. Still, we should move quickly. We have one more thing to do before I take you home."

Emerson walked back to his horse, removed the rope he kept tied to Kiitsoh's saddle and slung it over his shoulder. Then he helped Martha to her feet and led her to one of the mesquite trees. After she sat, Emerson used the rope to secure her to the tree.

"That ought to hold you," he said to Martha, then turned and walked back to Benny. "Now, my young friend, let's return you to your parents and contact the police, shall we?"

Emerson mounted Kiitsoh and Benny climbed up on his mare. As they started down the canyon toward the Chapo's place, Martha called out behind them.

"Wait! You can't just leave me here. What about the ghost? He'll kill me. Waaait!"

Emerson smiled and said, "Now she believes."

As Emerson and Benny rode away, a mournful shriek pierced the darkness, its echo dying slowly on the canyon walls.

† † †

JOANNE ZETERBERG is a professional writer working in the Scottsdale, Arizona, tourism industry. Her work is published regularly in *Experience Scottsdale*. Her short stories include "The Gift" (*How NOT to Survive the Holidays*, DS Publishing 2009) and "Death on the Intergalactic Seas" (*How NOT to Survive a Vacation*, DS Publishing 2010). JoAnne has studied with internationally known psychic medium James Van Praagh, is an active member of Sisters in Crime, and is currently working on a romantic suspense novel set in Alaska.

MOSHE GOES TO ARIZONA
HOWARD "DOC" CARRON

I'll never forget the date, April 4, 1871. The news was shattering. Papa told me his shop was failing and needed a large amount of cash to survive. My job as a detective trainee with Piedmont Investigative Services did not pay enough to help. Our cousin Otto, the big banker, would lend Papa the money, but he wanted me to go to *Arizona* to help with an investigation into robberies at his cattle ranch in the grasslands north of the Sonoita Valley.

"Papa, why me? I'm an apprentice investigator, not a real detective. Besides Arizona is over eleven hundred miles from here."

"Shah, Moshe, the last detective that was sent disappeared because he looked like a detective and asked too many questions. And you, thank heavens, look like a...a...well, you don't look like a detective."

"Papa, I'm not a cowboy either! Besides I can't work with cows because it's not kosher. That would be mixing meat with dairy."

"Very clever," Papa said, "I'm a butcher and I know the rules. Listen to me, Moshe, you will go there, Otto will tell them it's for your health—you do look a little undernourished—and you will listen. Make some friends and see what's what. Otto says, if you do a good job I won't have to repay the loan and Mama and I won't be, God forbid, out in the street."

Cousin Otto never did a favor unless there was something in it for him. I did know that he had a sweet spot for Mama and his bank had a big investment with two Englishmen in a 71,000-acre ranch. I guess he thought sending a tenderfoot like me (I'm sure he thought I was a real *schmendrick,* but fools can surprise you) would not generate any suspicion.

The only depot in Manhattan in 1871 was Grand Central which opened that year. I had a small valise, a knapsack, holding two changes of clothing, my *Tallis* (prayer shawl), my *Siddur* (prayer book), and the *Tefillin, a* strip of parchment inscribed with passages from the Hebrew bible encased in two small black boxes with black straps attached to them. Jewish men are required to place one box on their head and tie the other one on their arm each weekday morning. It was not much, but along with the railroad tickets Cousin Otto had given me, credit slips for food and lodging and instructions to the ranch foreman, my trip was laid out for me. Tearful goodbyes, a loaf of rye bread from Mama, a hug, an admonition to keep the Sabbath, and a dried sausage from Papa, and I started my journey.

The New York Central, in economy class (thank you Cousin Otto), took two days to get to Detroit, eight days to Omaha and on to Laramie and then Tucson. Food was a problem, of course. I didn't have access to kosher foods once I'd finished Mama's rye, but if there were no kosher food available—a Jew is obligated to nourish himself rather than die, the obligation to sustain our lives and care for ourselves overrides any conflicting commandment. So I was limited to bread, carrots, turnips, onions and potatoes. I know the meat wasn't koshered so I avoided it for the time being.

The Double C Bar Ranch was my destination. A waiting telegram at the Tucson station stated: MENDOZA WILL MEET YOU. An hour later, close to prayer time, a wagon loaded with supplies pulled into the station driven by a slim young man with a reckless face. He looked a little younger than me. I had never really seen a working cowboy except in Ned Buntline's Dime Novels of the Wild West.

"I'm Mendoza. You from the old states, no? Put your bags in the back and sit up front, camp is far."

We headed out at a fast trot. The noise from the horses and the groaning wagon put an end to my conversational attempts. Leaving town, Mendoza increased our speed to a modest gallop as I held fast to the bar on the side of the seat. The sun was starting to set when I tapped Mendoza on the shoulder signaling him to stop. I guess he thought I needed to relieve myself, but I said I needed to pray. I'm not sure if he understood, but he stopped and I pulled out my *Tallis* and *Siddur,* faced what I thought was east and, very quickly said the evening prayers.

I received a few curious glances when we arrived at the camp, but the ranch hands were only interested in getting their food. A tall, lean, red-faced man, in his early thirties, strode purposefully up to the wagon.

"I'm Red Corrigan, trail boss and you must be Moss."

"Well, actually the name is Moshe."

"Okay, but I think Moss will work better out here. I'm aware of your role here but since you can't ride a horse yet you'll be working with Jelly Belly, J.B. for short, he's our cook."

Did I hear him say *can't ride yet*? The only horse I knew was the one that pulled Rabinowitz's ice wagon back in Brooklyn. *Oy veh.*

"Well, sir," I said, "I can bake bread, make an edible stew and I'm a quick learner. I have some dietary restrictions, but I can manage. Oh, I hope this isn't a problem. I usually pray in the morning and the evening."

Red looked at Moshe for a moment, then said, "Let's go see J.B. and do something about getting you some working clothes."

The line in front of the chuck wagon had dwindled and the cook, a bald, very large black man, about two hundred and forty pounds, with lots of laugh lines around his eyes, looked at me like he was sizing up a side of beef.

Corrigan said, "J.B., this is Moss, from New York. One of the Big Bugs is his cousin. Sent him out here to improve his health and build him up." Corrigan added, "No special favors."

"Okay, boss, I'll put some meat on his bones, muscles in his arms and a lot of respect for hard work." Turning to me he said, "Let's go to the supply wagon and get you some working clothes."

Rummaging through a trunk full of clothes that had seen better days, I ended up with a high-crowned hat with a wide brim and a bandana needing a wash. I passed on the boots with their pointed toes and picked up the miner's boots and a flannel shirt. The trousers were canvas and we finished with a pair of soft, flexible gloves. We also found a relatively clean blanket roll and he told me I could sleep under the wagon or by the fire if I got cold. I was so tired that I just changed into my newly acquired clothes, crawled under the wagon, and was asleep in minutes.

Sometime later I was awakened by Rafe, who, it turns out, was the wrangler in charge of what they called a remuda and was on his way to see to those horses. J.B. was starting a fire and told me to get more wood from the wagon, find the scale and measure out two pounds of flour from the bin on the side. I retrieved a bucket of water from the barrel on the other side and so started my first cooking lesson.

We had ten cowboys to handle about three thousand head of

cattle. They worked in three shifts, a twenty-four hour job herding them in the proper direction and preventing stampedes. J.B. was also in charge of medical supplies and had a working knowledge of practical medicine. The rest of the crew, Matt, Ben, Harvey, Ephraim, Tom, Ray, Willard, C.L., Dusty, Leroy and Chester were introduced over the first week. I, of course, became Moss.

Everything was new to me. Rafe was working on this rope and I asked him what he was going to tie up.

"This," he said, "is a lariat. We use it to catch cows and horses."

"I see, and what do you use for bait?"

Of course that comment was campfire chatter for a week.

My new culinary skills included sourdough biscuits—woe betide anyone who messed with J.B.'s starter—mixing beans, bacon and homemade ketchup into what they named Fart and Dart Beans. We ate my potato pie, stew and lots of coffee.

I began to pay attention to the conversation around the campfire, especially during meals, and started to hear bits and pieces of information about the number of missing cattle. Ephraim commented on the smaller number of animals and different brands mingling with our stock.

When I had a chance, I asked Red if there were other ranches around and he said there were a couple of smaller spreads along the trail.

Ben and Harvey were closer to my age and I thought I might talk to them. Ben, dark eyebrows, black stubble and Harvey, thick lipped and heavy lidded, reminded me of the bullies I had encountered growing up. After a couple of attempts to talk about the missing cattle, Ben said, "Don't interfere with something that isn't bothering you none."

After a few weeks of riding an old crow-bait horse tied to the back of the wagon, I asked J.B. about branding. He said that Rafe might find me a quiet horse and we could take a look. We ventured out after breakfast.

I had never seen the process. Harvey and Ephraim kept the milling animals settled so that Rafe and Willard could cut out an animal with their horses, rope it, lay it on the ground, tying its legs together and applying a hot branding iron. Lots of smoke, bawling, a sizzle and the animal was running back to the herd, the brand standing out clearly. It was all dusty, smelly and exciting at the same time.

Ben rode up suddenly and asked the guys what I was doing there. J.B. waved him off. "To see the branding, Ben, not that's any of your concern. Get back to work or Red will have you on night patrol for a week."

On the way back to the main camp I asked about the other brands I saw. J.B. said, "Out here there are strays and ranchers who throw a 'long loop', which is why we brand in the first place. We run about three thousand head and a remuda of about two hundred horses. Those other outfits may have only a couple a hundred head. We'd best be getting back, need to make some Texas Butter tonight to go with the prairie oysters."

My stomach did a flip flop. I'd been introduced to this gem a week ago, steak grease and flour for the gravy and calf testicles, floured and fried.

At camp I put on my *Tallis,* and began to *daven. Davening* means rocking back and forth. I was putting my *Tallis* away when Red Corrigan came up. "Red," I said, "I heard Ephraim say that we have been losing some cattle. How does one lose a cow?"

"Yeah, we're losing quite a few head of cattle almost every day. With six or seven outfits on the trail headed for Tucson we can't be sure which of the unbranded calves are ours. To prevent rustling we pretty much brand everything we come across. Our brand is hard to change so what they do is called 'sleepering' calves. These rustlers put our earmark on the calves, cutting notches in their ears. We see the earmark and figure they're range branded. Then the rustlers come back, change the brand and drive them off. Have you heard anything?"

"Nothing. They've just barely accepted me." Red nodded and left.

J.B. had to move the chuck wagon the next morning to get ahead of the herd and since we packed the night before he let me take some time to practice my riding. I placed the blanket on the horse Rafe gave me, got the saddle placed properly, cinched up the girth and felt pretty proud of myself. I put my foot in the stirrup and found myself flat on my back, the saddle hanging below the horse's stomach.

Ephraim came up and instead of laughing he said, "Horses don' naturally accept the saddle. 'Til he understands who's boss he'll fill himself up with air when you tighten the girth. So when you start to tighten up the strap you give him a good knee in the stomach and as he lets out the air you tighten the girth. Oh, and when you mount the horse turn the stirrup to the rear, put your foot in, grab the reins and a chunk of mane and as the horse moves forward just swing into the saddle."

It worked. Flanked by the mountains I was off at a trot in the same general direction J.B. would be taking. As a beginning rider my horse had a hackamore instead of a steel bit in his mouth. With longer stirrups I was between standing and sitting and getting the horse's rhythm. I couldn't believe I was doing this. Me, Moshe, a Jewish kid from Brooklyn, a cowboy. Suddenly the horse's body tensed, he reared back and I lost the reins. A rattlesnake. The horse bolted. Hanging on for dear life, hands wrapped around the saddle horn, we were in a full gallop. I managed to grab the reins but the horse wouldn't stop. Pulling the reins, grasping with my knees, I pointed the horse up the hill. He ran out of steam and stopped. Just ahead was a grassy meadow.

I was back in control once the horse was calm. Walking now I marveled at such lush grass. A pond, fed by a spring gurgling from the rocks, was surrounded by about two hundred head of cows. The horse and I had a drink. I washed my face (the horse could wash his own face).

I found a tree stump to help me mount up, noticing that most of the cattle had been branded clumsily. I spied a trail of dust a few miles ahead and aimed the horse in that direction. I was a little ashamed and embarrassed to tell my tale of woe.

During the hectic serving period I was quite busy, but I did notice that Ben and Ephraim were having a heated conversation. With the last of the riders leaving the dinner line I asked J.B. what was going on with Ephraim and Ben.

"Ephraim's brother runs a small ranch and we're losing cattle. His brother Jethro Mason isn't too careful where he throws his rope. He always seems to have cattle to sell."

"J.B., where's Red? I have something to tell him."

"He's on the trail setting up our next branding corral and checking on the night crew. Why?"

"Well, it's probably nothing but, well, my horse got crazy this afternoon, spooked by a rattlesnake and before I could get him under control I ended up in a valley. It had lots of really green grass, a bunch of cattle and a big pond."

"Moss, until Red comes back, don't mention this to anyone. After breakfast tomorrow you show me what you found."

"Golly, J.B., I'm not sure I'll recognize the area but I'll try." I noticed Ben moving quietly out from behind the chuck wagon but it was time for my evening prayer. I put on my *Tallis,* and *Tefillin,* the little black boxes with the prayers in them, and began to *daven.* I was on a little knoll rocking to the beat of the prayers when a shot rang out. The box wrapped around my forehead exploded. Little bits of paper from the scroll swirled around my head and I fainted.

When I opened my eyes, J.B. was offering me something alcoholic. "Moss, Moss, is you hurt? Drink this." It wasn't kosher wine.

"I don't know what happened. I was praying and the next thing I knew my *Tefillin* exploded."

"Well my friend, the rocking, saved your life. A couple of inches and it would be your brains not the little box blown apart. Thought you were a goner for sure. The question is who wants you dead and why?"

The half dozen cowboys who'd gathered around me quietly dispersed, whispering amongst themselves. Ben stood there, looking at me with his dark, piercing eyes and then left.

I slept in the supply wagon and after breakfast J.B. and I took the trail toward the small mountain range where I ended up yesterday. At first everything looked the same and then I remembered the stump I had used to get back in the saddle. We followed a faint trail, strewn with rocks.

Just before entering the valley we noticed a small cave. There was a glint of some metal reflection and J.B. grabbed my reins and jerked us behind some rocks. He motioned for me to stay put. He brought out a pistol and crept around the rock. "Moss, it's okay. Come on over."

Scared witless, I managed to stumble over the rocks to the cave without falling.

"After last night's attack I didn't want you dry-gulched." J.B. saw my perplexed look. "I mean someone taking a shot at you again. The flash we saw came from a belt buckle that I guess a pack rat had dug up. I recognized it. There was a detective last seen out here before you came and he disappeared. I bet the rest of him is here, but we can't touch anything. We'll send for the U.S. Marshal in Tucson.

The floor of the cave was clean except for a boot mark near the wall.

"*Lamed*," I said.

"What?" J.B. looked at me as if I was losing my mind.

"Look J.B., that mark over there ל, looks like the Hebrew letter, *lamed*."

J.B. shrugged, unimpressed. "If you say so. Show me the valley."

There were no cattle to be seen, but the hoof prints around the pond showed recent visitors.

That evening, after dinner, we sat around the fire, drinking coffee, and discussing the angry comments Red had made about missing cattle and staying alert. We were ten days out from the railhead and he didn't want to lose anymore cows. Things became animated when Ben started in on Ephraim about his brother.

Lean, leathery and taciturn, Ephraim looked at Ben as if he just crawled out from under a rock. Ephraim spoke quietly. "Ben, don't know what your problem is, this blow about my brother is wasted on me. I work for this brand and Jethro does what he does. Maybe all this palaver 'bout Jethro has more to do with you than me?"

Ben jumped to his feet and then abruptly emptied his coffee near the fire and stormed off, followed by his constant shadow, Harvey.

"J.B.," I said, "this whole situation reminds me of Hebrew school when the Rabbi would use this technique called *pilpul* which meant that when something was 'true' it couldn't be disputed. What Ben said was irrational. He was trying to prove a point already established. Ephraim has a brother who has a small ranch. Looks like a suspicious smoke screen to me. Oh my. Look by the fire. Ben left the same mark we found in the cave."

"Slow down, Moss. You're using your *pilpul* reasoning to defend your own theory. Yes, it looks suspicious and we'll share this information with Red and the U.S. Deputy Marshal. Don't say anything to anyone else and don't leave camp."

Rafe returned from Tucson with U.S. Deputy Marshal Joe Evans. We went into the cave and found what was left of the detective's body, shreds of clothing, boots, belt and bones. The skull showed a bullet entry wound in the forehead and another out the back.

J.B. said, "The exit wound indicates a large caliber." I showed the imprint to Marshal Evans and told him about our discovery last night.

"Well, son. Not hard evidence but enough to question Ben. Show me the cattle."

There were about two hundred and fifty head of cattle with similar brands quietly grazing near the pond.

Looking at the brands now, Marshal Evans said, "Creative running irons at work here."

"Yup," J.B. said, "the brand is registered. These rustlers get them changed fast. Undersell the cattle, no questions asked."

Marshal Evans told us to go back to camp, report to Red and talk to no one. "I'll have a chat with this Mason fella."

I had a million questions but first we had to get out a meal which was a passel of t-bones. We started cutting up the side of beef. I kind of pushed J.B. out of the way and took over. He started to object but I said, in my least squeaky voice, "My pa is a butcher. I don't need any help from amateurs."

J.B. had this incredulous look on his face, half shock, half anger, and then he burst into laughter, saying when he caught his breath, "Moss, don't you beat all. If I'm not careful you'll take my job away."

Cooking the steaks was not a problem—couple of grates over the fire and since no one would eat an overcooked steak they didn't spend much time on the flames. We lounged around the fire after all the chores were done. J.B. was rolling his evening smoke when U.S. Marshal Evans rode in with Jethro Mason.

"Cup of coffee would do me right now," Evans said. "Me and Jethro is headin' to Tucson to look at the brand registry so we can answer some serious questions about the unusual brands we found. Even if the brands are registered it don't prove ownership of the cattle 'cause the brands aren't cleanly executed. Besides, this was not a one man operation."

Harvey started to say something but Ben stopped him quickly.

Without clearly reading the situation I blurted out, "Whoever was moving cows had to have help. The night shift always operates with two riders and it makes sense that the part of the herd that was farthest north, near the hidden valley would be suspect. We already know one possible person because of the clue we found in the cave and—"

Harvey jumped up and shouted at Ben, "I told you the cave was a bad idea."

Everything changed. Harvey drew his pistol from his belt, and Ephraim hit him on the side of his head with his big old Paterson. Ben drew his Colt and got off a shot. There was a loud clang as it hit the large cast iron pan I was oiling. Fire burst from J.B.'s fist and Ben dropped his gun and fell to his knees as a large red spot appeared on his upper arm.

J.B. put the .44 Derringer away. Turning to me he said, "You're one lucky shavetail, Moss. I hope that pan isn't too badly damaged, it's my favorite."

Well, I did my job for Cousin Otto, Red got the cattle back without a trip to Tucson in return for letting Jethro ride off (I think because of Ephraim) and Marshal Evans took Ben and Harvey back to jail. I was getting ready to turn in when J.B. and Red took me aside behind the chuck wagon.

Red said to me, "It's a wonder you didn't get yourself killed. I suggest being a detective is not your best career choice. J.B. here is a *real* detective for Pinkerton sent out by one of the other owners and he'll be leaving next week when we hit the railhead with the herd. I'll be needing another cook. You'd start at the ranch and be ready for the trail in six months."

"You can do it, fella," J.B. said. "And you can have my sourdough starter and the cast iron pan that saved your life."

"Me, a cowboy cook. Could be worse. Going back to Brooklyn to a cramped, dusty office, that would be worse."

† † †

HOWARD "DOC" CARRON - Born Brooklyn, NY. Married, 3 daughters. Author, photographer, musician, teacher, artist and craftsman, editor-in-chief of *Cigar Lovers Magazine*, librarian and chef. PhD. Taught in Southeast Asia, Mediterranean, Europe. Library Reference Supervisor. Publishing credits: "The Happy Cooker", "The Last Habano" (*Medley of Murder*), "A Favor for the Mayor" (*Medium of Murder*), "Christmas Came Late" (*How NOT to Survive the Holidays*), "The Old Miner," (*How NOT to Survive A Vacation*), "Tourado A Corda" (*Murder to Mil-Spec*), *Where There's Smoke* (Short Story Anthology).

NOT MY BROTHER'S KEEPER
MARGARET MORSE

After the cops let me go, I continued my nightly jog. I had my rhythm back when I turned the last corner. A patrol car flashed its lights in front of my father's house. *Dad had another stroke.* I dashed to the front door and slammed it open, stumbling into the sunken living room.

"Dad." The word bounced around the cathedral ceiling.

My father sat on the leather couch, between my step-mother Sallee and a uniformed cop. Jumping up, Dad staggered for a second. Sallee grabbed at him, but I was there, clutching his shoulders.

"I'm okay," he said.

I tried to lock eyes with him. His gaze slid away from mine. Having dropped some fat after his stroke, Dad's skeleton was close to the surface. Cheekbones defined his face. I felt his collarbone under my thumbs.

"Somebody tried to kill your dad when he drove through the entry gate," Sallee said, her voice high, her words clipped. "A bullet missed him by inches."

I backed away, noticed the cop check out my running shorts and mesh shirt. Damp with sweat, I breathed raggedly. I knew my face flamed brick-red.

Dad turned to the cop. "This is my son, Zane. He goes out for a run almost every night. He's been living in the guest house."

Dad had resumed his lawyer voice, the big one that made you want to take a step back. The cop, a burly guy with a shiny bald head, stood his ground. His radio squawked, and he walked over to the patio door to talk. He looked out on soft lights illuminating the swimming pool.

I swiped my hand across my face, tasted the salty sweat. "What happened?"

Dad sat stiffly on the couch. "I had just driven through the gate when I heard a crack. Next thing I know, there's a hole in the windshield. I stopped at the clubhouse, because I saw a security car there. The guard called nine-one-one. This officer just brought me home."

I kneeled in front of him. He still wasn't meeting my eyes. "What did the cops do?"

Sallee answered. She was as rail-thin as the girl who left her father's ranch thirty years ago. "They closed off the entrance. Patrol cars have been going up and down the streets, shining spotlights. Didn't you see them and the helicopter?"

"Yeah, they stopped me and patted me down."

Dad sat up straighter. His face took on the hawk look of a lawyer. "You let them—"

The cop rejoined us. "The detectives assigned to the case are on the way over to interview you."

"Did the patrol cars find anything?" Sallee asked.

"No. Your boy here is the only one the officers found outdoors."

Sallee sent me off to the guest house to shower. It didn't do much good. I broke into an extreme sweat after I saw the black pistol clip on top of my jumble of socks and underwear in the drawer. I emptied the other dresser drawers on the floor. When I didn't find anything else out of place, I crammed the stuff back. I kept out the plastic gloves I'd used to help dad with his bathroom needs after his stroke.

It didn't take long to search the small bedroom, closet and bathroom. I'd traveled light when I came home six months ago.

With the pistol clip in my gloved hand, I called my old friend Kelly.

"I was reading in bed," she said. "This had better be good."

"I need a lawyer."

"Don't say another word if anyone can overhear you."

"I'm alone."

"Give me the quick version of why you need a lawyer."

"Somebody tried to kill Dad when he drove through the gate tonight. I don't want to explain over the phone, but I could be facing an attempted murder charge."

"Is he okay?"

"Yeah, they shot at him but missed. I need you when the detectives come. Like right now."

"I'll be there in fifteen minutes. Keep your mouth shut except to ask to have your lawyer present."

I had to check my pickup, the one thing everyone knew I owned. Rusted, dented, holes in its seats, it was the outcast in the garage, parked next to Sallee's Lexus.

The pistol clip weighing down my shorts pocket, I poked through empty soda cans and tortilla chip bags on the passenger side. I located the gun under *The Complete Armchair Book of Baseball*, my emergency car read. Pushing aside paperwork in the glove compartment, I found the flashlight and shined it on the gun. It matched the one Dad once used for target practice, which he stored in a safe in his home office. I knew the combination, along with Dad, Sallee, and my step-brother Billy. I crushed five soda cans before I was calm enough to pick up the pistol in my gloved hand.

I figured Billy must be trying to frame me. The shining star of Sallee's life, Billy was seven and I was six when he and Sallee moved in. He and I spent the next ten years trying to kill each other, with periodic truces. Billy'd been suspiciously quiet since my return.

I had a good place to hide the stuff planted on me. This morning, Ronan Flynn, the next door neighbor, asked me to watch his place while he partied in Vegas. Ronan knew I wasn't too busy interviewing for reporting jobs lately. I left the gun and the clip in Ronan's sweater drawer, the plastic gloves with the bathroom cleaning supplies.

Free of incriminating evidence, I returned to our house, stopping to pop open a soda in Sallee's kitchen, bright with Mexican pottery and copper pans. From the living room came a honeyed low rumbling voice, one that could talk anybody into anything. Billy had the floor.

Dad and Sallee sat together on the couch, her hand resting on his forearm. Billy, curly blond hair trimmed short, wore a blue shirt and tan slacks. He stood a head taller than the man next to him, a squat, olive-skinned guy.

Dad got up without faltering. "Zane, this is Detective Farelli. My son Zane."

I raised the soda can at the cop. "What's going on?"

Dad moved away from Sallee to join the cop and Billy. "I've given Detective Farelli permission to search the guest house. I don't believe it, but the issue of your being involved in the shooting has been raised. Zane, do you also agree with a search?"

He was looking at me directly, the way an eagle spots a silver fish in the stream below. I turned away, sloshing soda on my hand. I put the can down.

"Consent to the search. It will show you have nothing to hide," Billy said.

I didn't deck him. My shoulder twitched. "Go ahead." I knew I wasn't acting innocent. I should be yelling, shocked and outraged, asking why they suspected me.

"Wait just a minute here." Sallee took a position between me and the three men. She put her hands on her hips. "This is wrong. Zane would never hurt his father."

Billy told the detective, "Dad changed his will last week at a belated welcome home party for Zane. For the first time since Zane was a kid, Dad included him in the will."

Sallee stepped closer to me, but talked to the cop. "We sent Zane to a military academy when he was sixteen. He didn't come home again for twenty years. Not one word from him in all that time." She rolled her shoulders back and lifted her chin. The wrought iron chandelier, with its ring of lights, crowned her. "When a friend told him about his father's stroke, Zane came home to help. That shows he loves his father."

Detective Farelli started for the door. "Okay, ma'am, I see how you feel. I still need to search his room."

"Hey," I said, "Wait for my lawyer. She's coming."

I could hear everyone's mind click: *He's already got himself a lawyer.*

The detective said, "Your dad and your brother are lawyers."

"I got my own."

The doorbell rang three sweet chimes. I opened up for Kelly. She wore black pants and a red shirt. Loose fitting, the clothes hid a body that was every inch muscle. She had on heels that took her height up to my chest, right where my heart should be. Dark hair jutted and spiked around her face.

"Good timing," I said, "Dad and I just told Detective Farelli here he could search my room in the guest house."

She pinned the cop with her eyes. It must be a lawyer thing. I'd never seen Kelly and Dad in action before.

"Detective, I'm Kelly Anderson, Zane Robert's attorney. Could you give me a moment with my client first?"

Lips pursed, the cop crossed his arms over his chest. "Sure."

Outside, at the fake rock waterfall that flowed into the pool,

Kelly stopped. "Did you forget the part about not saying anything except you wanted your lawyer present?"

"I want them to search my room now. They won't find anything." Over her shoulder I saw Billy shaking his head while he talked to the cop. "That weasel."

Kelly pivoted slowly, a graceful dancer's move. "What?"

"Billy told the cop about Dad including me in his will at the party. And before that, he must've said something else to make them suspect me."

"How like him." She whirled and grabbed a handful of my shirt. "I didn't call and inform you about your dad's stroke for this to happen. What aren't you telling me?"

"Something you don't need to know."

"You're sure about them searching your room?" I nodded. "I'm not going to waste time arguing." She released my shirt. "If this goes on past tomorrow, I'm getting you a different attorney. I can't think straight around you."

I followed, pulled by her energy. In the living room, she said, "Detective, I'd like to fight you on this, but my client consents to the search."

As he headed for the door, Billy said, "I'm coming along."

I bolted ahead of them. I can move fast for a big guy. Planted in front of Billy, I said, "You're staying here."

Billy charged forward with his hand out. The detective yanked him back. "Let's calm down here. I don't need anybody but my partner. He's out front talking to officers."

Sallee put her hand on Billy's arm. "Come in the kitchen with me. You can help fix your dad something to eat."

Kelly joined the detective. "I'm coming with you."

As soon as Billy stomped into the kitchen, I went to the back yard and grabbed the five iron Dad kept there to practice his swing. I whacked at an imaginary ball until I tore a divot out of the perfect lawn. When seven tufts of grass were scattered about, I rammed them back into the ground. The patio door slid open.

Dad said, "Are you all right, Zane?"

I leaned the club against the house, watched to make sure it wasn't going to slide away. My hands clenched, as if I were still gripping the shaft. "Sallee has guts to speak up for me like that."

"The reason the police wanted to search the guest house was that Billy brought out your bipolar history. The officer picked up on it, said you might be in a manic phase and—"

"When I was fifteen, one psychologist said maybe I was bipolar. After boot camp at the academy, I had no more incidents. You might give me credit for a good work record, seven years as a reporter for the *Hooverville Gazette*. No meds, no drugs. Clean, sober, sane."

"Once Billy brought up the idea, I had to follow through. A cover-up would mean I thought you were guilty."

"Having the cops search my room is your way of being supportive?"

"It shows I believe in you. They won't find anything. Any suspicion of you will be over tonight."

"You're a lawyer. You're good at explanations."

"I wouldn't want to live if I thought you wanted me dead."

I reached for the club. "I wouldn't want that." On the lawn, my slow swing gained momentum and slashed down. Dad left me, shutting the door behind him. I let the divots stay where they fell.

I stretched out on a chaise lounge by the pool. The lights of Phoenix washed out the night sky. I squinted at the few visible constellations, straining to see additional stars until Kelly stood over me.

She sat on the adjoining chaise lounge. "I agreed to stipulate you're a slob. They didn't find anything. You're not cleared. You could've ditched the gun in someone's shrubbery."

"Or thrown it in the canal."

"Billy must not have spent much time in the kitchen with Sallee, because he met us when we came back through the garage. He told the detectives he searched your truck and found nothing. He wanted to act like he was being fair to you."

I sat up abruptly. "All the years I was gone nobody tried to kill Dad."

"If you take off again, it will break your dad's heart."

I got up and kicked the red gravel that bordered the pool deck. "If I can keep Dad safe by leaving, I should go."

Kelly moved next to me. "You can't be sure going would do any good."

"I could be gone in an hour."

Kelly bumped me with her shoulder. "Then Billy wins. You can't let the bad guy win. He drove you away once. Don't let him do it again."

I stroked her spiky hair, then her silky skin, feeling her hot energy. "You need to leave. The legal part of the evening is over. If I'm going to outsmart Billy, I have to turn myself inside out."

The door to Dad and Sallee's room was closed. They wouldn't hear what I planned to do, because they used a fan and a white noise machine to mask sounds. I stood at the open door to Sallee's office and watched Billy negligently flick the remote.

When he saw me, he jumped up. "What happened?"

Blood trickled down my forehead. I backhanded my snotty nose. I shook all over. My eyes were teary. "I fell down or somebody hit me. Or something. There's a part I don't remember."

He came closer and peered into my eyes. I squinted at him.

He sniffed. "Besides beer, have you used any drugs?"

"I was afraid they'd make me say what I did."

He looked at the closed bedroom door. "Let's take it outside."

Going down the hall, I staggered and bumped into the wall. Billy grabbed my arm and steered me to the patio, guiding me to a chair at the table next to the barbecue.

I rested my forehead on the glass table top and groaned.

Billy sat opposite me. "How could you have gotten so wasted in just an hour on beer?"

I lifted my head and gripped the edge of the table, looking over my shoulder. "They keep lists. They have rules. The first rule? Don't tell Zane the rules." I smiled and covered my mouth.

Billy studied me. "They?"

I flipped open my phone. "Every day at twelve-twelve they give me instructions." I turned it off. "They can't hear us now."

"What did they tell you to do today?"

"Destroy the imposter." I pressed a hand over my right eye. "Only I can see the monster."

"Who?"

"The one who claims he's my father." I nodded three times.

"What are you supposed to do?"

"I failed to act. I'm in trouble. Big time. Huge."

Standing, I spread my arms as far apart as I could. I walked over to the edge of the pool and kneeled while I counted out loud to one hundred. After I got up, Billy joined me when I clutched one of the posts supporting the patio.

"You'd better not be taking over my skin," I said, releasing the post and grabbing his arm. I squeezed hard. "I've been watching you."

He stiffened, then pulled away. "What are you talking about?"

I backed up, wiping my hands on my shirt. "When I saw you, I knew what they meant."

"You didn't see anything."

"They thought I was in my room."

"You were supposed to be in your room when I got here tonight."

I paced up and down the patio. "I can be in two places at once. I was told to watch you." I sat down at the table and rubbed my forehead with my palm. "I'm getting that headache where my skull feels too tight."

Billy pulled a chair close to me. He spoke in a low, purring voice. "Here's an important secret. They told me to help you."

My heart sped up. I dropped my hand to cover my eyes and then my mouth. Billy had flattened his hands on the table. His long white fingers pointed in all directions.

"You're the secret agent," I whispered.

He nodded. "They sent me to finish the job. When you wouldn't get rid of that man who's posing as your father."

"You did it for me?"

"I took care of it."

"You missed."

He moved his face closer. "I took out the ghost who was haunting him. Now he's our father again."

"Our father? Which one? It's all going away." I retrieved the phone, turned it on, stared at the screen.

"Zane, shut that off. I have a way to help you fix this. That's why they sent me. First, tell me where you put the gun."

I pressed the phone to my forehead. "I put it where you put it."

His voice went up a notch. "You put it back in your pickup?"

"I saw you put it there. They gave me eyes to see."

"You couldn't have seen me. Nobody was in the garage. I— why am I arguing with you? I'll play along with your story."

I banged my head on the table. "I have to stop my head from exploding."

"I have a way to help. Sit here for two minutes. Don't move until I come back."

With my back to the patio door, I itched to turn around so I could keep an eye on him. I hoped shooting me in the back wasn't his idea of a headache cure. He returned and stood over me holding a yellow legal pad and pen.

"Zane, here's how you can feel better. Write out that you're sorry you shot at your father."

He lifted my hand and slipped the pen and pad under it.

"They can't be lied to," I said.

"You won't be lying. Truth is, you were inside my skin when I did it. You forced me to do it. Take responsibility for what you did. Go ahead."

Pressing as hard as I could, I wrote, *I'm sorry I got inside Billy's head and made him shoot at my father.*

Billy snatched the pad away and tore up the first several pages, stuffed them in his pants pocket. "Just write 'I shot at my father' and sign your name."

I pressed a fingertip on each of my eyelids. "Somebody is sticking pins in my eyes."

Billy dragged over a chair until it bumped mine. Before sitting, he slipped a pistol out of his pocket and placed it on the table between us. "This gun will end your suffering. Zane, don't torture yourself by making me call the cops and turn you in. When I tell them you confessed, you'll spend years in jail, no matter how your case goes. And you won't get any meds." He squeezed my arm. "Don't make Dad suffer again. I'll help you end this right here."

I turned to him, my shoulders slumping, and nodded. His eyes shone as he reached for the pistol. Snatching my hand out, I beat him to the draw. I clutched the gun flat on my chest. "They saw this coming."

His eyes raked my face. He leaned forward and pressed his hand on mine, digging the gun into my skin. His raised voice filled my head. "As long as you do the right thing, Zane. Do you want me to stay?"

"No, you keep twisting yourself around inside me. Go in the house and stand with your back to the patio door. I can't have you looking at me."

As soon as he stepped inside, I put the gun in the pocket of my cargo shorts. Reaching into the trash bin next to the table, I lifted up the paper bag covering the tape recorder I'd hidden inside. After I removed the cassette, I went into the yard next to

Ronan's fence, out of sight of the patio. I blew up the bag and gave it a quick slap; the sharp retort snapped the night air. The next sound was the patio door sliding open.

Billy stepped slowly onto the grass, stopping dead when he saw me holding the tape in one hand, and the torn bag in the other.

I threw the tape into Ronan's yard. "You might want to keep this from the cops."

Billy brushed past me and scrambled over the fence. He landed with a thump and a yelp. As I looked over, he was pushing himself off a mass of prickly pear cactus. Stripes of blood from the spines dripped down his arms. Three security spotlights flashed on.

I said, "If Ronan's alarm system is working, right now Prime Security's staff is watching you on a computer screen."

Billy turned his back to the lights and kicked at the prickly pear, finding the tape on top of one of the flat pads. With a grunt, he heaved himself back to my side of the fence, then headed for me. I stood my ground.

He confronted me, blood oozing down his arms. "How many back-up recorders did you have?"

"Call me paranoid, but I have two more, one for the cops, one for Dad and Sallee."

He lunged at me. I stiff-armed him so hard he fell back on the grass. Jumping up, he grabbed the golf club and headed toward me. I used a patio chair to shield myself. He banged on it with the club, arousing a neighborhood dog to bark.

"Knock it off," I said, "You want to wake Sallee and Dad?"

He tossed the club away. When I started to lower the chair, he snatched at it, but I tightened my grip and shoved, knocking him to the grass again. Heaving himself up, he tightened his fists and charged me. I punched him in the stomach. He curled into a ball and sucked in air, gasps and grunts that made me clench my teeth.

"That's for trying to kill my dad."

Billy staggered up and leaned on a patio post, one hand over his belly.

Far off, a thin wail broke into the silence between us. We froze until it faded away.

I wanted Billy gone. "Better make your getaway."

He slammed the door hard enough to shake the house.

Carefully, as if I could be heard outside, I opened the curtains a slit. A patrol car blocked the driveway as Billy unlocked his BMW. When the cops pinned him with a spotlight, he dropped his keys. I let the curtain fall.

"What are you still doing up?"

My father stood behind me, his voice echoing off the tile of the entryway. I sagged, swayed on my feet, but he gripped my arm and steadied me.

"You're safe now, Dad. That's all I wanted."

† † †

MARGARET MORSE lives near South Mountain in Phoenix with her husband Duane and nine rescue dogs. After working for twenty-five years as a public defender in adult and juvenile court for Maricopa County, Margaret retired to follow her dream of becoming a writer. Currently doing final revisions on an urban fantasy mystery, she has had stories published in *Arizona Attorney,* and the Desert Sleuths mystery anthology *How NOT to Survive a Vacation.*

ALL FOUR ONE
Virginia Nosky

The August sun settled behind the White Tank Mountains, streaking the Phoenix sky with plumes of gold. Camelback Mountain's ancient blocks of granite and red sandstone pulsed their residual afternoon heat into the handsome house clinging to its slopes. Indoors, air conditioning whispered around the identical Stratford quadruplets. The culmination of a plot that had occupied their pretty heads for over five years was at last coming into focus.

The door to the walnut paneled library banged open. "What's going on in here?" Jeremiah Stratford glared at his nieces, his dyed moustache bristling blackly with irritation.

Startled, the girls assumed their practiced innocence toward their detested uncle. Alicia glanced at the other three and quickly held out her hand, showing four yellow drinking straws of uneven lengths. The blonde quadruplets clustered around their uncle Jeremiah.

Amelia coaxed, "Hide the straws behind you, Uncle. It's a fun game we're playing. The shortest stick…um…loses."

"Yes, yes, Uncle Precious. Hold them. Help us play our game," the others cried.

Jeremiah's sour face registered disgust. *"Uncle Precious."* It was all he could do to keep from gnashing his teeth. *I can guess what goes on behind their angelic faces.*

But he'd be rid of the brats before long—his younger brother and sister-in-law's progeny were thrown into his life when the two had the selfishness to perish when their yacht went down in a Pacific storm. *Identical quadruplets. What are the odds of that? How did I get so "lucky?" Dumped in my lap when they were noisy four-year-olds. Seventeen years I've put up with them—from thumb-sucking to the whine of their hair dryers and now, regiments of hairy males hanging around. Won't be out of my life for four more years.*

They turn twenty-one next Friday, the first of September. Four more years before the money went to them. By then he should be pretty well set. He'd looted the estate over the course of his guardianship, but there was still plenty left. He should begin digging a lot deeper before time ran out. He nursed visions with his evening Scotch—kicking the Arizona dust off his shoes and sunning himself on pale sands teeming with raven-haired Tahitian beauties. He snorted. Blondes needn't apply.

He'd lived quite luxuriously as the quadruplets' guardian. As their only living relative the courts had dragooned him into raising them. He quickly found the onerous duty handsomely rewarding after being informed that, as their loving uncle, he had access to his brother's fortune. A string of nannies and household help had eased his pain. He'd found if he indulged the girls all their whims, he could indulge his own and the attorneys looked on with benevolence.

His brother and his wife had been pillars of the community, so the quads were newsworthy—their rare births, then as tragic orphans, their first day of school, their proms, beginning classes at Arizona State…all that crap. They were enormously photogenic and the newspapers and magazines loved them—inquiring now about photo spreads for their twenty-first birthday. "The Stratford Quads Are All Grown Up!" That kind of trash. He scowled at the thought.

Alana cooed, "C'mon, Uncle Precious. We need you to help decide."

Jeremiah didn't stifle his annoyance. "What, may I ask is to be decided?"

Amaryllis giggled. "We can't tell you yet. It's a secret. But you'll find out."

Alicia pulled at his hand and wrapped his fingers around the four straws. "It's a surprise. Arrange them behind you, hold them out. Don't be so grouchy, Uncle Precious. It's fun!"

Jeremiah grunted.

Each of the girls stepped forward and took one of the proffered straws from his liver-spotted hand.

Each one held up her straw. It was Alana who exclaimed triumphantly, "I got the short one."

Jeremiah glowered and sniffed suspiciously. "Nitwit. What are you so giddy about?"

Eight blue eyes grew round and serious. "We'll tell you

tomorrow. We promise."

"Bah. More idiocy." He turned and stomped out of the library of the beautiful house his brother had bought with, Jeremiah felt sure, ill-gotten gains. How else? He, Jeremiah was the smart one. He had lived a life of luxury because his oh-so-brilliant-brother rested on the bottom of the deep, deep blue Pacific Ocean. Yes, he, Jeremiah was the smart one.

Later that night the four girls in identical pajamas sat cross-legged in the middle of the floor of Alana's bedroom. They stared down at the gun—dull black against the white plush carpeting. They'd come across it in a drawer in the library gun case five years ago after they found a key in their parents' dressing room. Over weeks they tested the key on every lock and when, finally, it fit the display case drawer, they exulted. They hid the weapon in the folds of a party dress in Alicia's closet. Over the years there had been several plots to kill Uncle Jeremiah, but the plans had been formless, fraught with confusion—their young minds still immature to delicate scheming and nuances of the law. When they turned sixteen they began thinking in earnest.

Their uncle's malfeasance and nastiness had not tapered off as they had grown into teenage bloom—with limpid sapphire eyes, manes of golden hair, achingly beautiful contours. So their hate smoldered into shapeless plans that never jelled. But a year ago, aware their milestone twenty-first birthday was coming up, their plans had taken a harder edge.

They secretly loaded the gun, becoming at ease with the cartridges Father left. At first they worried the weapon would be missed, but Uncle ignored Father's collection, with only a comment from time to time that he would sell it. As the months passed Uncle apparently forgot his plan to dispose of the arms. Their plot began to take a concrete form. They studied criminal laws, researched murder cases on the Internet. What if a murderer could not be positively identified? They saw that the cases languished. Often forever.

They took the gun into the desert and practiced until they felt at ease with its feel in their hands.

How would they shoot dear Jeremiah Precious? In the back? No, he must die knowing his murderer. Well, not exactly know. He never could tell them apart.

† † †

They checked the television schedule and set the date of Thursday, August 31st. The eve of their birthday. Jeremiah would be home. He never missed *American Star*.

Alicia clapped her hands. "Okay sibs, Alana is the shooter. You'll kill Precious at seven o'clock, sweets, when he sits down to watch his program and slobbers over his Scotch. Now, Alana, here's your scenario. We all drive off at five thirty. Alana, split off and park your car around the corner at Carson's. They're out of town. Return home, kill Precious, leave the house, pick up your car, meet Amelia. She'll throw the gun in the canal just north of Hayden Road and McDonald."

Amelia added. "It's deepest there and they just finished draining and cleaning it."

"Right. Then you'll go to Fashion Square. Barney's would be good. Buy something fabulous. You can't dawdle. Our timing is tight."

Alicia continued with the overall plan. "All four cars leave, Alana splits, parks at Carson's. Amaryllis, Amelia and I will meet at the bar at the W. We'll mingle, flirt. Talk to friends. Be seen. Order crazy cocktails. Pay cash with hundred dollar bills. They always look you over. Amaryllis will leave to go to Neiman Marcus. Amelia leaves, meets Alana at the corner of Scottsdale Road and McDonald Drive and gets the gun. Amelia dumps the gun in the canal, then goes to Art Walk on Main Street. Buy something expensive, darling. Use Alana's check. Talk. To anybody."

Amaryllis looked at the other three. "I'll be at Neiman's buying tons of stuff. You'll love what I get. The new fall clothes are so, like, amazing. I'll try on just hundreds of shoes. And boots. The Manolos are so perfect—"

Amelia interrupted. "To the point, babes. To the point."

"Oh. Yes. I'll talk to people, collect lots of receipts."

"Alana, be noticed at Barney's. Hurry to Neiman's. Charge more stuff."

"I'll go to Dillard's from the W," Alicia said. "They have those little credit card thingies you sign and your signature looks weird. I'll swipe Alana's card, sign her name, show her license, then buy all over the store, sign both our names. All our handwriting is similar, but those scribbles could be anybody. Amelia, leave Art Walk and go to Styxx at seven thirty. Just be gorgeous. The bartender loves us. Use your credit card. Sign Alana's name on their little machine. Order another drink from the other bartender and sign your own name."

"Alicia, you'll go…" "Amaryllis, meet me…" "Alana, sign for…" And so they went over their comings and goings. Finally satisfied, they sat back, pleased. Amelia giggled. "Between six and ten there are going to be so many Stratford quads around Scottsdale everybody's heads will swim—they'll swear we were here or there and talked to us. Danced with us."

Alicia looked to the other three. "Dear Ones, why are we doing this? All four one…"

"…and one four all!" they sang.

"We'll synchronize our watches before we leave tomorrow," Alicia said. "Alana, after the big moment, when you leave the house, be *sure* you leave the pool door unlocked for the 'intruder.' Make sure the alarm is off. We'll all be at Styxx between eight and ten thirty and go home at the same time."

Alana smiled. "By seven-oh-two Uncle Jeremiah will be dead."

"Don't miss," said Amaryllis.

Alana held up her hand. "Not on your life. Not on our lives."

"When we get home, we call nine-one-one…" Alicia smiled. "…hysterical that our precious uncle Precious has been attacked by some cruel intruder. We think he's…ta da!…dead."

Peals of laughter floated down the corridors of the beautiful house on Camelback Mountain.

"And we're rid of the crooked bastard. And get all the money."

Alicia put her finger to her lips. "Shhh. We're not supposed to know that."

Amelia held up her hand. "Now. Everybody cry, like we rehearsed. Real tears. Pathetic sobbing. Now, one, two, three, GO!"

After a short sequence of sobs and wails, a cheer could be heard throughout the house. "All four one and one four all!"

At five o'clock, August 31st, all the girls dressed, identical outfits and shoes, careful makeup, blonde hair shining, brushing pearly shoulders. They extravagantly kissed their testy uncle good bye, faces radiant in expectation of the mayhem ahead. At 5:30 they left the house. A blazing sunset would soon settle over the mountains, blanketing the surrounding Valley of the Sun in a breathtaking symphony of deep oranges and golds as Jeremiah Stratford breathed his last.

Four yellow Mini Coopers wound down the drive. One veered off to a side street. The others continued on to the stores and clubs of Scottsdale.

At seven o'clock, Jeremiah Stratford settled in his leather wing chair and switched on his program. He took a long swig of his Scotch and sighed. He loved seeing these no-talent caterwauling oafs dispatched with such sarcasm. It tickled him to see the aching disappointment on their pathetic faces. Hilarious!

"Hi, Uncle Jeremiah. Precious." Alana glided gracefully into the room in her Jimmy Choo ballet flats.

Jeremiah still stared avidly at the screen where a gangly teen warbled something unearthly, unrelated to music. "Dammit, girl," he growled. "Are you still here? I'm never to be disturbed! Get out."

The girl cooed, "I have a present for you, Uncle Precious."

Jeremiah pulled his eyes away from the television. "Bah! I want nothing from you."

Alana peeked at her watch. "We all wanted to give you this in celebration of our birthday." The gun held steady in her hand, a dull black menace.

He stared at the gun. "You wretched brats. Which one are you?" His moustache curled like a small animal over his sneer.

She pulled the trigger. "I'm all of us. One four all."

Book-lined shelves and the luxurious oriental absorbed the sharp crack. A circle of blood bloomed on his chest. Jeremiah's hand reached out to her as he gurgled through the blood that foamed up in his throat. "What have you done? I was…a father to you."

Alana shot again. "Not."

The man crumpled into the widening crimson pool on the jewel-like oriental rug. The chair took the brunt of his head wound. Red gore splattered and smeared onto the dark green leather.

"Bye bye, Uncle Precious. Know you'd loved to have wished us Happy Birthday."

† † †

Detective Mike Hawthorne cleared his throat. "Girls…uh, Ladies, can you show us a room where we can talk? We'll be as quick as possible." He and Detective Jeff Mitford gently guided the weeping beauties out of the library. With backward glances at the shrouded corpse on the floor, they led the men across the marble-tiled entry hall to the living room. The quads crowded onto a cream-colored brocade sofa.

Meeting one of the sisters for the first time was stirring. Meeting four dazzling copies of each other all at once proved a bit unnerving for the policemen, particularly with eight aquamarine eyes brimming with tears.

Hawthorne cleared his throat. "Now, let's go over when you found the body of your uncle."

His words set off a heartbreaking ululation. He waited until they composed themselves. Hawthorne rubbed his Soul Patch, the postage stamp of brown fur he had recently cultivated on his underlip. He was not an unattractive man. Actually, he just missed being handsome—six feet two, blessed with thick brown hair and hazel eyes only a shade too close together. He thought the luxuriant Soul Patch might kick him over the line.

Mitford had given up being handsome a long time ago and got married so it didn't matter anymore. He held a pencil poised over his notebook. "Now, all four of you had been shopping and clubbing and got home at approximately eleven o'clock. Is that right?"

They nodded.

He looked at his watch. "It's now one o'clock. Which one of you found your uncle?"

"We all did," they chorused. Amaryllis broke in. "We all left Styxx a little after ten thirty, got our cars from valet and came home."

Alana swallowed her tears. "We'd *always* come in and give…gave…dear Uncle a goodnight kiss. He worries…worried so when we were out."

Alicia began to cry. "We were celebrating our birthday." She wailed, "Today is our birthday."

This revelation set off a new spate of tears.

Hawthorne squeezed his fur lip with his thumb and

forefinger. "Your birthday? All of you? Well. Uh. You'd all have the same birthday, right?" The girls nodded. "And you're how old today?"

In unison. "Twenty-one."

"So you've reached your...uh, legal adulthood today? Hmm." He scribbled a note in his book. "Mitford, go see if the coroner has taken Mr. Stratford...away." When Mitford had gone, Hawthorne turned a page. "Now, I'll need to know where you all were this evening. When you went out, where. Then I'll let you all go to bed. Unless you'd prefer to sleep elsewhere." The four shook their heads. "Is there someone, a relative maybe, who could come to stay with you? A neighbor?"

Amelia gulped down a sob. "We have each other. It will be all right."

"There will be police department people here, dusting for prints, and processing the scene. But they won't disturb you." He turned a page. "Now, who'd like to go first? I'll have to question you each separately."

Alana held up her hand. "I'll go first." The three others stood, kissed their sister and started for the door.

Hawthorne waited until they'd gone, then turned to Alana. "Now, when did you leave the house?"

† † †

The two detectives sat at the station leafing through notebooks. Hawthorne's chair squeaked as he leaned back, fingering his silky postage stamp. "The uncle sure lived large. Drove a Maserati that cost a buck and a quarter, hand-made suits and shirts. The works. Patek Philippe watch listed at forty-five thou. The girls spent freely, too. He raised them in pretty much the luxury they'd have had if the parents were alive. He kept them in the family home. House makes my place look like a bird's nest. Stratford didn't have a dime when he took over their guardianship as the only living relative. He'd worked sporadically at no end jobs, lived in a rental dump and drove a ratty Chevy. He made out here pretty well, I'd say." He made a note. "The girls are now twenty-one. Does that mean anything?"

"I'm working on it." Mitford frowned and went down a list. "No weapon found. Patio door unlocked. Nothing seems to be missing. Only fingerprints belong to the uncle, household help and the quads. The gun case was locked, nothing appears disturbed, but small arms aren't ordinarily kept on display."

"Yeah, yeah. The girls say they adored their uncle and that he was affectionate with them. Everybody else we talk to says he was a first class prick. We've got so many people who saw the girls the night of the murder, talked to all four of them—we could populate a small town. Everybody seems to know them, but where in hell would you normally find four identical quadruplets who would stop traffic if there was only one of them? Of course they'd be remembered. I doubt if *I'll* ever forget them."

Hawthorne riffled through a stack of receipts. "They sure as hell spent enough in the stores that night, before they hit the bars. Shoes, dresses. One of them, God I can't remember which one, bought a little knick-knack at an Art Walk gallery for two grand. All of them accounted for from a bit before six until ten thirty when they went home, called nine-one-one at eleven o'clock. Coroner says Stratford likely was shot between seven and eight." He flipped his chair up and slapped his hands down on his desk. "And why does this bother the hell out of me?"

† † †

The Stratford quadruplets drifted into the library. Dressed from head to toe in black from Uncle Precious's funeral, their eyes were riveted to where his body had lain.

Amelia was the first to speak. "CarpetDri did a fabulous job cleaning up where Uncle Precious...was. You'd just never dream, would you?"

All four tried valiantly to keep from smiling. They had promised themselves they would be the grieving nieces of their beloved Uncle Precious. All four one, one four all. No slipping. Ever.

Amaryllis wiped an imaginary tear. "I think I'll go to my room and touch up my lipstick before the crowd gets here. Caterers are in the kitchen."

Alicia laughed. "You just want to look pretty for that sorta cute detective."

"Oh God, Allie. He'd be cute if he shaved off that fuzzy hair on his bottom lip that he can't seem to let alone."

Alana laughed. "Yeah. It's stroke, stroke, stroke."

They all smothered giggles.

The four had arranged for drinks and a buffet after the cemetery—in tribute to their beloved uncle. So their grief would have to carry on the rest of the afternoon. Swallowed tears. Gracious replies to hugs and shoulder pats. Then they'd meet with the lawyer tomorrow to hear the good news about the money.

"Nobody who actually *knew* Uncle *Precious* cared enough to come to his funeral," Alana said.

"Despised by all." Amelia smiled. "Except by us, darlings. We *adored* him."

† † †

Hawthorne and Mitford questioned a parade of people again and again:

"Yeah, sure. I talked to both Amelia and Alicia. Bought them both a drink. Amelia gave me her phone number."

"Must have spent a half hour with Amaryllis. She's the quieter one. I can tell them apart. Not everybody can, but I can. "

"Saw Amelia I think it was. Could be another one. You know, talking with a guy."

"Sure I've got a receipt. See? Alana Stratford bought an Etruscan pot from us that night. We delivered it next day. Cops everywhere. What happened?"

"I was with Alicia most of the evening. Ask the bartender. And they danced a lot. Ask anybody. One time all four of them were there. Talk about hot!"

"I helped Amaryllis in the dressing room. The dress looked fabulous. Alana came in and wanted the same dress. I had to order three more. Wow, to look like that."

"I valeted two of their cars. Parked them right next to my stand. All evening."

"Yeah, they were all here. I mixed up kiwi martinis for them."

And more and more and more.

† † †

"Dammit, Mitford. Murders like that are ninety-nine percent by family. One of them had to have done it. But which one? There are dozens who swear they saw them all that night. Uncle siphoned off a bundle from the estate, nobody complained and there's a boatload left. Nobody liked him, but nobody seems mad enough to want him dead."

"The girls *were* to inherit the estate at twenty-five." Jeff doodled on his notes. "Their uncle would be involved managing the estate until then...so, he could still help himself for another four years."

"What happens now?"

"If something happened to him, the entire amount goes to the girls when they turn twenty-one. It doesn't appear they were ever told that. It was in a codicil. Lawyer says he had to look it up. The attorney who drew up the trusts with the parents died fifteen years ago. But the parents were young. Probably never dreamed they'd go at the same time."

"A body. No weapon, solid alibis, a motive we can't prove." Hawthorne stroked his bare underlip tenderly. "Are we looking at the perfect crime?"

Mitford eyed him. "Why'd you shave that off?"

"One of the girls told me I was better looking without it."

"Which one?"

"Beats me."

† † †

The quadruplets filed into the library, faces solemn. The lawyer motioned them to chairs. He sat behind Uncle Precious's massive desk and riffled through papers while they arranged themselves.

He cleared his throat. "I wish to inform you of the financial arrangements made by your parents when the four of you were born. As to certain conditions vis-à-vis the estate, with the death of your Uncle Jeremiah Stratford, what was to vest to you when you were twenty-five *now* reverts equally to each of you girls now that you have reached the age of twenty-one, as per the wishes of your parents."

The quadruplet's faces registered surprise, then smiles, excitement, as they whispered among themselves.

"Ahem. Your uncle appropriated the funds quite extensively for his own use. Your expenses took a large toll, this large house made further inroads. But your parent's estate is still worth over twelve million dollars. Each of you is now a wealthy woman."

After the lawyer had gone, Alicia shrieked, "We've got the money! We're rich!"

Alana stood. "About that." The other three looked up. "I deserve a *waaay* bigger share. I shot the bastard."

"Huh???"

Alicia's voice turned icy. "Just a minute, pussycat. *I* made all the complicated plans. I was the 'brains' of this little adventure. My share should be *huge!* You were all running around in dopey little circles. If it hadn't been for me—"

Amelia snapped, "*I* was the one who dumped the gun. That took *horrendous* chances. Except for me, it would have all fallen apart."

"My, my, my. Aren't you all greedy." Amaryllis stood and stretched, her smile sweet. Innocent. "Remember, darlings, all *I* did was shop and go clubbing. How was *I* to know you three had cruelly murdered dear Uncle Jerry."

†   †   †

VIRGINIA NOSKY has published seven novels, is an Independent Publishers Gold Medal winner, screenwriter and published poet. The author mostly sets her stories in Arizona and the Southwest. She believes its climate and topography are inherently theatrical and add drama to her work. Her latest novels are *The Fall From Paradise Valley* and *To A Certain Degree* (Champagne Books). She lives in Paradise Valley, Arizona with husband Richard, golden retriever Barkis and Lab Peaches. Visit her website: www.VirginiaNosky.com.

WHERE THE OLD AND NEW WEST MEET
KRIS NERI

People romanticize the Old West. The tourists I see play at living in an old Western town, though they're quick to whine when the cable goes out in their rooms. And the cowhands who work for the neighboring ranches—they look like the real deal on horseback, until you notice the cell phones hanging from their belts.

None of them would find Old West as much fun if they were condemned to a lifetime in it as I was. To break free, I made a deal with a very New West devil, and now I found my neck—and more importantly, my sister's—in a noose that couldn't get any tighter.

† † †

I'm Jessie Cartwright, owner of the Wilde West Town theme park near Camp Verde, Arizona, originally the creation of Dusty Wilde, the old cowboy film star. When Western movies faded in popularity, Dusty bid Hollywood goodbye and opened this park, which he ran it until his death at the ripe old age of eighty-two in the early 1960s.

Ten years ago, on a family vacation, we stumbled across the abandoned park. Dad, who'd always loved Westerns, spent hours striding up and down its wooden sidewalks and popping through the swinging doors of its ramshackle saloon. Too bad he hadn't noticed the holes in the roofs, or that sunlight streamed through walls that should have been solid. He'd tracked down Dusty's heir, an aging niece, and begged her to accept his and mom's savings for the rundown place. That was during my senior year in high school, when they dragged my younger sister Lindsay and me off to live in Wilde West Town.

Even if the Old West wasn't hugely popular anymore, the venture might have worked well enough. We'd begun restoring it and were attracting some visitors. But one cold, rainy night mom and dad were driving my sister to a school play when their car hit an icy patch and went over an embankment.

The police didn't find them until the next day. Poor Linds, who had to watch them slip away, went into a catatonic state from which she had still not emerged.

I discovered Dad had run up a mountain of debt, leaving me in charge of a theme park that few people wanted to visit, and the sole provider of a child who'd need constant care.

That was nine years ago. My sentence in the Old West had begun.

† † †

Today Wilde West Town was in an even more sorry state. Though Lindsay was now nineteen, the fragile girl with the straggly blonde hair still stared out of vacant blue eyes. I couldn't give up the rundown park, yet neither could I take a regular job. Not only did I lack job skills, having forgone education for the care and feeding of my sister and this blasted place, I couldn't afford to pay anyone else to care for her. Wherever I worked in the fake town, I kept her near me, until it was time to put her to bed.

The only sign of my frustration was that I stripped the place of any vestige of Dusty Wilde, the man who created the stupid town, starting with the grinning portrait over the hotel lobby fireplace. I couldn't bring myself to blame dad for sticking us with it, but I could blame Dusty for creating it. Now I couldn't even remember what Dusty had looked like. I only kept his name in "Wilde West Town" because I couldn't afford a new sign.

But I was losing my battle to keep us afloat. That morning, my cook, Ted, left the kitchen and headed for the barn, where we hid anachronistic things like cars that would intrude on our Old West mystique.

"Ted, please don't leave. I have a busload of tourists coming in tonight for a chuck wagon dinner and saloon show."

"Jessie, I don't want to go, but my last three paychecks have bounced."

"I'll have money again soon," I said, scarcely above a whisper. Could he see how ashamed I was of how I'd be making it?

"Kid, I can't feed my family on promises. The coffee shop in

Camp Verde will start paying me for real today." With that he climbed into his minivan and drove off.

Though I'd never before admitted defeat, I started pounding the ground. Hot angry tears flowed, and I screamed, "Noooo, I can't take anymore. Mom and Dad, do you hear me up there? I need a break. No, I need a miracle."

†   †   †

After I cried myself dry, I went to the hotel kitchen to see what I could accomplish on my own. My staff had abandoned me, but there were a couple of guys in town who would fake a shootout on Main Street, if I let them drink enough booze. I didn't know how I would serve a chuck wagon dinner in the churchyard while simultaneously playacting as the dance hall girl in the saloon, but I'd figure that out later.

In the kitchen, a man stood beside my unseeing sister. Dressed in Western garb, he took off his white cowboy hat, and gave me an appealingly crooked grin, saying, "Miss Jessie, I hear you need a new cook. I'd like to apply for the job."

When did he hear that? Ted had just left. "Sorry, pal, but I can't pay you."

"I'd be plumb happy to take the job for room and board. I'll bed down in the bunkhouse."

We'd never gotten around to fixing up the bunkhouse. Springs popped out of mattresses decades past their expiration date and so much dirt had accumulated it drifted like snow. "You'd better find a bed in the hotel." Though where I'd fit that busload of tourists if he took a room, I couldn't say. "The bunkhouse..."

"Don't worry about it, Miss Jessie. I'll clean it up."

I shrugged. His funeral. "Drop the 'miss,' okay? Keep the Western gibberish for the guests."

"I reckon I could do that."

When was he going to start? "What's your name?"

He hesitated. "You can call me...Duncan."

Should I trust this cowboy? What choice did I have? Even if he was a serial killer, I had to accept his help.

†   †   †

We made it through the bus visit. The gunfight the local boys had staged wasn't pretty—they passed out on Main Street, dead drunk before firing a shot. Fortunately, the tourists regarded it as fun.

The next morning in the office, where Dad's papers were boxed against one wall, I worked on our finances. Even after depositing the tour company's check, I couldn't cover this month's bills.

The ping of a new email sounded in my Mac. That computer was one of the few good things I owned. A geek friend in town gave me his castoff gadgets when he bought the latest electronics.

Duncan wandered in, still dressed in the same cowboy duds.

"Ooh-eee, what is that?" He stared at the aluminum MacBook Pro.

He was kidding, right? With him watching in fascination over my shoulder, I clicked on my browser.

"I told you, pal, drop the cowboy act." I opened the lone email in the box, which read, "Coming Wednesday. Five thousand dollar payment." It was unsigned, but I knew too well who had sent it.

Five thousand bucks would keep us afloat for a couple of months. But it would also plunge me into the depths of hell, knowing what I had to do to make it. I hung my head in shame.

Duncan lifted my face with his finger and said, "Miss Jessie, why don't you tell me what kind of trouble you've gotten yourself into."

† † †

My deal with the devil. "A coyote contacted me," I said softly. "Enrico Morales."

Duncan frowned. "A coyote? Them wild dogs?"

"No, the people who bring in illegal aliens from Mexico."

He frowned, confused. Did he live in a cave?

"I guess most of these coyotes do what people pay them for, but not Morales. He brings in young girls and sets up temporary bordellos in various hotels around the west. Morales has an email list of johns, and once he and the girls arrive, those bastards come in droves. The other illegals—the men and older women—they stow in the barn, until others come for them.

People who pay for lifetime servants." I felt my own face twisting with distaste. "They sell human beings, one way or the other. And I help them. I've tried to get out of the arrangement, but they've threatened to use Linds in their brothels."

"Ain't there any lawmen in this town you can turn to?"

"The cops would arrest me—and they should. But what would happen to Lindsay?"

Duncan thought for a moment. "Can you shoot?"

"For real, you mean? No, why would I? We use blanks—what does it matter if we can't really aim?"

"What are they teaching you young'ns today?"

He wasn't that much older than me. Maybe early thirties or so, though he did act more like an out-of-touch old man.

After a while, he said, "There are tunnels downstairs, right?"

How did he know that? "More like connected basements, but yeah." That was where I had stashed all the Dusty Wilde memorabilia.

A slow smile crept across Duncan's face. "Miss Jessie, I might have an idea how we can drive your varmints away."

† † †

I'd forgotten how much memorabilia was piled up down in those basements: movie posters, Western clothes, loads of antique guns and the original reels of Dusty Wilde's films. I even spotted the portrait of Dusty that I'd taken from the hotel lobby. It was turned toward the wall. I didn't have the heart to look at it.

We don't often see basements in the sandy Arizona soil, but Dusty Wilde had the good sense to not only include them in his design, but to connect them. If this had been a vibrant theme park, with lots of staff, the modern world could go on below, without destroying the illusion up above.

"What are you thinking, Duncan?" I asked, watching him paw through boxes of guns.

"If you could rustle up even a few more men, they could use these connected basements to pop up in different parts of the town, to make those outlaws believe we have a small army here."

"There's nobody left I can call on for help. I've had to ask for so much since our parents died." I looked at the reels of old Western movies and felt the first glimmer of hope I'd known in a long time. "What if we just made them *think* we have an army?"

† † †

I did have one friend I could turn to, my computer patron, Casey. Casey was a teddy bear of a man with a shy smile hidden behind a black beard.

When I told him about my troubles, he said, "Jessie, why didn't you tell me things were this bad. I could lend you—"

I waved away that suggestion before he could make it. I'd learned my lesson about being beholden from my deal with Morales. Even for Linds, I wasn't doing that again.

"Casey, it's enough if you can help me execute my idea."

Here was my thinking: we had TVs all over Wilde West Town. In the hotel rooms, as well as the hotel lobby, the saloon and other public spaces. But they were hidden behind wooden panels, to keep modern life from intruding too much. They were also all connected by an internal network that Casey had set up, which allowed me to screen some of Dusty Wilde's old films in particular rooms.

I pointed to the old reels of movies we hadn't yet transferred to DVD. "What if we record the sounds of men's voices making threats, as well as gunfire? If we orchestrate our selections right, and play them on the TVs behind the panels, when Morales and his thugs are asleep, they might believe they're under attack and go."

"But really you and Duncan will be here alone with Lindsay?" Casey asked. I'd already refused to let Casey stay. He was a computer wizard, not a fighter. I was also hoping to get Duncan to hide out.

"Do you have any sleeping draught, Miss Jessie?" Duncan asked.

Sleeping draught? Was that like sleeping pills? "Why would I? Hard as I work, I fall asleep as soon as I hit the pillow."

He tented his fingers over his nose and thought about it. "A Yavapai medicine woman once taught me how to make a real good sleeping draught."

"Give me the ingredients. We might be able to find them in a health food store."

"Health food? Isn't all food healthy?"

What was wrong with this cowboy?

He shrugged sheepishly. "Anyway, Miss Jessie, it's kind of a secret recipe. The Yavapai rez is near here, right? I should be able to pluck up everything I need if I just wander in that direction."

Picking weeds in the desert? Whatever. "What would we do with this potion once you make it?"

"We'll mix it into our varmints' drinks." Duncan said with his crooked grin. "These bad ol' boys won't know what hit 'em."

"Not a bad idea, Duncan," I said. Could he really create a knockout solution? "Maybe I can use some on the johns, too. You know, to give the girls a break."

"That's the spirit, Miss Jessie," Duncan said.

"What about you, Casey? Can you make us a DVD with the sounds of threats and gunfire?" I asked.

"I *can* do it." Casey rattled off some techno-babble to explain how he'd carry it out. "But I don't feel good about it. The odds of this working sound slim to me."

Slim chances were always better than none.

Casey said he'd work faster if we'd leave him alone. Duncan insisted we sprinkle some of the old guns in places around the town. I couldn't see why we needed them—there was plenty of Western crap everywhere—but I felt too anxious to argue. To be honest, even with my crazy plan, I didn't think we'd survive.

I never saw Duncan cook his brew, or even pick his weeds. He must have worked on it while I was placing guns all over town. Mixing recipes from Indian medicine women was a little too Old West for my taste anyway. Later that afternoon, Duncan brought me a jar of a nearly clear liquid that he assured me wouldn't change the taste of the drinks. We hid it behind the bar.

Morales and his crew showed up the following afternoon, along with the vans of frightened immigrants. Morales didn't look like a thug. He was tall and strikingly handsome, like the Spanish don in some gracious old movie. Only his gray-brown eyes looked as cold and dead as stones.

His men were as thuggish as you'd expect, though. They grabbed me and made disgusting sounds whenever I came near.

Not Morales—he limited our contact to the same threat he made every time. He squeezed my arm so hard, it brought tears to my eyes. "Don't go getting any *loco* ideas, Jessie. No *policía*. Behave and you'll be five grand richer when we leave. Otherwise, that pretty little sister of yours will become one of my girls."

His men opened the doors of the van, and the frightened immigrants stumbled out. It was the haunted looks in their eyes that devastated me, the knowledge that their American dream had taken a detour from which they might never return. Mine too.

†   †   †

In my dancehall girl garb, I poured drinks in the saloon for all the brothel customers. Casey had gone, after having set his DVD to play in the hotel's rooms tonight, operated from a computer in the basement. I made Duncan promise to stay down there, too. I sprinkled a good helping of Duncan's brew into all the drinks I poured.

My gut was knotted like a fist. I didn't begin to relax until I saw how fast the buzz came on in the johns. I prayed they'd pass out before they forced themselves on those girls. I also took a beer to the guard in the barn who kept a rifle trained on the men and older women.

I foisted dosed drinks on all of them, though Morales himself never touched a drop. To my surprise, Duncan came into the saloon carrying a sandwich, which he placed down before Morales; a watery mayonnaise dripped out from between the slices of bread. This was a different Duncan. Instead of flashing his usual irreverent grin, he seemed remarkably submissive.

"I thought you might like something to eat, sir," Duncan said.

Morales ignored the sandwich. "I haven't seen you before," he said.

"I'm Miss Jessie's assistant."

"Assistant, huh? So Jessie's putting my money to good use." Morales tore a bite from the sandwich.

When Duncan turned away, he winked, and I knew some of that medicine woman's potion made into that sandwich's mayo.

The nights the bordello operated out of Wilde West Town were the worst—loud and raucous. But this night became eerily quiet, with every man in the town fast asleep. To my surprise, the girls in the hotel and the people in the barn didn't run away when they could have.

Right on schedule, Casey's DVD began to play. Thugs and johns in drugged and drunken stupors awoke to sound of threats and gunfire. Not surprisingly, the johns stumbled off first. The thug brigade didn't last much longer. I would have thought Morales could have recruited stronger soldiers, but they caved fast. Before we knew it, Duncan and I faced each other alone.

"It actually worked," I said, sighing in relief. What was in that stuff that Duncan made?

"It sure did, Miss Jessie."

"Don't celebrate yet," said a voice from behind us.

Morales. He hadn't left along with his men. He dragged Linds, holding a gun to her head.

"This little *chica* and I are going to party upstairs. If either of you try to stop me, she won't leave that room alive."

Before I could react, Duncan pulled a gun from his holster and fired, missing Lindsay by mere inches. Blood spurted from Morales's shoulder. With a gasp, he dropped my catatonic sister.

I was so stunned by the fact that Duncan's pistol was loaded with live ammo, and that he drew and fired with such ease and accuracy, I didn't even go to my sister, who had collapsed on the floor.

"Señor Morales, you best leave now. And if you ever come back this way, you're gonna find the law chasing you," Duncan warned.

"Yeah? You and what army?" Morales demanded. His hand clutched his wounded shoulder, but we couldn't count him out yet.

"This army," Duncan said with a flip of his thumb over his shoulder.

Many of the illegals Morales had brought here stepped forward, with guns cocked and ready to shoot. The guns Duncan had insisted we spread about. If anyone had reason to shoot Morales, they did. Morales accurately read himself outgunned. He stumbled out of the hotel. Minutes later, I heard his van's engine fire up outside and drive off. I didn't care where he went, as long as he left.

Filling the silence that followed was the sound of weeping. Who...? Huddled on the floor, Lindsay was crying. All these years and nothing had broken through the walls of her mental prison, until now.

Duncan gently stroked her hair. "Miss Linds, you've seen the worst this world has to offer. If you put it all behind you now, I think you might be surprised by how much better it can be."

† † †

The next few days passed in a blur. Lindsay's connection to the world grew stronger every day. Duncan and I offered Morales's prisoners the option of staying with us or leaving. Most decided to help us to spruce up the place.

Duncan spent some time alone in the office every day. I had no idea what he did in there. Since I suspected he was trying to teach himself to use the Mac, I decided not to intrude, so as not to embarrass him.

Weeks later, when he told me he was leaving, I felt a pang of regret.

"You and Miss Linds, you'll be fine now. It's time I move on. But if you two ever need me, I'll know it and come back."

I watched him walk away with more sadness than I'd felt since our parents died.

At the hotel door, he turned back. "Oh, Miss Jessie, you should look through some of them papers your daddy left. When he passed on, he was working on getting certified by some historical group. That should allow Wilde West Town to secure some grants." With that he walked out the door.

I noticed that Dusty Wilde memorabilia was now scattered around the hotel lobby again. Dusty's portrait hung up over the fireplace. I stared at it. No! It wasn't possible. Same crooked grin, same cowboy clothes. Duncan looked just like Dusty Wilde. But Dusty Wilde had died fifty years ago, as an old man, not a young cowboy.

I remembered the day I'd cried, the day I screamed to the heavens that I needed a miracle. Was it possible? I drew closer to the portrait and saw the name under the portrait: Duncan "Dusty" Wilde. I staggered away in shock.

I ran to the bunkhouse. It looked exactly as it always had, caked with decades of dirt. Duncan couldn't have been sleeping there. Where…?

I went to the road. Off in the distance, I could see Duncan walking by the shoulder. Not Duncan—Dusty. If that could be believed. Who would have thought Dusty Wilde would return to save his town, and us?

"Dusty," I called.

He turned my way, and with a flash of his crooked grin, he waved. Then he just faded away. Maybe Dusty, but maybe also... an...angel.

I returned to the office in a daze, just as the phone rang.

The caller identified herself as Ms. Howard, from the Arizona Historical Foundation. "Miss Cartwright, I wanted to let you know that your theme park has been approved for a sizeable grant. Your father began the paperwork years ago. We never understood why he didn't follow through until your assistant called to explain."

"My...assistant?"

"I need to review some of the material with you, however. My connection with your assistant was bad, like a cell phone call from a long distance."

I laughed. "Ms. Howard, it was long distance, all right. You can't imagine *how* long a distance."

† † †

KRIS NERI's latest novels, *Revenge for Old Times' Sake*, the newest adventure in her Agatha, Anthony, Macavity Award-nominated Tracy Eaton mysteries, and the first book in her paranormal series, *High Crimes on the Magical Plane*, were both Lefty Award nominees for Best Humorous Mystery. Kris has published some sixty short stories and is a two-time Derringer Award winner and a two-time Pushcart Prize nominee for her short fiction. She is co-owner of The Well Red Coyote bookstore in Sedona.

DIABLO RANCH
ISABELLA MALDONADO

We rounded the edge of the wash along the bottom of the parched floodplain. Majestic saguaros stood sentinel on the banks above us, reaching toward the turquoise sky. The heat was palpable, and our horses were eager for the last leg of our ride to the stable.

"All right," Earl called out to us. "Let 'em fly!" We barely touched their flanks and the geldings exploded into a full gallop. Hot air blasted my face as I fought to stay in the saddle. Born and raised in South Phoenix, I had ridden horseback on my grandfather's farm in Mexico. A rush of adrenaline coursed through me.

Ethan Averly galloped beside me, looking smug with his perfect show ring form and ridiculous English riding boots. "Tallyho!" He laughed and spurred his mount.

I leaned forward on Corona, a chestnut and white paint, gripping with my knees, and surged ahead. We raced over the uneven ground back to the stable. The other three riders thundered in moments later, kicking up a plume of dust as they reined in hard.

"I didn't know you were such an experienced rider, Miss Cruz," Ethan said.

"I'm a cop in Phoenix. I really don't have much time to ride."

He looked at me speculatively. "Equestrian unit?"

"Never had the pleasure. I'm a homicide detective."

Four pairs of eyes stared as if seeing me for the first time.

When I arrived at Diablo Ranch earlier that morning, we introduced ourselves over breakfast. I didn't elaborate about the details of my work. I simply said my name was Veranda Cruz and that I worked for the police department.

"What do you do with the police?" Troy Merchant, another guest, asked as he passed a basket of muffins across the table.

I'm a 33-year-old Latina who looks ten years younger. They'd probably assumed I was a file clerk. "I go where I'm needed," I said, closing the subject. I didn't say I was here because my partner, Jason, had called his Uncle Earl for a favor. Earl owned a dude ranch in Wickenburg, Arizona and was happy to accommodate an extra guest for the weekend.

I also needed to clear my mind and make a decision that could change the course of my entire career.

The other guests were with Averly Enterprises, an import-export business based in Los Angeles. The four top executives had come to the ranch for a strategic planning retreat. Ethan Averly was Chief Executive Officer and his younger brother, Colin, Chief Financial Officer. There was a strong family resemblance between the brothers. Both in their late forties, they were slightly built and pale. Ethan's fair hair was almost completely gone on top, while Colin's noticeably receded.

As we chatted during the meal, I learned that the brothers had inherited the multi-million dollar company from their father, who built the business decades ago. His two sons and daughter had grown up knowing nothing but private schools, designer clothes, and of course, riding lessons.

Troy Merchant was Vice President in charge of exports. Tall and athletic with thick brown hair and hazel eyes, his dimpled smile was quick, if somewhat forced. He mentioned he was married to Ethan and Colin's sister. "We like to keep things in the family at Averly Enterprises," he said.

Ruby Pierce was the VP for imports. "I'm not in the family," she said, looking steadily at Troy, "I earned my position through hard work, not by birth or marriage." There was an uptick of tension in the room as her pinched face tightened in a frame of short-cropped red hair. Breakfast had ended on that note, and we all prepared for a long outing in the desert.

Now in the late afternoon sun, I patted Corona's soaked neck. My saddle-sore haunches protested as I swung my right leg over and down. Earl's main ranch hand, Miguel, took the reins from us and led the horses into the barn.

Earl looked at his watch. "You can all shower up and relax for two hours. Cookie will ring the triangle for chow at six o'clock. When you hear the call, food'll be on the table in ten minutes."

Our tired group shuffled toward the main hall. After a long, cool shower, I slipped into fresh jeans and a T-shirt, pulled on cowboy boots, and went looking for Earl. I found him in the stable with Miguel, grooming the horses.

"Want some help?" I asked.

Miguel smiled. "We don't let guests do this kind of work, Miss Cruz."

"I'm not afraid to get my hands dirty."

"I'm sure that's true from what I hear," Earl cut in. "But you'll be sore enough tomorrow without addin' to it."

"Tomorrow! I'm sore now."

Both men laughed. "You need somethin'?" Earl asked.

"I wanted to thank you for your hospitality."

"No need. That nephew of mine told me you just arrested a real psycho serial killer after trackin' him for six months. He also said you've got some thinkin' to do. A dose of fresh desert air should be good for what ails you."

I was touched by Earl's insight. My partner had obviously told his uncle about my dilemma. I had recently taken the Sergeant's exam and had been notified that I was in the next group to attend supervisor training. If I accepted the promotion, I'd leave homicide and be on a management track for the rest of my career. I had to decide by Monday. I confided to Jason that, while I felt murder investigations were my true calling, the grisly death scenes took a toll on me. Intruding into the private grief of victims' relatives was like salting an open wound. Sometimes family members learned ugly truths about their loved ones. The facts ultimately had to come out, even if it caused more pain in the process.

Miguel interrupted my reverie. "We're planning a nice demonstration after dinner." He pointed toward four beautiful horses, two black and two white, snuffling in their hay bins. "I'm getting ready to tack 'em up when I hear the chow bell." Ornately tooled black leather bridles and saddles waited in front of each stall.

"They're gorgeous," I said.

"My pride and joy," Earl said. "I don't rent them out for trail riding. They're competition horses. You won't believe the maneuvers they can do. You'll see this evening. We have a lighted ring all set up and the horses are ready to go." Earl smiled. "Why don't you look around at the main hall entry area while we finish up here? There's a display case full of interesting local history."

"Thanks, I will." I headed back to the large building with a façade like an old west tavern.

I lost track of time in the foyer of the main hall looking at an enormous row of glass cabinets with sepia photos, worn clothing and yellowed news clippings from over a hundred years ago. I heard the chow call and realized I was famished. Within ten minutes everyone sat at the table except the two brothers, Ethan and Colin. Cookie, a stout rough-hewn man wearing a denim apron covered in barbeque sauce, went outside and rang the triangle again.

Ruby rolled her eyes and plopped her napkin down beside her fork. "I'm going to get them." She got up and stalked out of the main hall toward the guest wing.

The rest of us looked at the heaping platters and bowls laden with T-bone steaks, potatoes, salad, corn bread and baked beans. Everything smelled heavenly.

A shrill scream jarred me from all thoughts of food. Everyone shared a moment of stunned silence, then chair legs scraped the floor as we scrambled to jump up. I rounded the corner to the guest wing first and saw Ruby standing at the end of the hall, frozen in place. Her mouth was wide open, though no sound escaped. She pointed inside the doorway to the guest room in front of her.

As the others tried to calm Ruby, I looked inside the room and saw two bodies lying motionless on the floor. Ethan was crumpled in a heap, his head so badly bludgeoned I could only recognize him by his clothing from earlier that day. A branding iron lay next to him.

Colin was sprawled on his back nearby wearing a bathrobe, a massive gash across his throat. Blood had sprayed on the floor, walls, and furniture and pooled under his neck. He held a large, bloody knife in his right hand. I ran into the room, bent down next to Ethan and laid my fingers across his carotid artery. His skin felt cool to the touch. I found no pulse.

My stomach clenched. The metallic smell of blood assailed my nostrils as pictures of mutilated bodies from the recent serial killer case edged into my mind. I pushed them back, swallowed the lump in my throat and forced myself into detective mode. I narrowed my eyes and looked more closely at the bodies.

As the others stood in the hallway, Earl elbowed his way into the room. "Should we start CPR while someone calls for an ambulance?"

I pointed at the underside of Ethan's exposed arm. "See that dark purplish coloring beneath his skin?" Earl nodded. Then I indicated Colin's leg. "That's called lividity. Gravity has caused the blood in their bodies to pool at the lowest point. Both of these men have been dead for at least half an hour."

I stood and spoke to the group. "This is now a crime scene. I'll be in charge until I'm relieved by local authorities." I turned to Earl. "Is there a landline here for emergencies?"

"Yep, in the kitchen."

"Call nine-one-one and advise them we have two deaths. Tell them there's a homicide detective from Phoenix on scene. Let them know first indications are that it's a homicide-suicide, but make it clear I'm not definite on that yet."

"Got it. Anything else?"

"Gather everyone in the main hall. Be sure no one leaves. Have Miguel stay with them and come back here with a first aid kit if you have one."

Earl left the room and began shepherding the group toward the main hall. I turned my attention back to the scene in front of me.

A few minutes later, Earl returned and handed me a small box with a red cross on it. "Emergency folks are about twenty minutes away. I told 'em what you said, but they're sending an ambulance anyway along with the police."

I nodded. "That's standard procedure." I opened the kit, retrieved a pair of latex gloves, and snapped them on. "I don't like this."

"How so?" Earl asked as he started to come closer.

I held my hand up, palm out. "Don't go any farther. I'm used to working around crime scenes. I need to check some things to make sure we aren't in danger, but we don't want to contaminate potential evidence any more than necessary. Something's not right."

"Such as?"

I blew out a long breath. "I've been on a lot of suicides. I've never seen anyone slash their neck open like this. It's not impossible, but it's improbable." I pointed to the walls. "His jugular was cut. That causes a lot of blood spatter, which helps to determine what happened."

I carefully walked to Ethan's body, bent down and lifted his arm. An outline of the arm was defined on the floor by droplets of blood surrounding it. "You see? There's no blood beneath Ethan's body, which indicates he died first and wasn't moved after he was killed."

"So you think Colin killed Ethan and then himself?"

"Appears that way." I noticed a thin stack of papers near his body and pointed. "That looks like some kind of financial report. I'll wait for the local PD to check that out." I crossed the floor carefully. "It appears Ethan was killed with this branding iron." I bent over and squinted at a wrought iron rod with a decorative letter D on one end. There were clumps of hair matted with blood stuck to the lettered end. "There's one of these in my room, but it's in the shape of a triangle."

"Every guest room has one propped against the window sill," Earl said. "For atmosphere."

"I wonder what Ethan was doing while Colin grabbed the branding iron."

Earl waved to get my attention. "What's that piece of paper lying on the bed?"

I tiptoed around coagulating puddles of blood to the edge of the bed and leaned over a handwritten page. "This appears to be a suicide note. It's signed, Colin Averly."

"What's it say?"

I scanned the message quickly. "Basically, that Colin was embezzling from Averly Enterprises. Ethan discovered it and confronted him. Colin freaked out and killed him. He then apologizes and says he has to end it." I straightened up and shook my head. "This note is crap."

"How so? It spells out what Colin was thinkin', right?"

"It sounds way too contrived." I turned to the bed again and squatted down so I could peer underneath the note. "Now that's interesting."

"What?"

"The note is propped against the throw pillow. There are two small droplets of blood just visible on the bedspread beneath where the note was placed, but none on the note itself."

"Naw," Earl said. "That would mean Colin put the note there after he cut his own throat. Not possible, right?"

I nodded and bent down to examine the floor near the edge of the bed by my feet. "Bingo."

Earl looked exasperated as he craned his neck to see over my shoulder. "What?"

"It's a highly technical police term. It means I've spotted something important." I grinned as he raised his eyebrows. "There's some blood on the floor with a smudge that resembles the toe of a shoe. If a third person, the killer, was in this room, he or she would have to stand about here to put the note on the bed."

"You mean there's a killer here?" The color drained from Earl's face.

"I believe there is." I thought about my service weapon, a Glock .40, secured in a gun safe at home. "Look, Earl, I need a gun. Do you have anything here?"

"Sure, we have shotguns for pest control."

"No, I need a sidearm."

"My granddaddy's Colt forty-five Peacemaker is locked in the display cabinet out front."

"Is there ammo for it?"

"Sure 'nuff."

"Would you mind loaning it to me?"

"My granddaddy was a Deputy U.S. Marshal. I think it's just what you need." Earl left the room and returned a few minutes later carrying a Colt with a seven and a half-inch barrel. He half-cocked the hammer to free the cylinder, loaded one round, skipped a chamber, then loaded four in a row. He closed the loading gate, pulled the hammer back and let it fall on an empty chamber.

"This gun's an antique single action revolver. You don't load all six chambers, and you have to cock it to shoot each time," Earl said. He held up a thick leather gun belt, its loops loaded with twelve additional bullets. "Granddaddy was a tall skinny guy. They used to call him 'Slim.' Should fit you okay."

I put the belt around my waist, cinching it as tightly as I could. It still fell down around my hips, but stayed there, thanks to my Latina curves. I took the Peacemaker and slid it into the holster.

"I look like Calamity Jane," I said, rolling my eyes.

"Hey, it's better than trying to carry that hog leg around stuffed down your pants."

He had me there. "Let's go to the main hall. I want to ask a few questions before the local police arrive."

When we entered the room, all eyes turned to me, then dropped to the gun on my hip. "Here's the deal," I said without preamble. "This was not a homicide-suicide. It was a double murder." I delivered the news bluntly for shock effect.

Carefully watching their faces, I went on. "The killer made a mistake. A bit of blood was smeared by a shoe. All of your shoes will be collected for evidence. They'll be analyzed for trace amounts of blood at the DPS forensic lab. There's a chemical called luminol that will show blood stains invisible to the naked eye."

Troy lurched forward and grabbed his stomach. "I think I'm going to be sick." He jumped up and ran from the room.

I glanced at Earl. "Stay here and watch everyone. I'm going to keep an eye on Troy."

Earl pulled me aside and whispered, "Let me go with you, I don't trust him."

"I don't either. There are really only two suspects, Ruby and Troy. They're the only ones here with enough information to leave that note. My whole speech about the shoe print stain was really only to sweat the culprit."

"You mean you can't find the stain?" Earl asked.

"Crime scene investigators will be able to. I just wanted to see who got twitchy when I brought it up. I need to check on Troy. Stay here. If he's the killer, he's feeling cornered and very dangerous right now."

I walked to the edge of the hallway leading back to the guest wing and peeked around the corner. All of the doors were closed. Troy's room was across from mine. I knocked and called his name. No response. I twisted the doorknob. Locked. Not waiting for a key, I kicked the door open. The room was empty. I looked out the open window and could barely make out a figure on horseback galloping away under a darkening sky.

I raced out into the main hall and grabbed Earl's arm. "Troy's got one of your horses and he's heading west." The others stared as Earl and I ran out to the barn. One of the black competition horses was missing. The other three paced restlessly in their stalls, agitated by the commotion.

"Damn! They were all tacked up for the program. He took Fiero," Earl said. His jaw tightened as he grabbed a shotgun from a rack on the wall and strode toward the other three horses.

"Earl, it's not safe for you to go after him. He's already killed two people and he may be armed, we don't know. Just tell me which of these other ones can catch Fiero and I'll chase him down."

"First," Earl said through clenched teeth, "that bastard killed my guests and stole my horse. I'm goin' after him no matter what you say. Second, you'd get lost. It'll be dark in a few minutes, but I've known this place since I was a pup. I'll find him."

I only had seconds to make a decision. Earl swung up on a white horse as I hesitated. I didn't like taking a civilian along on a manhunt, but I knew I had no chance of finding Troy on my own. "All right," I said. "Which is the fastest one left?"

"Take your pick."

I walked over to the black gelding. Tactically, I'd have preferred we both had a dark mount to present less of a target in case Troy was armed. Darkness was falling fast, and I could hide in the shadows better. Leaning into my horse's stride as we pelted across the craggy ground, we rode out hard to the west.

A short time later, I heard the loud crack of a gunshot as we galloped into a narrow ravine.

"He's doubled back to ambush us," Earl said. "Follow me!" He circled his horse around a nearby outcropping of rocks for cover and pulled up.

"Your white horse is too easy to spot."

"I know. Let's go on foot."

I nodded and we both quietly swung down. "Well, now we know he's armed and still homicidal," I whispered. "Let's try the direct approach." I yelled, "Troy, put down your weapon and surrender! Don't make things worse than they already are."

"It's you or me, Lady!" Troy called out. "I'm not going to jail."

I scanned the area in the direction of the voice and noticed furtive movement in the shadows a few yards away. I saw a small spark of light followed by a deafening gunshot. The air near my head whirred. A rock behind me exploded, showering me with stones. I aimed my weapon at the spot where I had seen the muzzle flash of Troy's gun, cocked the hammer and fired. The Colt sounded like a cannon going off.

My ringing ears couldn't make out any sound, but I saw a

shadow tumble down from halfway up the embankment, then pitch forward onto the ground. Cautiously picking my way, I approached with my gun trained on Troy's motionless form. I spotted a semiautomatic handgun lying near his hand and kicked it away before squatting down.

Earl scooted over and snatched the pistol, stuffing it into his waistband before coming up next to me. "Looks like he's gut shot."

"Do you have anything we can use to apply direct pressure?"

Earl pulled a bandana out of his back pocket and handed it to me. "It's gonna be tough gettin' him back to the ranch," he said as I put the cloth on Troy's stomach and pressed down. A dark pool was rapidly spreading beneath him.

I looked at Troy, who clutched my hands over his abdomen and moaned. "We need to get you medical attention, can you ride?"

"No," he gasped. "Need to confess what I did. Don't think I'm going to make it."

I knew he was right. I gentled my voice. "I'm listening."

"I killed Ethan and Colin," he said. "I was embezzling. Knew Colin would catch me. Decided to get rid of both brothers. Only way I could inherit the company. I'm just an in-law." Troy's speech slowed and he looked like he might pass out.

"You don't need to say anything else," I said.

His voice dropped to a whisper. "Made it look like Colin had embezzled rather than me. Practiced Colin's handwriting... wrote a suicide note. Planned this trip...assumed small town cops wouldn't figure it out." He looked at me and smiled weakly. "After the ride, told Ethan I needed to talk about finances. Gave him spreadsheets to distract him. Grabbed the branding iron. Hit him over the head. Kept going until he was dead."

"Save your strength," I said.

Troy groaned and began to pant. "Went to Colin's room next. Told him his brother was hurt. Followed him to Ethan's room. Came up behind him. Cut his throat." Troy coughed. "Put the knife in Colin's hand. Note on the bed. Cleaned up." Troy focused his gaze on me. "So stupid. So sorry."

After this, Troy passed out. I held him until I felt him slip away moments later.

After a long silence, Earl cleared his throat. "He led the

kinda life most folks would give their eye teeth for, and it still wasn't enough."

"Some people don't appreciate what they have," I said. "His jealousy and greed drove him to kill. All for nothing."

"Well I, for one, am satisfied with my lot in life," Earl said.

I looked up at the starry desert sky and contemplated the death and misery I had witnessed as a homicide detective. Then I thought of the photograph I'd found in the serial killer's home after the arrest. It was a snapshot of his next intended victim, a pretty young mother pushing her baby down the street in a stroller, oblivious to the predator stalking her. A sense of calm settled over me.

"Me too," I said. The knot in my stomach loosened, and I knew I wasn't going to take the promotion.

†   †   †

ISABELLA MALDONADO, PhD, is a retired police captain. She attended the FBI National Academy in Quantico. She worked as a patrol officer, hostage negotiator, interpreter and recruit instructor at the police academy. She commanded the Special Investigations and Forensic Division, Public Information Office and a patrol district station. "Diablo Ranch" is her first short story to appear in print. She is currently working on a novel featuring Veranda Cruz and her efforts to hunt down a serial killer in Phoenix.

THE DANGER OF IMPULSE SHOPPING
SUSAN BUDAVARI

"You be very careful out there, Miss," the turbaned store clerk said to Lydia in a hushed voice as he handed back her charge card and a credit slip to sign. He pointed out an article on the front page of the newspaper she'd placed on the countertop. "Last night a lady was killed two blocks from here. The Strangler, again."

Lydia had dashed into the convenience store for bottled water and a newspaper on her way home from work, but then had lingered loading up on snacks and other nonessentials. Impulse purchases at obscene prices. *A dumb thing to do with money so tight...and a madman on the loose in the neighborhood.*

She nodded to the clerk. Her hand trembled as she dropped her credit card in her purse. "Thanks, I'll be careful." She tucked the newspaper under her arm, grabbed the four plastic bags filled with her purchases and walked out the door.

The wind howled. She shivered. There had been barely a breeze when she'd entered the store. She grimaced. It was cold and nasty, atypical for Phoenix in late April. Even the weather had turned on her.

Her car was parked on the side of the building. She looped two of the bags around her wrist, and holding the top of her jacket closed, looked around to be sure no one lurked nearby as she hurried to her car. The wind blew her hair into her eyes. Strands stuck to her lips left sticky by the sugary drink she'd finished while waiting on line to pay.

When Lydia reached her banged up five-year-old Impala, she set the bundles down beside the car to get her keys from her purse. She gave another quick look around, then unlocked the vehicle and opened the back door wide. As she rushed to load the groceries, a sudden gust of wind knocked the door into her. A plastic bag split and her purse spilled. Mumbling curses, she grabbed the loose items and threw them into the car, then tossed the newspaper onto the front seat. In the process her fingernail bent back and she shrieked. She grabbed her purse, slammed the back door and got behind the wheel.

Lydia locked the car doors then sat for a moment staring at her angry reflection in the visor mirror. The lines in her forehead grew deeper each day. She smoothed her brow and pushed stray blonde strands behind her ears. She fished a brush and an emery board from her purse, ran the brush through her hair and began to file down the jagged fingernail. She felt bone tired. Lately, she lay awake nights trying to decide whether she'd be better off leaving Phoenix and moving back East.

As she turned the ignition, she read the headlines in the newspaper lying on the seat next to her:

FIFTH STRANGLER VICTIM
TEACHER FOUND DEAD IN PHOENIX HOME

That poor woman.

The beeping of a car horn startled her. The sound came from a red Yukon one space away to her left. The driver, wearing a shiny green windbreaker, gestured wildly to her. Had he been sitting there watching her? *Ignore him.* She turned the radio on loud, needing some good music to lift her spirits. Glancing again to her left she saw the Yukon-man lower his passenger side window and shout something at her. She couldn't make out what he said over the music, and wasn't about to engage in a conversation with him. As he slid over from the driver's side and stuck his head out the window, she gunned the engine and took off. *Were guys always on the prowl for any woman alone?*

When Lydia was younger, she enjoyed the attention she got from men. Memories popped into her head and made her chuckle. She'd been hot, but that was a long yesterday ago. Some interesting dating scenes had started in parking lots— others ended there. Now she was over forty and glad for the lifetime gym membership, bought when she had money. Despite a few extra pounds around her bottom, her body still looked strong and fit, although most of the men interested in her were north of fifty and she hadn't met any recently with whom she wanted to spend time. Especially not after the exhausting days she'd been putting in at work. Low pay and a demanding boss, criticizing everything and dangling a pink slip at her. Times were hard, but she didn't have to be reminded of it three times a day.

If she'd known what lay ahead for her, she wouldn't have been so quick to leave Charles. He was no bargain, but he'd brought home a decent paycheck. *Who am I kidding? Once he started hitting me, I had to leave him.*

A woman alone isn't safe. Maybe buying a gun would be smart. Having grown up back East, she couldn't let go of the idea that good people didn't carry guns. *Hey, not everyone who carries a gun is a criminal—at least not out here in Arizona. Right?* Back home, it *was* the bad guys who packed weapons. Here, the good guys *needed* to pack. It's still the Wild West. To stand a fighting chance, a person has to have something to even the odds. *But could I shoot anyone, even if my life depended on it?*

Lydia pulled onto the main road and checked the rear view mirror. No sign of Yukon-man. Road rage stories on the nightly news terrified her. Confrontation was something to be avoided. Her rule was: never make eye contact with other drivers and step on it to get away from any situation that could turn threatening. Fortunately, she was only a short distance from her home.

After a few minutes on the road, she began to relax. She didn't know what made her check the mirror again, but when she did, the red Yukon followed two cars behind. She made a quick right without signaling and pulled into the car wash line behind the takeout restaurant.

Twenty minutes later she was back on the road, her car sparkling. She'd been meaning to have it washed for weeks, so this encounter with Yukon-man wasn't all bad.

The rest of the way home Lydia kept looking in the rearview mirror. When she turned onto her street, a frown settled on her face. The neighborhood had once been friendly and bustling, now several houses were vacant, foreclosure and bank-owned signs stood in front of them.

She pulled into the garage of her rented two-bedroom bungalow and hurried inside. After making sure that the front door off the living room was locked and peeking out the side window, she took the groceries from the car and put them away. She went to the bedroom, changed into jeans and a T-shirt, and slipped on comfortable shoes. What she needed was a cool glass of chardonnay. She poured some from an open bottle in the refrigerator and took a sip as she headed back to the living room.

Why am I always letting my imagination run away with me? Next, I'll be thinking Yukon-man is the Phoenix Strangler and I'm going to be Number Six.

Lydia told herself that Yukon-man was probably a jerk who hoped to make small talk and overwhelm her with his charm. With no response to his catcall, he decided he'd show her—scare her by following her. No matter how old or ugly they are, men seem to think they can make eyes at every woman within whistling distance. Then they get vindictive if their overture isn't welcome.

She plopped down on the sofa and flipped on the television to catch the evening news before starting dinner. Minutes later the doorbell rang. She jumped up and peeked around the shade, spotting the bright green windbreaker at the door. *Yukon-man.* His car was parked across the street. At first she wondered if he'd found her from her license plate, but remembered the car was still registered to Charles at their old address.

He's got to know I'm here—the lights are on and he can hear the TV. He won't go away so easily. What should I do?

A knock on the door. Then pounding. A chill ran down Lydia's neck and spine. She stood frozen in place, stifling the involuntary sounds in her throat.

Call the police.

She wondered if every frightened female in Phoenix thought she'd spotted the strangler and got on the phone. Would the police pay attention to her call? Could they get to her in time? Where was her phone? On the cocktail table. She snatched it up and punched in 911. She whispered her name and address and told the dispatcher a man was trying to break into her house. The phone went dead. *I must have left it off the cradle too long.* She hurled the handset on the sofa.

Lydia hurried back to the window and, just as she glanced out, Yukon-man started around the house. She could run out the front door. But if he caught her, she'd be at his mercy. She was safer in the house until the police came. *The kitchen door. I never fixed the lock.* Only a hook and eye kept it closed. A few tugs and the door would give way. Then he'd be in.

Noises at the kitchen door. She raced to the kitchen and looked around for something to use to defend herself. *My cast iron skillet!* She grabbed it from the sink and positioned herself against the wall. *When he gets in, his back will be to me.*

A couple of shakes and the hook gave way. The door opened. She saw his green sleeve. He paused facing the living room. "Hello. Ma'am," he called out. "You—"

Her heart jumped in her chest. *Do it now.* She took a deep breath, lifted the frying pan and slammed it over his bald head with all her strength. He crumpled forward onto his stomach, his arm outstretched.

His hand grasped something.

She knelt beside his body. Blood trickled from his mouth. His hand relaxed.

A plastic card slipped from it. She picked it up. *My credit card. The one I used at the convenience store.*

She touched the side of his neck. No pulse. *Dead?*

She crept away and leaned back against the counter, her head in her hands, whimpering. *Oh, no. Did he come to return my card? What did he shout in the parking lot?*

She pulled herself up and began feverously pacing. *Did he pick my pocket in the store? No, he wasn't inside. Besides, if he stole my card, why return it? Could that be how the Strangler gets inside a woman's house?* Stomach in a knot, she took a deep breath and let it out slowly. *Think Lydia, think.* Could her credit card have fallen out when she dropped her purse? If so, did he see it, yell to her, then pick it up after she drove away? She was listed in the directory. Knowing her name, he could have looked up the address and driven to her house. *Why didn't he call me? Omigod! Maybe he did. I never checked my voice mail.*

She broke into a cold sweat and started shaking. Tears streamed down her face.

Did I just kill an innocent man?

If they prosecute people who shoot criminals robbing their homes, what chance do I have?

I don't want to go to jail!

She gasped for breath, ran to the bathroom, knelt by the bowl and threw up.

When she finished, she blew her nose and splashed cold water on her face. "What do I do now?" The police had to be on the way.

Back in the kitchen, Lydia sat on the floor, hugging herself and rocking, her eyes focused on her knees. She heard the approaching sirens. *My life is over.*

†   †   †

The policewoman placed a glass of water in front of Lydia and sat down across from her at the kitchen table. The officer's young face held a look of concern. "We've finished here for now. How are you doing ma'am?"

Lydia adjusted the blanket draped around her shoulders and murmured, "I was so scared. I thought he was The Strangler. I had no idea...he came to return my credit card." Still shaking, she rubbed her cheek with the wad of tissues in her hand.

"His name's Russ Kirby," the officer said. "We found duct tape in the pocket of his jacket and these." In her gloved hands she held two photos for Lydia to see.

Lydia's eyes opened wide. "That's me. I wore that outfit last week." Her stomach quivered. "But...but...I never laid eyes on him before today."

"You said he called out to you in the store parking lot. Then he showed up at your door?"

Lydia nodded. "I didn't like the way he was acting in the parking lot. I beat it out of there right away. Then I spotted him on the road behind me, so I tried to lose him. I thought I did." She wiped a tear from the corner of her eye. "I'm wary of strange men. I'm divorced, you know, and live alone." She reached for the water with a trembling hand and took a swallow. "I heard him pulling on the kitchen door. I was scared...to death."

The officer's cell phone beeped and she stepped away to take the call.

When she returned, she said to Lydia, "Kirby was a convicted sex offender. With his record, things could have gone very badly for you." After a beat she added, "You'll need to come with us to the station to give a full statement." She locked eyes with Lydia for a long moment, looked around, then said, "Don't worry, it's standard procedure."

A tremendous weight lifted from Lydia's chest. She could breathe again. She hadn't killed an innocent man. She had a future.

As moments passed and calmness set in, Lydia knew she'd changed.

I took care of myself.

The Wild West no longer scared her.

That instant she made up her mind. She was staying put in Phoenix.

First chance she got, she'd go shopping for a gun.

† † †

SUSAN BUDAVARI has completed the first two books in a psychological mystery series featuring a Scottsdale P.I. and his physician wife. She has written over 30 short stories and co-edited and contributed to several award-winning anthologies, including three from Red Coyote Press: *Medley of Murder*, *Map of Murder,* and *Medium of Murder*. Previously, she worked in chemical research and scientific information management in the pharmaceutical industry and was Editor of *The Merck Index*, a bestselling encyclopedia of chemicals, drugs and biologicals.

BLOWHARD
BARBARA GOODSON

A clay-white cloud of dust surrounded Marla as she threw the last shovel of dirt on the grave. Ducking her head she roughly dragged the sleeve of her shirt across her eyes. The shriek of the desert wind masked her sob. At thirty, her face reflected an intimate knowledge of grief and disappointment.

"Damn it." Wiping away tears, Marla stared at a rugged, treeless landscape that stretched for miles down an empty valley.

Cradling the shovel in the crook of her arm, she made her way across the patch of dirt surrounding her doublewide. The trailer was a battered wreck that shook with every gust of wind. The truck tires she'd stacked on the roof kept the place from toppling off its concrete blocks, but they didn't keep the wind from tearing through hundreds of cracks and gaps in the aluminum siding. A layer of grit coated everything, inside and out.

Marla tossed the shovel on the ground and opened the door. The wind ripped the door from her hand and slammed it back against the outside wall. She wrestled it closed. The trailer was isolated, hot and ant infested. The place held no fond memories. Everything about it reminded her of destruction and death. If she stayed much longer she was afraid she'd grow old, die, turn to dust and blow away.

Marla grabbed her purse and car keys, slammed the door shut and left. Leaning into the wind, she skirted around the side of the trailer, past the water tank, to where she parked her truck.

A fierce blast of wind rocked the pickup as she settled into the sagging driver's seat. The old Chevy smelled of wet dog, cigarette smoke and despair. She narrowed her eyes against the glare of the setting sun, turned the key and revved the engine.

Roaring along the rutted, dirt road that followed the electric transmission line, she got the old truck up to a rattling fifty miles an hour. A plume of dust chased her through the gate that her daddy put up thirty years ago. Tumbleweeds huddled along the fence line that marked her property. A half- mile farther and she turned left onto the paved highway. From there it was twenty miles to her job at Hunter's Hotel.

The hotel was a relic of the boom years when the mine was running three shifts a day and even the ranchers were making money. In 1980 the interstate highway bypassed the town, the mine closed and so did the hotel. Long haul truckers on their way to L.A. still rumbled down Main Street. But they didn't stop at Hunter's. The bar managed to stay open serving a weather-beaten collection of men with nothing much to do but drink until they were drunk.

Marla knew them all. She knew what they drank, what they ate and where they slept. She ignored their crude jokes, rude noises and gross habits. She picked them up when they fell down and mopped up what they spit, spilled or pissed on the floor. She hated the job but she needed the paycheck.

It was after five-o'clock when she parked the Chevy around the corner from Hunter's. She was late. Climbing out of the truck, her shirt clung damply to her back and a fine layer of grit covered her face. She didn't care what she looked like and neither did the five half-drunk, disheveled men who swiveled around to watch her entrance.

Dwight Grimel, the owner, stood behind the bar. His narrow face went red and the scruffy patch of a beard under his lower lip bristled. "You're late," he said in a flat, angry voice.

"Family emergency," Marla said, twisting her wind-blown, faded blonde hair back to the nape of her neck and adjusted her plastic hair clip. Stepping behind the bar, she shoved her purse onto a shelf under the cash register.

Snapping a gray bar towel at her butt, Dwight sneered. "Family emergency? That's the third one this week."

Marla jumped back. The drinkers perked up, waiting to see how this little drama would play out.

She shrugged, "It's been a bad time for me."

"Far as I can remember you got no family. Your ma died of the cancer twenty years ago and your pa killed himself two years back. That's all the family I remember you havin'. How can you have a family emergency if you got no family?"

Shaking her head, she didn't answer.

Dwight jutted his face toward her. "You understand I'm

runnin' a place of business here. I gotta be able to count on you."

The drinkers watched, waiting for her response.

Marla looked at her feet and mumbled, "Billy died."

Dwight shook his head. "What? Who died? I can't hear you."

The man nearest Marla stretched his tattooed arm across the bar and held out an empty beer glass. "She said Billy died."

Dwight scowled. "Who the hell is Billy?" He grabbed the drinker's empty glass.

Marla took a breath and gave Dwight a defiant look. "He was my dog. A damn good dog—better'n most people I know," she paused. "I had to bury him. Wouldn't be right not to."

Embarrassed, the men shifted on their stools and studied their drinks. These were men who understood the importance of a good dog. There wasn't a man among them would say a bad word about a person's dog.

Dwight fiddled with the beer tap, slowly topping off the glass and pushing it back across the bar. He dried his hands on the front of his T-shirt and avoided looking at Marla. "Well hell, I didn't know." He shifted his feet and tugged at his belt buckle. "So, you gonna get to work?"

Marla nodded.

"Okay then." Dwight turned his back on her and popped open a can of Coke. After carefully pouring it into a glass, he took it to a booth in the darkest corner of the bar. He was settling in to spend the night watching a baseball game on the wall-mounted television.

Two of the drinkers held up empty glasses. Marla pulled beers for them. She hoped they wouldn't ask about Billy. Her dog was the only reason she'd stayed in this blown-out, no-hope dusty town. Except for Billy she would have moved two years ago when she'd been forced to leave the house she grew up in. It, along with almost everything else, had to be liquidated to cover her daddy's bad investment. She might have moved to Phoenix then, maybe tried to get a real job. She didn't because Billy was getting old and kind of smelly. He'd developed a heart murmur and he was going blind. Even worse, he'd begun to growl and snap at people. Besides, he was a big black Lab; she couldn't drag him off to some tiny apartment in Phoenix.

Her only option was the old trailer sitting smack dab in the middle of the windiest, most barren stretch of land in all of

Arizona. It was the only thing her daddy owned that she hadn't sold.

Leaning against the bar, she thought about her options. With Billy gone, she could leave. She mopped the sticky bar-top and tried to picture a new life for herself. One of the drinkers impatiently tapped the rim of his empty glass. He needed a refill. She got his beer and slid it to him. He wordlessly pushed a few dollars at her and gripped the glass with a callused hand. Marla realized there was no fear of conversation. The drinkers had gone back to the serious business of getting drunk.

Shifting into her usual routine Marla refilled glasses, mopped up the beer slop and kept an eye on Dwight. If he thought she wasn't keeping the drinks and the money moving he could get mean. She wasn't in the mood for a confrontation.

She was rinsing out a glass when the door opened and a tall, barrel-chested man wearing a yellow sport shirt and khaki pants strolled in. He ambled over to a table in the center of the room and settled on a wobbly chair. At the sight of him Marla's heart pounded and a sour bile rose in her throat. She put down the glass and stiffly walked over to the table.

"Jim Beam straight up?" she asked.

The man grinned up at her, "You remembered."

With undisguised contempt she said, "Yeah Emery, I remember. You and Daddy always drank your Jim Beam straight up."

"That was a while ago," he said, ignoring her attitude. Eying her up and down he added, "You're still lookin' good."

Marla wheeled around and walked back to the bar. Emery Anderson shrugged and slicked back his thick, dark hair. Looking around the room, he spotted Dwight. "Dwight is that you? What the hell you doin' hidin' out in the corner? Come on over here and drink with me."

Dwight raised a hand in a half-hearted wave. "Hey," he said, not indicating that he planned to move.

Then Emery said the magic words. "I'll buy."

Dwight gulped the last of his drink, stood and wiped his hands on the back of his jeans. "Marla, bring me a rum and Coke," he shouted.

There was no need to raise his voice, the men at the bar were silently nursing their beers, the TV was on mute and the juke box hadn't worked in years. Hunter's was as quiet as a tub of turnips.

Marla could hear the wood floor creak with every step Dwight took.

As Dwight approached, Emery stood, stuck out his hand and smiled like a politician, all teeth and twinkly eyes. "How ya doin'?" he asked, enthusiastically shaking Dwight's hand. Without waiting for an answer, he dropped back onto the rickety chair.

Dwight pulled out an equally damaged chair and sat across from Emery. "I'm doin' okay," he said.

"Well good," Emery said cheerfully. Before he could continue, Marla brought two drinks to the table. She set the Jim Beam down hard. "You wanna run a tab?" she asked, looking at a point somewhere over Emery's head.

"Let's do this, sweetheart." He said pulling a fifty dollar bill out of his shirt pocket. He slapped it down on the table. "Let's see how many drinks General Grant can buy."

She snorted and snatched the bill. Placing the other glass on the table, she gave Dwight a little nod. If some fool wanted to buy Dwight a drink he'd order a rum and Coke. Marla knew he wanted the Coke the way it came from the can and no expensive rum added. Dwight looked on it as an opportunity for revenue enhancement.

Emery held his glass up. "Here's to good times," he said with boisterous good cheer.

"Yeah, sure," Dwight said, listlessly raising his glass an inch or two off the table.

Emery took a quick swallow and set the glass down. "So, what's the news around town? What's goin' on?"

Dwight shrugged, "Same old crap. Suppose to be some deal in the works to build a solar power plant out by Burro Mountain. Probably not gonna happen. Other than that we're just sittin' around watchin' the wind blow. One of these days it'll blow the whole damn town off the map."

Emery looked over his shoulder as though he thought someone might be listening. "Don't kid yourself, there's money to be made here."

Dwight brought his glass to his lips and didn't say anything.

"Hell," Emery continued in a confidential tone, "I think you know what I mean. I always said you were the one man around here smart enough to recognize a real opportunity." He grinned and watched for Dwight's reaction.

Dwight leaned back, pulled at the patch of hair under his lip and nodded. "Maybe."

"You're no fool." Emery finished his drink and set the glass down with finality.

Dwight and Emery sat in silence while Marla brought two more drinks and picked up the empties.

Dwight took a gulp of his fresh Coke and burped loudly.

Emery rested his elbows on the table, leaned toward Dwight and lowered his voice. "I got something goin' that I think you'd be interested in, somethin' that a smart investor like you would appreciate."

Dwight rubbed his chin again and waited.

Emery slapped a hand down on the table. "Wind power. That's where the money's gonna be." He nodded, agreeing with himself. Wiping a bead of sweat off his forehead, he continued. "I've been thinkin' about puttin' together an investment company. Get in on the ground floor with the energy business."

Dwight shook his head. "This gonna be like that last investment company you started? What was it called? Magic Man Investments? I don't remember that workin' out so good. Although you did make a lotta money disappear." He called across the room. "Marla wasn't it Magic Man Investments that your daddy sunk everything into?"

Marla wiped the bar and took a minute thinking about what she wanted to say. People around town knew what had happened. Her daddy'd been talked into cashing out his company retirement benefit, taking a second on the house and borrowin' money from all his old friends. Within a month it became obvious that his drinkin' buddy, Emery, had led him down a fool's path. All the money was gone.

Her daddy was a proud man. He couldn't live with the shame of being so stupid and he hated owing his friends money. Even worse was feeling their unspoken pity. The first warm day of spring he took a rope to the garage and hanged himself. He left a lot of debts and a note saying he couldn't live in such a sorry way. Twisting the bar towel, Marla said, "Don't believe a word that comes out of his mouth."

There was a low mutter of consensus from the drinkers at the bar.

Emery shook his head and held up a hand to stop potential dissent. "It was Sunset Investments and I was never convicted of anything. An indictment isn't the same as a conviction. Marla's pa got himself in a predicament all on his own. I didn't make him do anything he didn't want to do."

Irritably pushing his drink away, Dwight scowled. "Yeah, well I'm not givin' you a dime."

Emery feigned surprise. "I'm not askin' for your money." He reached into his shirt pocket and pulled out a business card. "I'm offerin' you an opportunity." He held the card out to Dwight. "Look at this."

Dwight took the card. "What's it say? It's dark as hell in here. I can't read this damn thing."

The only light in the bar came from the one light bulb and the two beer signs that hung over the cash register.

Emery finished what was left of his drink and leaned forward. He spoke in a voice filled with greed and alcohol. He grew louder with each word. "It says these guys are developers, big time developers. They got more money than God. They just need help locating the right piece of land."

At a signal from Dwight, Marla came back to the table, her face hard and her voice tight. "You ready for another?"

Barely acknowledging her, Emery shoved his empty glass across the table. "Yeah."

Snatching the empty glass, she turned on her heel and headed back to the bar.

Dwight rested his forearms on the table and leaned forward. "You got some developer's business card. So what?"

"So I'm the man in the middle. I can find what they need. It'll be easy money. It's a no-fail deal."

"Then why do ya need investors? Sounds like you got it pretty well worked out."

Emery spoke with the conviction of a true zealot. "Think about it. Right now you could buy land around here for next to nothin'. In six months, when the developer wants to make a deal, we could double, maybe triple, our investment."

Marla came back with a fresh drink. Emery took a long gulp and leaned back.

Dwight shook his head. "What makes you think people around here want to sell?"

Emery laughed again. "Are you kiddin' me? They'll sell so fast it'll make your head spin. The hicks around here are too dumb to figure out that wind is a sellable resource." He moved his chair a few inches closer and dropped his voice to a low growl. "I'm tellin' ya, we could make some real money together. You got the cash to buy up the land and I know the developers."

Dwight signaled for Marla to bring two more drinks. Narrowing his eyes, he silently stared at Emery. Finally he said, "People aren't as stupid as you think."

Emery's face flushed pink and his voice rose until he nearly shouted with enthusiasm. "But they are! There was an old gal who worked at the Safeway." He waved a hand to indicate the direction of the grocery store and then gulped the rest of his drink. "I told her for two grand she could save a puppy rescued from Afghanistan. Who'd believe that?" He grinned and lifted both hands in a palms-up gesture. He chuckled. "Well I'm here to tell ya she did! I gave her a sickly twenty dollar mutt and I laughed all the way to the bank."

Without warning the silent man at the end of the bar slammed his glass down and spun around. His face was a mask of fury, his body tense with rage.

"That was my Ma," he said as he slid off the bar stool. "The damn dog died two weeks later after she spent another five hundred on vet bills. She took it real hard. You think that's funny?"

Hitching up his jeans, the obviously pissed-off man hunched his shoulders and crossed the room in two strides. Without a word, he grabbed a handful of Emery's hair and slammed his face onto the table. The cartilage in Emery's nose broke with a loud snap. He screamed and a bloody puddle spread around his face.

The man released his grip on Emery's hair. Emery raised his head. His eyes were round with fear. Blood poured from his nose, his face contorted with pain.

The other men at the bar watched in stunned silence. Dwight hurriedly stood up and jumped away from the table. "Hey, take it easy," he said in a strained voice.

Emery's attacker pulled his sagging jeans up to the bottom of his beer belly and turned to face his buddies, there was a look of drunken determination on his face. "Reckon I'm gonna have to teach this lyin' blowhard a lesson."

He unbuckled his wide leather belt and struggled to pull it through the belt loops.

Emery saw his chance. He rolled off his chair, wiped the

blood out of his eyes and bolted for the door. The angry drinker muttered something. He seemed to forget about his belt and started after his prey. Whimpering, Emery yanked the door open. With a terrified glance over his shoulder he staggered out to the sidewalk. The big drunk gave a laugh and followed.

Dwight, Marla and men who rarely moved off their bar stools crowded around the open door. Dwight made a half-hearted attempt at reason. "Hey man, take it easy," he said, and then grudgingly added, "Come on back inside I'll buy you a beer."

The furious drinker ignored Dwight. He repeated with extra emphasis, "I'm gonna teach this blowhard a lesson."

Spitting a stream of tobacco juice at Emery's feet, he stepped forward. Emery protectively covered his bloody face with his hands. His attacker puffed out his belly and gave Emery a violent two-handed shove. Caught off balance, Emery toppled backward off the curb and into the street. His head hit the pavement with a hollow thud.

Coming down the hill at sixty miles an hour, there was no way the driver of the eighteen wheeler could avoid the man lying in the street.

Everyone, even the police, agreed that Emery was drunk. Falling in front of the semi was an unfortunate accident. The driver felt real bad about running over a man. The police assured him he wouldn't be held accountable. When he drove off toward L.A., he was looking pale and kinda rattled.

Back in the bar, Marla mopped the blood and whisky off the table and pocketed the business card. She waited for the police to finish taking statements. When the last flashing lights were gone, she leaned back against the bar and scanned the gloomy room. She knew if she didn't make a change soon she could find herself spending the rest of her life with these sullen, dirty, and sometimes violent men.

Walking over to where Dwight was closing out the cash drawer, she unfastened her hair clip, wiped her hands on a bar towel and said, "I quit." Without looking back she walked straight out the door.

† † †

The wind blew just hard enough to rustle the leaves of the palm trees around the pool. Marla sat with her feet up on the lounge chair and watched Hugo, her black Lab puppy, chase a lizard. It had been three years since she'd bought the house in Phoenix. Six months since she'd felt able to bring another dog into her life.

As she enjoyed the warm afternoon breeze, she thought about Emery. It was hard to believe that his beer-soaked business card would be her ticket out of the two-bit town where she'd been born. There was no doubt that Emery had been a blowhard, a con man and a liar. But he'd been right about one thing: wind was a sellable resource. People with money were looking for places where the wind blew hard. Her land supported one hundred wind turbines. She'd leased it to a developer with the condition that one small plot be left untouched. When she cashed her first check, she put a marker over the spot where Billy was buried.

† † †

BARBARA GOODSON is a graduate of the University of California, Irvine. Her short story "Hell to Pay," is included in the mystery anthology, *How NOT to Survive a Vacation*. She is currently working on a contemporary mystery, EARTHQUAKE WEATHER. Over the years she has worked as a graphic designer, illustrator, and teacher. Barbara now lives in Arizona and is a member of the Desert Sleuths chapter Sisters in Crime.

THE PRINCESS GUARDIAN
Lori Hines

Alara slammed on her brakes—hard. Her SUV slid to the right, the wheels narrowly escaping a fifty foot drop off. Massive sharp boulders, barrel cactus and a herd of javelina stared up at her. Stunned, Alara looked at the plastic bottle of soda precariously balanced in her cup holder. Splattered, sticky brown liquid had sloshed on the dashboard, driver's side, the passenger seat and beige carpet.

Shaken, hands gripping the steering wheel, she stared at the Native American woman on horseback who had crossed in front of her car and watched Alara intently. Sitting atop a tan palomino, she looked like an Indian princess. Two long, dark braids trailed down the front of her elaborately decorated tan leather dress. Alternating red, yellow and blue beads topped her moccasins.

Alara wanted to back up and keep driving in the remote section of land off Interstate 17 near Phoenix, but she sat there, frozen. The mysterious stranger's eyes pierced Alara's from ten feet away. After a few seconds, the horse reared up, then leapt off the road and into a shady riparian area opposite the ravine.

She quickly pulled the keys out of the ignition, got out of her car and ran to the side of the road. Hooves pounded against stones and water as the horse raced past sycamore and cottonwood trees. After a few moments, the beautiful Indian halted her horse in the shallow stream that paralleled the road and looked over her shoulder at Alara.

"Who are you?" Alara yelled, pushing her long brown bangs off her forehead, cautiously following the mare as it continued to trot along the water's edge. She hesitated, glancing back in the direction of her vehicle. There were two blown-out tires on the right side. She groaned. "Where can I find help out here?"

The Native American woman had stopped again, watching her. Alara felt drawn toward the stranger. Abandoning her SUV, she followed along the shady creek, picking up her pace.

Now twenty feet away, the woman and the horse transformed into a light pink mist. The vapor-like entity hung eight feet above the ground for a few seconds, then vanished before Alara's eyes.

She couldn't believe what she had seen. Terrified, yet curious, she continued to follow.

When she reached the area where the dark-haired woman had morphed into the bizarre fog, Alara noticed a clearing in between two ten-foot-tall Palo Verde trees. The tallest of the branches on both trees bent over, entwined, creating an oval frame. Massive Swiss cheese-like holes covered a whitish colored canyon wall—natural formations created by time. The apertures were tall enough for a human to walk under. Shadows passed back and forth between the openings, twenty feet above the ground.

Twigs broke behind her. Alara whirled around, but could see nothing. Her eyes focused on the carpet of leaves and twigs, a narrow dirt path leading along the other side of the stream and a stand of mesquite trees. She saw no one, yet knew someone, or something was there—watching.

No birds sang. No insects chirped. No breeze created a conversation among the trees. The trickle of the water beside her even seemed to cease as Alara stood under the Palo Verde's unnaturally bowed limbs.

She turned to run back to her vehicle, but then remembered the flat tires on her SUV. She looked up at a pueblo that had been built into the canyon face a hundred feet above the desert floor. A group of people stood near the edge of an open ruin, observing her intensely. A little boy took a step forward. Alara gasped as the figure hovered just over the precipice of the ruin.

Alara stepped out from under the trees onto an overgrown path that led to a steep incline toward the massive ruin. A clopping sound echoed throughout the stillness, somewhere ahead of her. She had not lost her stunning Indian guide.

Twenty minutes ago, she was on a relaxing weekend getaway, her two kids in Texas to visit their father. Alara wanted—no needed—some time to herself. This may not be the trip to Italy she always wished for, but she seemed drawn to a different journey.

Due to her mysterious mishap, the only hope of rescue was her cell phone, inside her purse, which she had abandoned along with her SUV. She felt herself being led to an adventure beyond her control. Only she had no idea how it would turn out.

A rattling noise made her glance down to see a blue-gray striped tiger rattlesnake coiled in the middle of the path, her foot poised directly above its head. Instinctively, she pulled back. But it was too late. The venomous serpent struck. She expected the pain of sharp fangs, but she felt nothing.

The reptile darted under a creosote bush. Alara glanced down at the inside of her leg. There were no puncture marks on her skin. *How the hell could it have missed?*

"That's enough. I'm going back."

She turned to go back, but an invisible force prevented her from moving ahead. Alara stepped forward again and met the same wall. She walked off the narrow trail and tried to get around to the riparian area nearer to her vehicle. It was no use. She could go no farther. An unseen solid force in front of her blocked her path.

"This can't be happening." She pounded frantically against the mysterious barrier. Alara collapsed to the ground, sharp rocks digging into her knees. "Please, I want to go home."

The sensation of a firm hand placed itself on her right shoulder. She stood up quickly and looked behind her. No one stood there, but an eerie calm determination swept over her. She would see this mystery through.

She squared her shoulders. "Okay, damn it! I'm not sure why I need to be here. Or what I'm supposed to do. But let's get this over with so I can get out of here." Alara charged ahead full force on the narrow trail. A deep canyon awaited beyond gently sloping hills dotted with creosote, prickly pear, desert grass and various sized boulders. An old windmill sat atop the tallest bluff.

Twenty minutes later, she gazed up at the massive pueblo. There were no people watching her from there as they had earlier. Or so it seemed. She wondered if they could still be there. She couldn't see all the way up the ruins. The steep hill only went to one of the eight-foot-tall holes in the side of the canyon wall.

Children's giggles came from somewhere to her right.

"Hello!" She glanced to either side of her, and up into the natural, cave-like apertures and ruins, but didn't see anyone.

"Is anyone here?" Complete silence answered her.

Alara climbed up the steep section of trail, arriving at the entrance to what appeared to be a series of interconnected caves. Brilliant light filtered from the other round openings in the rock. Golden rays crisscrossed each other, highlighting geometric spirals and crosses, stick figures, animal shapes, and the shape of a mask etched on the stone walls.

The hair on Alara's arms stood on end. The temperature suddenly dropped—drastically. Something passed by directly behind her. She whipped her head around. Nothing was there.

Rocks and dirt began to fall on her. Looking up, she saw a six-by-four-foot fissure and backed up to see if she could distinguish anything through the opening. She bumped into something behind her and turned to see a wooden ladder leading to a space above.

"That wasn't there a minute ago. What is going on?" Alara observed the ancient rungs carefully. Terrified of heights, she tightly gripped the sides of the ladder, glancing up one more time before starting to climb. A ball of orange light streaked directly across the second story. She glanced at the hole-like entrance of the cave, tempted to run. Dark, mysterious entities floated back and forth where she came in.

Alara gripped onto the ladder tighter, her hands moist against the aging wood.

I'm trapped.

She took a deep breath and proceeded to the room overhead. *Don't look down, Alara. Come on, you can do this.*

Laughter echoed from below—a little boy's voice.

She gasped, leaning against the ladder. She looked down. It was only ten-foot drop, but felt to her like fifty. Her head began to spin. Alara closed her eyes and took a few deep breaths.

"That wasn't nice," she snapped. "You could have made me fall." Her anger guided her more quickly to her destination. Alara reached the top, then stepped off the top rung and onto the dirt floor.

She trembled, thinking of the strange illumination of only minutes before, wondering if the light could have been an entity, how many spirits inhabited this place, and what did they want with her?

Sunlight poured into a series of what used to be smaller rooms, leading to a twenty-by-twenty-foot open ruin. She stepped over the remnants of a two-foot stone wall into the larger room. There were remains of a firepit containing the bones of a small animal. Etchings on a protrusion of rock showed a white mask, a snake and an image of two trees with their limbs reaching toward each other. The images faced the direction of the stream far below.

Alara held her hand up within an inch of the Palo Verde arch drawing—a replica of the trees far below. A brief electric shock tore into her fingers and palm, up her arm and throughout her torso and legs. She grabbed her hand and held tightly, trying to alleviate the pain. Backing away, she continued to stare at the petroglyph in amazement. Afraid and confused, Alara slowly stepped away from the rock art and toward the cliff's edge.

Without warning, a powerful breeze pushed her backward and she started to lose her balance. Regaining her footing, she whirled around and jumped back—now only a step from the edge of the fifty-foot drop off.

The Palo Verdes stood proudly in the distance, their tallest branches entwined. As the sun started to set, the last of the rays penetrated through the two stately trees, under their limbs and onto the prehistoric drawing of the trees in the pueblo. The branches of the Palo Verde petroglyph shimmered and bent slightly, as if a breeze had blown through them.

Alara approached closer to the rock, not sure what she was seeing.

The Indian princess on horseback appeared out of nowhere on the path below, watching Alara, waiting. Her eyes bore into Alara's, a sly grin across her face.

Alara could see her SUV in the distance. She glanced back toward the mystical woman who had guided her into the canyon, but she had vanished again.

"How the hell am I going to get out of here?" Panicked, Alara ran back to the ladder—it too had vanished. If she took a risk and leapt down she could break a leg, both legs. Or much worse.

Dressed only in shorts and a T-shirt, she knew she must find a way out before sunset. In a panic, she saw a man passing in between the very same trees with their branches entwined. He stopped and stared up at her.

She waved her hands in desperation and called out. When the man reached the point with the steep incline leading up to the hole in the rock, Alara gasped. This same man with wavy brown hair and a dragon tattoo on his arm had been in her dreams the night before. Now she knew the dream represented something more.

"Are you all right?" he yelled.

"Y—yes." Alara rubbed her arms with her hands, cold from the gradual decrease in temperature. "But I can't get down from here."

She thought he would ask why she couldn't escape the same way she climbed up. Instead, he followed the narrow path up to the natural opening in the canyon wall. Then he disappeared for a few seconds.

He reappeared and brought the ladder over and placed it beneath her. "What's your name?"

"Alara. Thanks for your help," she said, descending to the ground floor. "I was beginning to think I would be stuck here."

He took her hand in his. "I'm Shaun." He watched her intently.

"Can you help me get back to my car?" She nodded her head toward the dirt road.

Shaun looked into the distance toward her car. "Sure. Let's get you back safely. Seems you've had enough excitement for one day." Shaun's tone had changed from cordial to cold. She wondered how much this stranger knew about her recent outings.

With trembling hands, she pushed a long strand of hair behind her ear, glimpsing at a brilliant black and orange Gila monster perched on a rock, right next to the path. The creature peered back at her. "You could say that."

Shaun followed her back down the steep trail and to the embankment with the enigmatic Palo Verde trees. A hawk with cream colored wings and reddish tail glided gracefully on the currents. The bird of prey observed her with the same steely gaze as Shaun.

"So, what have you been doing out here?" he asked.

Alara stared straight ahead, quickening her pace the closer they got to her car. "Oh, just driving around, enjoying the beautiful scenery. Then something strange happened. An Indian woman appeared out of nowhere. I swerved to avoid her and ended up with two flat tires."

"There's definitely some interesting things to discover out here," Shaun said. "Though temptation looms close."

Alara felt his eyes boring into her as they approached the place of her accident.

She ran to her vehicle and got behind the wheel, grabbed her keys out of her pocket and shoved them into the ignition. "Thanks so much for helping me get back." Panicked, she turned the key, but realized she couldn't go anywhere.

"Darn it!" She slammed her palm against the steering wheel. She glanced in the rearview mirror to see Shaun looking at the pile of ceramic artifacts she had taken from an ancient burial site two weeks earlier.

She had been sloppy and hadn't covered her find carefully enough. The sudden stop earlier must have dislodged some of the items under the tarp.

She thought about running, but had a feeling she wouldn't get very far. She started to cry as she walked to the back of her car. "Listen, I only took the pottery because I lost my job six months ago. I don't have any prospects and I'm about to lose my house. I heard it would be easy and I didn't know it was that big a deal."

"There's a myth about this place. Whoever is led through that," he glanced back toward the path and arched Palo Verde trees, "has been lured to face a silent jury for their sins." He stared up at the pueblo on the cliff. "The guilty are led by a beautiful Native American woman who lies in a burial site twenty miles north of here."

Alara wiped her eyes and stood next to Shaun at the back of her vehicle. "You knew...back at the pueblo, didn't you?" She couldn't breathe. She thought she had been alone during her excavation at the primitive settlement a few weeks ago. But she was wrong. Someone had been watching. Someone had followed her here. The princess guardian spirit. Could she have taken some of the very objects owned by the vengeful phantom?

Shaun held up Alara's right palm so she could see. She gasped. A two-inch image of the trees was imprinted on her skin. She remembered the shock she had received from the petroglyph.

"Let this be a constant reminder. I'm not the jury here. Only the harbinger of justice."

He showed Alara his own hand—it had the same symbol of the Palo Verdes embedded into his palm. A glint of brilliant light burst from the ruins as he held it up. She gazed up at the pueblo. Had the display of radiance come from the mysterious petroglyph?

Just then, an image of Shaun invaded her mind. A picture so vivid and the sound of a gunshot so real Alara collapsed on her knees. He stood over a man's body, a pistol in his right hand. Earthen-colored pottery and ancient knick-knacks were scattered around. Shaun turned away, hurriedly grabbing ceramic pieces and packing the artifacts into a duffel bag.

The vision ended as abruptly as it began. Could the symbol somehow etched into her hand be uniting her thoughts with his? What did Shaun mean when he said he was "the harbinger of justice?"

Alara glanced from the pueblo on the cliff, to the Palo Verde arch and back to where Shaun had been standing.

He had vanished. Along with the artifacts.

†   †   †

LORI HINES' publishing credits include the paranormal mystery novel *The Ancient Ones*, published by Aberdeen Bay. Short stories include "Tragedy in the Pines," published in the 2010 Sisters in Crime, Desert Sleuths anthology, *How NOT to Survive a Vacation*. Awards include honorable mention for "A Glimpse Beyond" in the Desert Dweller Short Story Contest. She is a member of Sisters in Crime, Desert Sleuths Chapter, the Arizona Archaeological Society, Aqua Fria Chapter, and the AZ Authors Association. Visit her online http://lhauthor.wordpresscom.

CINNAMON CHURRO
MARTIN ROSELIUS

Sitting at the kitchen counter, I absently reached for the ringing phone while my concentration remained focused on the Diamondbacks box score in the sports section of the *Arizona Republic*. "Hello, this is Alexandro."

A gravelly voice from my past, reached out, taunting me. "Terrible thing about your daughter. She was such a pretty little cinnamon churro."

My arm dropped as I shot upright, my fresh cup of steaming coffee smacked the tile countertop and shattered, releasing a flood across the surface, some of which was quickly absorbed by the newspaper. I summoned the strength to speak. "Chagall?"

"Understand there's another young churro in your house now. Can't wait to meet her." There was a light snicker. The line clicked. The voice, gone.

Fingernails dug into my palm. Black liquid flowed over the edge of the counter and burned my thighs. I stared blankly at the puddle, then closed my eyes. The face remained, forcing a scream. "Chagall!"

I sat in stunned silence. The phone call ripped at my core as memories dark as nightmares burst to the surface. The pedophile and child molester, Brian Chagall, had entered my life nearly ten years ago, forcing his obscene violence upon my family. My wife, Maria, and I had testified against him in court. Helped put him away. He vowed he'd be out one day. Exact his revenge.

My rage subsided. I began to think more clearly. Accept the bitter reality. Chagall had been released from prison. How could they allow that? Is there no justice for victims?

Maria was at work and our four-year-old daughter, Angelina, in kindergarten. I contacted the Phoenix Police Department and spoke with a Sergeant Bartlett of the Family Investigations Bureau. He called back, confirmed that Brian Chagall, convicted sex offender, had indeed been released. How will I tell the mother of our second child that the man responsible for taking our first had been set free? Though we had welcomed a new baby, Angelina, named for a sister she'd never meet, we hadn't forgotten Teresa. No child can replace another.

That evening, after Angelina had been put to bed, and before I left for my shift, I told Maria of the disturbing phone call. She responded as if a hand had reached out of the pits of hell and slapped her. She had lived with deep dread this day would come. After the shock wore off, the tears flowed. I pulled her against me, her body shaking.

"What do we do now?" She looked at me, her face red, puffy, tear-streaked. "I can't live like this. We can't hide Angelina from that man forever."

I held her tight as my eyes drifted to the gold-framed portrait of Teresa in her softball uniform, bat across her shoulders, a big smile on her face. A happy time, before her life had been reduced to a few photos and cherished memories.

The thought of Chagall living in our Phoenix community tortured me. Maria was right. We couldn't live this way. The system had released that bastard. He had all but killed my daughter. Raped her. Held her in his basement for three days. She had escaped through a window but not before he had sucked out the vibrant breath of her youthful existence. Three years later, a deeply depressed teenager, she had taken her own life. Now this man threatened my second child.

I couldn't stand by and let it happen again.

Due to my call to Sergeant Bartlett, the police brought Chagall in for questioning and tried to establish probable cause for a parole violation. Chagall denied making the call and no evidence could be found to corroborate my complaint. The DA's office was hesitant to press charges. The police were instructed to simply advise Chagall not to have contact with us. I felt outrage. I couldn't sit back and wait for Chagall to carry out his threats. I had to protect my family.

That night I lay awake, fighting barely controlled anger and uncontrolled fear, when an ugly idea formed. Chagall had forced my family into a burning room with only one exit. The only escape, the only path to peace of mind, was through the front door. And Chagall had planted himself in the doorway. I had lived the worst kind of nightmare of any parent. I wasn't going to see my family face that kind of terror again.

The next day I drove across town to an Internet café. For a modest fee I used an onsite computer and accessed the Web. I had already checked out cruise itineraries from home. But now I needed to research airline flights and other information without leaving a trail of evidence that led back to me.

After leaving the café, I located a rare working public payphone and dialed my long-time friend in San Diego. "Carlos. It's Alexandro."

"Alex. How are things, *amigo*?"

"Not good. Listen. We need to talk."

"What's going on? You sound on edge. Nothing's wrong with Maria, is it?"

"No. She's doing…Well, she's okay."

"What's that supposed to mean? You're not having marriage problems, are ya?"

"No. Nothing like that…"

"Well?"

"Listen," I said. "We have always been like brothers. I need to ask you to do something. It requires you to trust me big time. And we must keep this between us. No one can know anything of what I'm about to tell you. We take it to the grave."

"Damn, *hombre*! You sound serious."

"I am."

Carlos and I went way back. Grew up in the same neighborhood in San Diego. Stood up for each other at our weddings and were godparents to each other's kids. He was like family, only closer than most. We had bailed each other out a few times, but never found ourselves skirting serious trouble.

That was about to change.

"You know I'm here for you, brother," he confirmed. "Whatever you need."

"Okay. Listen carefully. Here's what I need you to do. Within the next few weeks you have to fly to Puerto Vallarta, board a particular cruise ship and spend the night. The following morning when it arrives in Mazatlan, you'll leave the cruise ship, take a bus back to Puerto Vallarta, then fly back to San Diego."

"What? What the hell are you talking about? Fly to Puerto Vallarta. Spend the night on a cruise ship. Take a bus. Fly home? That sounds crazy, man. What's this all about?"

"I know it sounds crazy, but I can't say much more than that, so don't ask."

"This a joke?"

"No! It's no joke. I'm serious as hell. Listen, I wouldn't ask you to do this if it weren't important." I paused, knowing I was asking a lot of my friend. But under the circumstances, I was willing to risk anything. "Look. The less you know, the better. Trust me on this." I hesitated a moment. "Though there is one other thing…"

I could hear his skepticism. "Yeah?"

"Maria and I are taking a seven-day cruise down the coast of Mexico. When you board the cruise ship in Puerto Vallarta, I'm getting off. Then when you leave the ship the following day in Mazatlan, I'll be getting on. For those thirty-three hours…you'll be pretending to be me."

I told Carlos not to call my home or cell. I'd contact him in two days. I wanted to give him time to think it over. It was the least I could do.

Carlos could be a believable stand-in for me. Besides being a life-long friend I could trust, we had comparable physical features. We were nearly the same size, though he was an inch taller and had broader shoulders. We also had similar facial features and skin tone. With matching haircuts, we could be brothers.

When I contacted Carlos two days later, he agreed to help. He knew I was up to something, but put his confidence in our deep friendship. I doubted he could even begin to guess the reason behind his involvement. It was hard enough for me to grasp the truth.

The end result of my plan jabbed at my conscience. I continued to talk to myself. Look deep within me. Struggle with the answers. Am I no better than rogue vigilantes south of the border? When this was over, could I live with myself? Could I look at my daughter's face and not feel shame, disgrace? Would guilt reach out, continue to tear at us until finding its own justice? What about my Church? I knew full well the Catholic viewpoint on capital punishment. Can I break with my faith?

When I told Maria about my surprise booking of the cruise, she was thrilled, but questioned the timing.

"We've both been stressed these past few weeks," I said.

"Our nerves are shot." She knew what I meant. "It'll do us good to get away. We'll leave Angelina with your family in San Diego. I already called and set it up with your brother."

"I don't know, Alex. I'm not sure this is a good time to leave her. Why now?"

"What better time than now? The weather will be perfect in Mexico, and besides, we need some alone time."

"Just you and me?" She moved in close, wrapped her arms around my neck, lifted her head up and pressed her lips against mine, whispering, "Like a mini honeymoon."

I returned her kiss, held her head in my hands, stared deep into her eyes, and began to unfold the hard truth. "Maria. There's more to this cruise than I've told you."

"More?" She picked up on my serious tone and studied me with questioning eyes.

I brushed her hair back. Gave her a thin smile. I didn't know how much to tell her, or how much she would want to know. Would she understand there was no other recourse? The thought sickened me. But the thought of doing nothing, waiting for that bastard to come for my daughter, was . . .

"You know I love you and Angelina. I can't bear the thought of anything happening to either of you." I leaned down and kissed her once more, then told her about Carlos's involvement. I could see confusion settling on Maria's face. She opened her mouth, but I placed my finger over her lips to silence her words.

"I'll rejoin you in Mazatlan and Carlos will disappear. The remaining two days of the cruise it'll be just you and me. We'll enjoy each other like nothing ever happened. I was never gone. Carlos was never there."

Maria's face could not hide her shock. "What are you talking about? You're disappearing for two days and Carlos is going to take your place? Have you lost your mind?"

I leaned back and held her shoulders. "Please trust me on this. There's good reason for it. Carlos has already agreed."

"Carlos has agreed? What about me? I haven't agreed to anything! What are you going to be doing in Mexico for two days?" She stared at me a moment, then pulled back a bit. "Wait...it's...it's Chagall, isn't it? Alex, what are you planning to do?"

"Please, don't ask. Carlos has to stand in for me. Everyone must believe I've been aboard the entire time. No one can know any different. It's very, very important. Believe me, it has to be."

"*Dios mio*, Alex. Don't do this. There must be another way." She reached up, brushed my hands off her shoulders, turned, walked across the room and stared out the window. After a few moments, she spun around, tears in her eyes. "Alex, don't do this!"

Over the next few days we had brief conversations on the touchy subject of the upcoming cruise. Maria wanted to know more of my intentions, but instinctively knew where the boundaries were. She remained on edge and apprehensive. As did I.

I finalized my plan, reviewed every detail countless times. When the day arrived for our departure, we packed our luggage, along with a special bag I had prepared, and headed for the freeway. After six hours we arrived in San Diego, dropped Angelina off with Maria's family, then drove to the cruise terminal, boarded and settled into our cabin. During the two days at sea, tension grew between Maria and me, but we deliberately avoided discussing my impending departure.

The early morning sun glistened off the calm water of the harbor surrounding Puerto Vallarta. The ship was a flurry of activity. Passengers eager to sightsee, shop, eat and partake of their first Mexican margarita in the bustling port formed noisy lines in the halls and gangways while waiting to disembark. Maria and I returned to our stateroom after a quiet breakfast to pick up the bag I'd be taking. Her eyes were tearful as we embraced. "Are you sure you know what you're doing?"

I nodded.

She squeezed me tighter. "*Please, please, please* be careful, *corazón*. Angelina needs her daddy."

"I will." I swallowed a lump in my throat. "Don't worry, everything will be okay." I lowered my head, and in an attempt to relieve her anxiety, whispered in her ear. "I know Carlos is a good friend, but don't forget to wear those really ugly flannel pajamas tonight."

Maria leaned back and slapped her open palm against my shoulder with a light tap. She smiled as tears rolled down her cheeks.

We spotted Carlos at the same time. He was waiting outside the bar where we agreed to meet, far from the terminal. At this early hour, tourists hadn't yet begun to pour through the doors. He was dressed as I was in jean shorts, tropical flowered shirt and sandals. We headed for a table in the corner. After brief greetings, we exchanged driver's licenses and passports. I gave him my cruise ship photo ID card that on-board security scanned each time a passenger left or returned to the ship. He passed me his house key. I handed him a pair of glasses with frames that matched mine, but with clear glass. I removed my Jose Cuervo baseball hat, held it out to him, stood up, extended my hand, then leaned over and kissed Maria.

She reached up, held me tight, whispered, "I love you."

I kissed her again, then headed to the bathroom to change into jeans, a solid color long sleeve shirt and black boots. When I returned, they were gone. My heart flipped once or twice while I paused, stared at the empty chairs, then headed for the door.

I took a cab to the airport where I exchanged dollars for pesos and bought a one-way ticket to Hermosillo, Mexico. There I arranged for a small private plane to fly me to Puerto Peñasco, a small town on the Sea of Cortez quite popular with Americans who had purchased homes and condos in and around this beach community. Carlos's family was no exception. They had a home there and an unremarkable dark-green Subaru parked in their garage.

Upon arriving in Peñasco, I caught a cab to his vacant house, located the car keys in the kitchen drawer, cranked the vehicle and was soon heading up Mexico Federal Highway 8 to the border at Lukeville, Arizona, an hour away.

I checked my watch. 3:13 p.m. By 4:02 I hit the border station. Only two cars were ahead of me, so there wouldn't be any delay. Time was critical. I had to drive to Phoenix, take care of business, and return to Lukeville before the border closed at midnight. It wouldn't reopen until six the next morning. If I didn't cross back into Mexico before midnight, I wouldn't have enough time to work my way to Mazatlan before the ship sailed.

I had anxiety concerning the border checkpoint, even though I had the necessary credentials and I made a pretty decent Carlos. I pulled up, stopped, and a Border Patrol officer immediately circled my car with his trained German Shepherd sniffing for contraband. A second officer stepped out of the booth and extended his arm. I handed him the passport.

"Where you headed?"

"Phoenix."

He stepped back in and flipped through the document before entering Carlos's information into the government's database. He leaned out, glanced in the rear window, scanning the inside of my vehicle. "Purchase anything?"

"Nope."

A few minutes later, after studying the computer screen, he reached out once again and handed over the passport. "Drive safe."

"Thanks."

The drive to Phoenix was uneventful on the single-lane road that wound through the barren desert landscape. A highway with little traffic. Darkness fell. I thought of Maria and Carlos. They'd be having dinner now in the ship's intimate Pinnacle Grill. The wait staff there would not recognize either Maria or me by sight, but there would be a reservation and a charge to our cabin confirming we had eaten there. I had planned their evening so they could avoid sitting with our assigned tablemates in the regular dining room. For thirty-three hours they had to maintain a low profile.

I became more anxious with every passing mile, running my plan through my head again and again. What if something went wrong? What if Chagall wasn't home?

Then the big question…what if I can't do this?

By 6:52 I was on I-10 and soon entered the city limits. Lights of the metropolis lit up the sky. Traffic was heavy but moved at a lively pace. I jumped onto the freeway loop that circled the greater Phoenix area before exiting at Indian School Road.

After stopping by a Mexican bakery and a sporting goods store to make purchases, I parked in a spot at the outer fringe of a shopping center. Climbing into the back seat, I opened my bag and removed clothes and accessories: black tights that slipped over my feet and covered my legs, a black long-sleeve leotard and a red Arizona Diamondback jersey. I put on tennis shoes and batting gloves, plus a shoulder-length black wig and a pair of ladies bling-encrusted sunglasses that automatically adjusted to light.

With some earlier research I knew Chagall's address. He had

taken up residence in a house his mother left him. With an open carport it blended in among a modest neighborhood of ranch-style block stucco homes. During the past weeks I had risked driving by on two consecutive Tuesday evenings. Each time, a car had been sitting in his carport and lights were on in the house. I drove there now. The same car was there. The lights were on. Knowing I was under a tight timeline allowed less time for doubt to creep in. I had to move fast.

I parked against the curb a block away. The neighborhood remained quiet and dark except for a few widely spaced streetlights. I would have to pass through the soft light beneath three of them to reach his house. I turned off the ignition. Sat for a moment. Retrieved two photos from my wallet. My girls. I held them in my hand, traced their faces with my finger, took a deep breath. "For you my angel in heaven." I glanced at the second one. "And you, my little sweetheart." I raised the photos to my lips, gave each a light kiss, then replaced them in the wallet before slipping the billfold into my folded jeans pocket.

Glancing down the street, I satisfied myself no one was around. I looked in the mirror and swallowed. I knew, from this moment on, my life would never be the same. I fought with my conscience long enough. Better I fight the demons that would surely haunt me, than allow them to torment my child. I picked up a paper sack soaked with fresh cooking oil stains and the newly purchased Louisville Slugger baseball bat, opened the car door and stepped out.

My tennis shoes made a soft, rhythmic thump against the uneven sidewalk. Within moments, I approached the door and knocked three times. Footsteps. The door flew open. A burly silhouette filled the doorway. A gravelly voice, smelling of alcohol, broke the silence.

"Who the hell are you!"

I was sitting at my kitchen counter when the doorbell rang. "Just a minute," I hollered as I set the morning paper down, rose and headed toward the entrance hall with coffee cup in hand. I opened the door and stared at two men in suits. The taller one held out a leather billfold to display a polished badge. "Mr. Alexandro Espinoza?"

"Yes. I'm Alexandro."

"I'm Sergeant Bartlett. Phoenix PD." He gestured to the other man. "This is Detective Gonzalez. We'd like to ask you a few questions. May we come in?"

I studied them for a moment, but revealed no anxiety regarding their visit. "Ah, sure, please." I swung the door wider, led them to the living room, and pointed to the couch. "So, what's this about?"

"We're investigating a felony assault. Man named Chagall. Brian Chagall. We understand you know who this man is."

I looked straight at the Sergeant. "Yes. Yes I do."

"And I recall you and I discussed Mr. Chagall on the phone several weeks ago. I'm sorry your family had to endure that..."

I remained silent as he trailed off.

"Your wife, Ms. Maria Espinoza, is she home?"

"No. She's at work."

"We need to talk to her and anyone else, for that matter, who might have had a motive to assault Mr. Chagall."

"Can't say I'm upset. I'd have preferred someone kill the bastard. But personally, I don't believe in capital punishment."

The Sergeant studied me a moment then pulled a small notepad out of his coat pocket. "Can you tell me where you and your wife were last Tuesday evening?"

"We were both in Mexico. My wife and I took a seven-day cruise." I rubbed my chin, squinted toward the ceiling. "Tuesday night, huh? Believe we were in Puerto Vallarta. No, sorry, the ship left Puerto Vallarta that night, heading to Mazatlan."

The detectives glanced at each other, then the Sergeant dropped his eyes to his pad as the pen did a rapid salsa across the page. He asked further details about the cruise line and the dates. I filled him in.

"We'll have to confirm this, of course." The detectives stood and I escorted them to the door. The Sergeant turned and stared at me. "You never inquired about his condition."

"Is he still capable of assaulting children?"

The detective studied my face. "Someone beat him severely. A woman reportedly, although the victim is a rather unreliable witness to his own beating. He was inebriated at the time. Allegedly, a baseball bat was used. Really did a number on him. Shattered both kneecaps. He won't ever walk again. Probably be pissing through a tube the rest of his life."

The detective shook his head, started down the steps, then turned back. "Funny thing. The assailant forced him to eat cinnamon churros before he was assaulted. Wonder what that was all about? Couldn't eat 'em now though. Have to put 'em in a blender, drink them through a straw."

I watched the officers' vehicle as it turned down the street, then glanced up and stared off toward the peaks of South Mountain. I took a deep breath, knowing I could breathe easier now. The winds of justice had cleared the air and removed a foul stench that had settled upon the community. I followed the little wisps of cloud that started in the west and stretched across the sky, pulling my eyes higher, to a place I thought about every single day.

We got the bad guy, my angel. He won't ever hurt another child.

† † †

MARTIN ROSELIUS, following a career in graphic design/illustration, has channeled his creative energies into the art of writing, having completed a memoir, SAND IN MY SHOES, ROCKS IN MY HEAD, and his first novel, an espionage thriller, YELLOW BLOOD, RED FEVER. His publishing credits include: *Caribbean Travel + Life* magazine, the *Mystery Readers Journal* and short stories published in anthologies by Sisters in Crime and the Society of Southwestern Authors, the latter which took third place in SSA's 2010 writing contest.

THE TUMBLEWEED MYSTERY
CR BOLINSKI

When Sasha suggested the campout I gagged as if a fish bone were caught in my throat. "You must be kidding," I told her. "I don't do campfires or overnights outside." I had a reputation to keep. Especially one contrary to what my peers were doing, like dirt biking or rafting down the Salt River. It was the west's answer to recreation. While living in New York, mine had been hanging out at art museums, specifically the MOMA, for relaxation. Even though I now lived in Arizona, my mantra still had not become "do as the westerners do."

But Sasha being Sasha had her own agenda and insisted I play chaperone to her and Tony, who was the "utmost hunk"— her words—and if I didn't, well, she'd just "die."

"What?" I roared. "I'm not going to be a third wheel out in the middle of nowhere. And I certainly won't participate in anything kinky. Besides, you're too old to go camping. It's for kids who don't know any better."

"Come on, Jayne. What's gotten into you? There'll be others there too. Tony's daughter and older brother...and another couple, friends of his brother. Also, I think his brother's boss may show up...or somebody's boss." She gave me another pleading look.

"You want me to be a babysitter too? How old is this brother?" Maybe this won't be that bad.

"He's a year or two older than you and...it isn't a fix-up, I promise. He's even cuter than Tony. Vincenzo, but they call him Vinny. Please? He's seen us together and really wants to meet you."

"Our first date is under a pine tree? I don't think so." How much more was she leaving out?

Sasha finally convinced me to go. It was actually blackmail. She remembered the favor she did for me a few months ago— lending me money so I could visit my boyfriend who became my ex when I found out he'd been cheating. She just happened to remember my words, "I promise I'll pay you back." The favor not the money. Never have a friend with a good memory.

It was evening and we sat around a campfire getting roasted by the crackling flames. No one told me what kind of clothes to bring. I thought camping clothes, right? So I packed everything brown I owned. I didn't realize there were certain western getups like boots and cowboy hats, and particular jeans and T-shirts that gave one the ins to being a camper. When I asked Sasha about shoes, she said boots. So I got a pair of Gucci hiking boots. I thought, they're brown, and of course they'd be hip enough. No. The rest of the group looked sloppy and unkempt. When I spoke, I tried to roll my native Bronx accent back into my throat, and I seethed that my first rule of not doing campfires was broken.

Tony sat next to his daughter, Gia. She had wide blue eyes and dark long hair. A quiet kid, but charming. Maybe I felt we had something in common since we both were strangers around other strangers. Sasha sat on the other side of Tony, her "hunk." Vinny sat near me. Vinny's friends, Roberto and Maria, were nestled across from us on the other side of the fire.

"Wasn't someone's boss supposed to join us?" I asked.

Maria loosened her arm around Roberto, "Roberto's boss. But that didn't work. Right, honey?"

Roberto kept his eyes on his food. He didn't answer.

We were finishing bowls of chili. Mine was excruciatingly hot, as in acid hot, so I gave it to Sasha. Now rolled up in blankets sitting on tree logs in the desert night under a cool western sky, our conversation dwindled into silence. The stars were intense and under all their twinkling brilliance, I expected Gene Autry, my grandmother's hero, to come riding through the brush singing "Back in the Saddle Again."

I had to admit, Sasha was right. Vinny was better looking than his younger brother and we hit it off right away. His brown eyes were happy and engaging; dark eyelashes emphasized them even more. His skin was the color of burnt sienna and he smelled of pine needles and campfire smoke.

Roberto had on his Stetson and boots with silver tips. He rolled his cigarettes, something I thought was a forgotten art, and had a western drawl the size of Texas. His wedding band and Maria's matched perfectly. They must have married recently.

Roberto said, "This is living. Out in the wilderness—God's country. Nothing gets better than this." He hugged Maria, then looked over at me, "Hey, city girl. What happens when you get your boots dirty? Do you send them to the cleaners?" Maria giggled. He was just one big riot.

"No. I spit on them. Just like you do," sarcasm oozing from every pore of my body.

Sasha got in the middle. "Take it easy. We need to get along."

Roberto's chest puffed up. "Yeah, but we don't have to sound like Bronxie over there."

"Roberto!" Maria chimed in. She looked coyly at me, "Please don't mind him. He got laid off yesterday…then got into it with his boss—that's why he's not here."

"Don't even mention him, Maria. He's a lowlife." Roberto looked annoyed and walked away.

Vinny told me, "Roberto and I work for the same company. Roberto's boss is one big racist dude. He even got into it with me earlier today, and he's not even my supervisor. Nobody likes him. But last week Roberto asked him along thinking it would help their relationship, help change his boss's view of Mexican-Americans."

Maria added, "Roberto usually has a great sense of humor. Always plays practical jokes on everyone."

I started to say something else but Sasha shushed me… probably afraid I'd say something about Roberto's obvious chip on his shoulder. But if I just lost my job, maybe I'd feel similar.

I could think of a hundred things better than being here. But these were Sasha's friends, I kept telling myself. She'd singled me out earlier when we were getting settled, said I should be friendlier. Thought I'd try her advice. It would keep the peace.

The fire popped and pieces of red ash landed on my new hiking boots. I blew them off and noticed the sky seemed darker. Where did all those stars disappear to? What's happening? The wind picked up and sand blew in my face. I swallowed its dryness and, for the first time, knew what arid tasted like. Air currents howled in the distance and a bit of adrenaline ran through my veins.

Vinny seemed to take the oncoming weather as an excuse to get closer.

"Hey," I may have said a bit too loud. What was it about

campfires that brought out notions of romance? I was dying out here in the wilderness and felt about as attractive as a spiny cactus.

Vinny murmured, "Just trying to let you know I'm nearby and that you're safe." He had a knack with words. For all I knew safe with him may have been the same thing as being curled up next to a mountain lion.

I looked around our cheery group. You could tell Vinny and Tony were brothers because of similar skin coloring, and each had a dimple in his chin. Sasha was right, they both were good-looking men, and I agreed with her depiction of "hunk." Gia, Tony's daughter, looked about twelve. She and her father bundled up in a serape and practically sat in Sasha's lap. The preteen knew how to warm up to her father's girlfriend. Maria and Roberto were still wrapped up in each other. Good reason for my exit.

"Think I'll call it a night." Vinny started to get up too. I looked at him with conviction. "I'm capable of going to the tent myself." He smiled that smile that said it wasn't the tent he was interested in. I pushed him back onto the log. "See everyone later."

When we first arrived at the campsite, I thought we were going to do the whole outside thing, sleeping under the stars, smelling nature. Thank God for saving me from that. My second rule of not doing overnights outside remained intact. Although the last time I visited a tent was for a wedding, not for sleeping. This one was a lot smaller. I would have preferred individual sleeping areas, but what could happen if we all were together? Maybe it was better.

Gia followed me. I guess the adults wanted to be alone. We unfolded our sleeping bags, Gia moved hers closer to mine.

"I'm always the one left out," she said. "Glad you're here." Well, that made my night. "I didn't want to come but my dad thought I should get to know your friend."

"Her name's Sasha."

"Whatever." Gia stripped off her outer layer of clothes. Underneath, she already wore flannel pajamas. Doggy paw prints were sprinkled along a light pink background. She crawled into her sleeping bag.

I felt for the kid. "It's probably tough being with different women your father dates. At least they want you along. There are plenty of children that don't get that offer."

"Maybe. At least my father isn't a total loser like my mom. She left us. Haven't seen her in five years. So, I'm not that lucky."

I told her I had a mother like that too. Gia didn't seem to care.

I wanted to change the subject and thought the weather would be a safe topic. "That wind seems so loud to me. Does it usually sound like that?" I curled up in my sleeping bag and zipped the side seam shut.

She said her father told her earlier it was probably moving around forty miles per hour.

How the hell could the tent stay up in that? As soon as my head hit the pillow I didn't care about wind anymore.

During the night I'd occasionally hear wind whistling against the flaps. Sometimes the sound was so intense it seemed to roar and then subside into whispers. I didn't know if I was dreaming or if those thunderous sounds that came ripping through our campsite were for real.

Morning came too soon. It was quiet when I moved the blanket inside the sleeping bag away from my face. My mouth tasted like dried scallions. I swallowed my first yawn, hoping my sweatpants, three layers of sweaters, tights, gloves and scarf would be warm enough for me to go the latrine. Everyone else was sleeping. Gia was still on my right and Vinny, snoring like a drunken sailor, a little too close on my left. Very carefully, I tiptoed out into the dawn.

Once outside, I discovered the wind had settled and my anticipation along with it. I started to walk toward a clearing where the piñons and cottonwoods led into a dense forest. The area smelled like fresh pine and although everything looked withered from a long winter, here and there were spots of green that indicated spring wanted to come through. I heard light footsteps following me. Turning around, I found Gia. "I need to go to the bathroom, too," she said. Together we looked for the obvious holes in the ground.

I noticed a large wall of sagebrush piled into a huge bundle. I'd never seen anything like it. Grabbing Gia's hand, we walked toward this tumbleweed mountain that caught my curiosity because of its humongous form. I slowly inspected the dried-out thorny limbs and clumps of twig-like branches entwined in each other. Spellbound by this desert oddity, I moved closer still clasping Gia's palm.

I was trying to figure out where all these tumbleweeds came from when Gia cried out, "There's a hand sticking out of that brush!" I looked where she pointed, eye level for her, and felt sick when I spotted bloated fingers with discolored, blister-like formations on its knuckles.

Covering Gia's eyes, I turned her around in case there were other parts of a body stuck in the shriveled spines. I had to get her out of there, pronto.

"Come on. We'll get your dad to come back and see what's going on." As we turned to leave, I took one more look and saw those distended fingers hanging through a clump of dead weedy limbs. I let go of my grip across Gia's eyes and dragged her back to camp as fast as I could, forgetting about the toilets. She must have forgotten too because she didn't complain as we broke into a run. I discovered my designer boots were pretty good for sprinting. Thank you, Gucci.

When we got back to our campground, everyone was up except Roberto. I waved my arms frantically and gasped, "We think we saw a hand in a mound of tumbleweed."

"Think? You think? Did you or didn't you?" Vinny asked.

"Gia found it and I wasn't about to let her stay to examine it. But I'm sure it's there."

He glared, then said, "Well, you should have made sure."

"Vin, lay off." Tony said to his brother. "I'm glad she did that for Gia. That was good."

Vinny and Tony scrambled in front of me. Gia ran to her dad, who said to me, "Show us where." He turned to Gia. "And you, young lady, stay here with Roberto. He's inside the tent. We'll be back as soon as we can."

"Why can't I come too? I was the one who found it."

"I said stay here." Tony raced in front of everyone.

Sasha and Maria wrapped blankets around their shoulders and we all jogged toward the clearing. I turned and saw Gia's head droop as she stood in her pink PJs.

We came to the clearing where I last saw the bundles of dried weeds. "The hand was inside that tumbleweed, over there." I pointed to the biggest pile at the far corner of the opening. The group gathered around the mass of tumbleweeds expecting to see some part of the human anatomy caught in twining bristle. But there was nothing. I looked around to see if there was another big mound of tumbleweed that could have moved since we were last here.

Vinny said, "I don't see any hand." His lips rolled into a skeptical smile.

"Actually, I'd feel better knowing there wasn't one," I said. "But I'm sure I saw it." I went over to examine the brush; touched the outside of the limbs and poked my head into the maze as close as I could without getting thorned. I looked for evidence, any evidence that would indicate there was something human stuck in those dried-up needles, but found nothing.

"Here it is!" Sasha screamed from beside another jumble of tumbleweeds. "I found it!" But as she looked closer, "No. Sorry. I thought I saw something solid but it's nothing."

Sasha looked at me. "Maybe you saw an animal like a squirrel or a gopher."

"It was a hand. Right where we're standing." I wondered if maybe this was some kind of sick joke that dear old Roberto was playing. I looked for Maria. "Is this something that Roberto would do? Is he playing with me?"

"I don't think so." She seemed to be studying the scene, rolling the blanket tighter around her shoulders. "But early this morning, real early, before anyone else was up, I didn't see him. He wasn't in the tent." She hesitated, "Are you sure the hand was real?"

Although I nodded my head in agreement, I wondered if it could have been some type of plastic or rubber.

I promised myself this was the last time I'd ever go camping with Sasha. If this was some kind of initiation to the west, I didn't like it. Not one bit.

Vinny suggested, "Look. None of us are finding anything. Let's go back to camp and make breakfast."

"You okay with that, Jayne?" Sasha asked.

They were all waiting for me to say something and I wanted to leave. "Sure."

Tony reminded everyone we needed more wood for the fire. "If all of us bring a couple of more logs back, we should have enough to make it through one more meal."

I said to Sasha, "You're coming with me. If I discover another tumbleweed with a different human part, I don't want to be alone."

"That would be something, wouldn't it?" she said.

"Yeah. Something."

Sasha and I walked into the dense woods. We each grabbed a couple of downed tree limbs and hustled back to camp.

We sat on one of the camping logs deep in thought. The morning was sunny and the fire knocked off the stiff chill. Gia stood outside the tent waiting for her dad.

Tony ran out and said, "Roberto isn't here! Maria, I thought you told me he went back to sleep. I better go look in the van."

I gave Sasha a mood altering stare. "Here we go again. Something else to get excited about. What is with this cowboy?"

Maria heard me, "He should have been in the tent."

Tony came back and told us he didn't see Roberto in the van either.

Tony looked over at Maria, "Weren't you the last person who saw him?"

"Yes, but that was awhile ago. He said he was going to use the 'hole,' then go back to camp and get more sleep."

Tony asked, "So you didn't actually see him go inside?"

"I thought I did," Maria said. Then pointing to me added, "But then that's when Jayne came back and told us about the hand." She looked around at our motley group. "I thought someone said they saw him go into the tent. Wasn't it you, Tony?"

I thought it was Vinny. But I wasn't sure about that either. Something didn't settle well with me. I became more convinced that Roberto was playing with us. Me in particular. It went through my mind that he may have gotten up before me and put a fake hand in the tumbleweed for me to find. Unfortunately, Gia found it first.

Sasha said, "Vinny, didn't you tell us Roberto was in the tent?"

Everyone looked at Vinny. His eyes glinted in the morning light. He looked too happy. Was he in on it too?

"Nope. That was Tony. Remember he told Gia to stay put until we got back."

"How could we have left his daughter alone without knowing for sure if Roberto was here or not?" I asked. Some group of responsible people we turned out to be.

Tony took charge. "Everyone stay here. I'm going into that

clearing again and look around. Just stay together. And look after Gia."

Maria took a sack of chewing tobacco out of her pocket. "Before he left earlier, Roberto asked me to hold onto this." She opened it up and inside was a latex glove shoved into its crushed leaves. "Do you think this means something?" Her high voice cracked and she looked on the verge of tears.

Now I felt for sure Roberto was our antagonist. "I think it means we've all been suckered." Sasha stuck her elbow in my ribs. "What?" I raised my eyebrows at her. "It certainly sounds like he was the one that put that hand in the tumbleweed, figuring someone would find it."

Gia's words rang through my head, *I'm always left out.* It looked like both of us were the odd ones out. "I wonder if anyone else was in on Roberto's plan?" What and who should I believe?

Sasha confirmed, "I knew nothing about it." She was waiting for Maria to say something. But Maria was pacing back and forth.

My hungry stomach needed nourishment. It put a stop to our current bickering and I passed around stainless steel plates with plastic spoons.

Halfway through a huge hot cake covered with syrup, Roberto and Tony came into view, Roberto laughing his head off.

He looked at me, "You thought I did what? Place a hand in the tumbleweed?" He couldn't control his hysterics. My cheeks felt as red as the fire. "Lady, you haven't been around our parts for too long, have you?" His laugh kept him from saying anything else. Maria whispered something in his ear. He stopped giggling.

"Oh. I see you found the plastic glove. Okay. Okay. It was me. I did it." He confessed much too quickly.

Still suspicious, I added lying to the list of reasons of why I didn't care for Roberto.

I didn't know what to believe now. No one else mentioned the hand again.

It took about an hour to pack up and start back to civilization. I was more than ready. Now I'd probably have nightmares about hands, even plastic ones. If I did I would call Sasha and wake her up.

We were about a mile from our campsite when the traffic started slowing.

Sasha broke the silence, "Is there an accident up ahead?"

Before any of us could answer, our van stopped behind a number of cars in front of us. I really wanted to get home and put this experience behind me. I thought about the people in the van who were now avoiding me. So far there was Vinny, and I didn't understand why, Roberto, and maybe Maria, out of loyalty for him. Gia seemed to be my only friend, and, Sasha, of course, who says I should be more charming. While ruminating on this, fifteen minutes passed and it looked like we were in for a longer wait.

Tony, our designated driver, decided to get out of the van and see what was holding up traffic. I told Gia, "Sasha and I will be right back." Maria fell into step behind us and Vinny behind her. Roberto stayed in the vehicle with Gia. We shoved our way through the crowd until we could see what all the commotion was about.

"Oh my gosh!" A woman covered her mouth with her hand. She had on a big sombrero; her eyes wide open. I heard murmurs through the crowd and a man tried to stop us from getting closer.

"Jayne, help me push through the crowd." Sasha wanted me to shove a family over so we could get into the circle of people.

"Hold onto me. I'll do my best." I elbowed my way past the mother and father and then through two motorcyclists wearing black leather and ponytails. Finally we were able to break through some kids standing in front of the gathering. We looked in the direction where everyone seemed to be focused. I grabbed Sasha's wrist. She had her mouth opened wide and then I saw what she stared at. On the ground was a body stuffed inside a thicket of tumbleweeds. An arm with a missing hand dangled out of its prickly limbs.

Maria pushed her way in front of me. Vinny still right behind her. She bent down to get a closer look at the body and then turned toward us, "Oh, no! That looks like Roberto's boss."

"It sure does," Vinny agreed. His smile had a little curl of mischief when he said, "Looks like that hand was for real."

† † †

CR BOLINSKI (aka CR Seldin and C Rose) writes in many genres and has published poetry, flash fiction and mystery short stories. Some of her work can be read in several anthologies, among them, *How Not to Survive the Holidays* (DS Publishing, 2009), and *Medley of Murder* (Red Coyote Press, 2005). She presently lives in northern Arizona.

FOWL PLAY
AMY SCHUSTER

Manuel entered through the familiar French door. He was Puerto Rican and partial to cockfighting. That's how the trouble all began.

Earlier that evening he'd placed a bet on Conche, the rust colored bird that was all the rage. He'd watched him in the preliminary scrimmage and he was red hot. "A sure thing" as they say. Problem was Manuel placed his bet on margin. Tito took the action, making notes in a spiral bound notebook and tucking it into his belt. Conche fizzled, then Tito came looking for him, wanting the dough. Manuel slipped into the darkened alley and fled until enough ground had been made between them before slipping inside the aforementioned French door.

The old man lay upon flannel sheets, a fan spinning above him. The smell of Ben Gay wafted through the air. The off-duty Chihuahua snorted upon its pillow, too tired from the day of barking to make a fuss. Manuel slowed his pace as he skirted past the bed to the floor safe. He lowered himself into the corner, his eyes straining in the pale light as his fingers tumbled the lock. He pulled the door and it opened with an eerie creak.

The old man stirred, hoisting himself up on one elbow to turn on the bedside lamp. "Back again, I see," he said in Spanish.

Manuel stood, his overalls bagging. "Papa, I've run into a spot of bad luck. I need money to satisfy my debt."

"So you come to me, in the cover of darkness to make your world right?"

"Shut up, old man. I don't need your lecture. Tito's hot on my trail. I'll just take what I need and be on my way. There's plenty here, you won't miss it."

"Lucky for you my legs are weak. If I could, I'd get out of this bed and beat you silly with my bare hands," the old man said. "One day all I have will be gone and you'll have to take your thievery to another man's door. He pulled on the chain to hush the light before lying back down.

"Oh, Papa, so tired and full of fear. It's always the same."

"It's true I am tired. Your *madre*, God rest her soul, she worked her fingers to the bone for you. We did without so that you might go to college and have a better life. And here you are pissing it away on gambling. Will you ever learn?"

"I can double the money here at the fights. What do I need college for when the cocks might pay so well?" he said, closing the safe and taking his leave.

Manuel walked back through the alley, the soles of his shoes crunching in the quiet of the night. With a flick of his lighter he lit the cigarette pursed between his lips, the small flame illuminating his bronze face. Tito stepped into his path from the recesses of the darkened corridor, stopping him.

"Why'd you run? Don't you know nobody runs from Tito?"

"I...I needed to go get the money so I could pay up," Manuel said with a stammer

"We're all professionals here. You could have just explained yourself. I'm an understanding guy. But you don't run from Tito. That was your first and last mistake," he said, palming the brass knuckles that adorned his right fist.

"But, I have the money, all of it. It's right here," Manuel said tossing the cigarette to reach in his pocket. Tito pounced, pummeling his face and gut, the brass splitting the flesh that covered the crunching bones. Manuel crumpled to the ground in a heap like an imploding building, his face a shambles, oozing blood. Playing dead, his teeth wobbled inside his closed mouth, tainted saliva trickling down his throat. Through the haze of shock he felt Tito fishing the cash from his pocket, his snakeskin boots inches away from his fractured face.

"Don't come back," Tito warned as he sauntered back down the alley.

Curled into the ferocious pain of the beating, Manuel lay there motionless except for his thoughts which moved through space like a time machine, pausing at points of failure that troubled him. He felt his life slipping away as he lay there in the dirt, his breath a grating rattle as he silently mouthed the rosary, his *madre*'s favorite prayer. Her spirit came and knelt beside him in the hellish alley and chased his remorse away. He could feel the warmth of her as she cradled his broken face in her thick arms, the sight of her flawed grin a vision that calmed his heart. By the time he finished the Hail Holy Queen, he knew what he had to do, his father's words from earlier that night ringing in his swollen ears.

† † †

Manuel's plane landed in Lubbock, Texas. From there he caught a bus that dropped him not far from campus. He hoofed it from there, shouldering his pack, smoking a cigarette as he went. He paused before the ornate brick entry that stated: WELCOME TO THE INTERNATIONAL SCHOOL OF CLOWN PERFORMING ARTS.

He corralled his nerves as a mixture of emotions seized him. A sense of duty conquered the ambivalence as he proceeded with the realization of his parents' dream. He made the sign of the cross before going through the entry and on to the admissions office, which was a lopsided tree house perched precariously upon the massive branches of an old oak. He set his pack down and climbed the uneven boards nailed to the tree, each one giving beneath the weight of him. Once upon the slender porch he saw a sign over the door: DEAN OF ADMISSIONS. He rang the bell which released a stream of seltzer water into his face. He spat and reached for his handkerchief.

"Come on in," Manuel heard from the other side of the door. He hesitated, before turning the knob and pushing only his head through the crack to scout the scene.

Seated at the desk with his feet up inside the small cell was a clown. His afro was rainbow colored and stood out like a halo against the backdrop of the tree trunk that lined the back wall of the room. His lavender eyelashes batted the chub of his white cheeks when he blinked. His painted on smile widened when his lips parted revealing yellowing teeth. "Come in, come in," he ushered with his free hand, the other one resting on the sable colored rabbit that sat in his paisley lap. "You must be Manuel. We've been expecting you."

Manuel released his breath, the tension ebbing at the sound of the man's voice. He pushed the door all the way open which popped a balloon, which dropped a rock tied to a string, which tipped the bucket of water that doused him all the way down to his feet. He stood there, rocking on soggy shoes, waiting for direction.

"You're not laughing, that's good. We like our clowns to be complete novices. We will construct you from the ground up, one clown idiom at a time. It's much easier to engrave the elements of fine clowning onto a blank slate rather than try to correct poor clowning habits that developed from God knows where. I can see you've had no formal training and that's what we prefer," he said stroking the rabbit.

"Have a seat on that unicycle there. We've rigged it so it's secured at times but intermittently it's released, which will train you rapidly in the art of balance. Before you know it you'll be riding it with the greatest of ease," he said as Manuel straddled the unicycle.

"They call me Homey, and this here is Bunny Foo Foo, sometimes Foo for short, depending on my mood. I see here on your application that you are the first person in your family to attend college."

"That's right, it was my parents' dream that I attend," he said teetering on the unicycle seat.

"Lofty goals indeed. Listen pal, it's no cakewalk making it through this institution of higher learning. People think its all cream pies, banana peels, and floppy shoes but it isn't. There are long standing traditions in the clowning profession that must be adhered to. You can never lose sight of our mission statement and the Clown's Code of Conduct." He pinched the rubber nose tighter onto the end of his own. "Have you decided on a major?" he asked honking the horn mounted on his desk with his fuchsia colored fingernails.

"Rodeo clowning," Manuel replied with conviction.

"Ahh, I see, a cowboy at heart," Homey said with a wink. "It's one of the toughest fields and dangerous to boot. Those bulls mean business. Look there," he said, pointing to one of the photographs mounted on the wall. "That's Hokey Pokey, one of our finest rodeo clown alumni. He was the first to elude the bulls on stilts, it was his signature move. It wasn't easy trekking through all that crap on stilts. He had some great runs until Lawrence Welk, the bull, not the quintessential big band leader, stopped him in his tracks. Pokey took a nasty fall and Lawrence Welk sat on him, like a man waiting for a bus. All the life was squeezed right out of old Pokey. He died doing what he loved," Homey said wiping away the single tear that pooled on his pasty face.

Manuel coughed, interrupting the mournful tone that had taken over. "I understand the risks and I take them on wholeheartedly. Could you direct me to my dormitory? I've been traveling all day and would like to rest before dinner."

Manuel began his trek across campus to his room. He missed Puerto Rico with its cobbled streets, candy colored houses, and tropical breezes. Here the dust rose with the fall of each boot, the confusing twang of the Texan's dialect, the flags, the crew cuts, the ten gallon hats. It would all take getting used to.

He pushed the door open to reveal the room. It was small like a cracker box and he, the crumbled sleeve of saltines. A twin bed hugged the far wall with a bland spread and thin pillow on top. There was a folded futon, a sink and a hot plate next to a door that led to the dingy bathroom. It wasn't much and it made him long for home and his stuff. Out of sorts, part of him wanted to walk right back out the door he came in and return to his life in San Juan. He could almost smell the pork roasting over the barrel fires that lined the streets, the charred fat sizzling. He thought longingly of the hibiscus in bloom, a pot of strong coffee on the stove, a line of freshly laundered clothes snapping in the air, the smells of comfort.

There was a knock on the door. Puzzled, he answered it. In the hall stood a man about as big around as he was tall. His arms ballooning out from his girth, in his left hand a fist full of churros. He wore polyester pants pulled tight against his fat, harnessed by a leather belt stretched to its limits—a colossal silver buckle, glimmering. A white Stetson rested on the tips of his ears, a pronounced overbite fought with pink lips, the soul patch graying. Black, round rimmed frames slouched on the bridge of his pug nose, begging to be shoved back into their proper place, the lenses smeared with a greasy sheen that blurred the crows feet behind them.

"Hi, I'm Frederick," he said, offering his hand. "I'm the welcome wagon here at Clown U."

"Hi, I'm Manuel," he said shaking his hand. "This is great. I didn't even know they had a welcome wagon."

"Well, I sort of started it myself, it's not official or anything. Just a small gesture I make towards the new arrivals. You know, to make them feel at home. I've been studying here for quite some time. It's hard when people graduate and move on. I sort of keep losing my friends. Churro?" he asked holding out the bundle.

"Sure." Manual reached for one and took a bite.

"I'm working on my third PhD, in case you're wondering why I've been here so long," Frederick said before biting his own churro.

"Exactly how long have you been here?"

"Fifteen years," Frederick said with his mouth full.

"Oh, wow, I had no idea one could study here that long. When do you figure you'll be done?" he asked.

"My parents keep asking the same thing. Look, I keep telling them it's all about being the best you can be and for me, my genius needs to be stoked. I'm not happy unless there's something new for me to learn. My dissertations include Tricycle Riding for the Portly, Stilt Walking the Tall and Short of It, Cream Pies versus Fruit Pies—the Clown's Conundrum, and Coulrophobia—Fact or Fiction."

"It sounds as though you've covered just about everything," Manuel said.

"What's that supposed to mean? Are you implying that I'm spinning my wheels? Just wasting time? You sound like my mother, the witch. Oh yeah, she sends the tuition check and the room and board, but trust me, it all comes with a price. Every month her ridiculous handwritten notes come on floral stationary spritzed with Chanel Number Five. It's torture the way she coddles me. She can't stand me being gone, she wants me back at home with her and Father so I can caddy for him while he cheats at golf. Have you ever watched a man cheat at golf? It's twisted," he said as his neck began to twitch and sweat settled beneath his nose.

Frederick grew more agitated as he let loose his story, the words filling the space with dread that painted a picture of instability, hard for Manuel to avoid.

"Hey man, I didn't mean to upset you," Manuel said. "I'm sorry. These churros are real good, can I have another?"

"Yeah sure, help yourself." Frederick raised the fat hairy fingers that held them. "Sorry I went off on you. She gets the best of me sometimes. Where are you from?"

"San Juan, Puerto Rico. It's really nice there. Very different from Texas."

"Yeah, Texas is, well, Texas. It's unlike anything else. You'll get used to the dust before long, it's everywhere. What did you do back home?"

"I was into cock fighting. It's in my blood. I gave it up. The gambling losses were taking their toll, but that's in the past. It was my parents' dream I go to college, so here I am."

"That's nasty business," Frederick said. "Lacey likes cock fighting."

"Who's Lacey?" Manuel asked.

"This girl I know. A good friend. She's stopping by later for a drink at my place. Why don't you join us around eight?"

"I don't want to intrude."

"Oh, she won't mind at all. In fact, if you play your cards right, she might even get you into the fights later tonight."

"Really?" Manuel gushed as saliva swished over his tongue and his palms began to itch. "I don't know. I'm supposed to be done with all that. This is my new start. I left all that behind. I better not."

"I didn't say you had to take her up on it. Tell her no. Besides, I'm not even sure she'll invite you. Come on, it'll be fun. She's a real looker."

"I suppose it wouldn't hurt."

"Excellent," Frederick said as he hoisted himself up from the futon. "I'll see you around eight then."

Manuel closed the door as a familiar euphoria bathed him. There was no doubt that he'd follow sweet Lacey to the cock fight. The impetuous burn of his addiction erased all the concerns he held about Frederick's volatile whims, his thoughts instead tiptoeing toward the thrill of the fights. He reached for his wallet and counted out his cash, his fingers dallying there on the familiar bills, the coarse weave, the tell-tale smell, delighting his senses.

Aroused, he wasted time throughout the early evening, going through the motions as he made a bowl of ramen noodles and sang a happy song. He thought of calling his father to tell him that he'd arrived safely, but talked himself out of it as he sat watching reruns of *Love Connection*. Each time Chuck Woolery said, "I'll be back in two and two," Manuel's eyes darted to the clock on the wall, willing the hands toward eight.

Answering Manuel's knock, Frederick opened the door at five 'til, with a heavy beer stein half full in his left hand. "Come in. Would you like a beer?"

"That sounds great. Wow this is some set-up. What is it? Two bedroom?" Manuel asked, looking around at the tastefully decorated space.

"Yeah, Mother sends her decorator every year from Corpus to update. I use the other bedroom as my office. It's where I write my dissertations," he said, handing him a beer.

Manuel's eyes shot to the vintage cuckoo clock on the wall. "Where's Lacey? I thought you said she'd be here at eight."

"She's always late. Relax. How's that beer taste?"

"It has a bitterness to it. I like it. It's different," he said taking another sip.

"You'll get used to it," Frederick said with a chuckle as he waddled into the kitchen. He returned carrying a platter of party sausages and bite sized chunks of Velveeta. "Hungry?" he asked as he placed the platter on the table and grabbed a handful.

"You know I was, but I'm not now," he said as an unfamiliar buzz coursed through his veins. "I guess the beer is filling me up. This couch is really comfortable. I feel like I'm sinking down into it. My feet feel heavy, too, like I'm wearing gravity boots." He rested his head onto the high backed sofa. "I must be more exhausted than I realized. Where's Lacey? I really wanted to meet her. If I can catch a second wind I might take her up on the cock fights," Manuel said as he noticed he was alone in the room.

"Frederick, where'd you go?" he mumbled through thick lips. He tried to raise his hand but couldn't. His whole body was slack, each command his brain dispatched went unanswered. His eyes circled the room, wearily. His respiration slowed, and no sweat broke the surface of his skin even though his insides raged with fear. Incapacitated, he waited.

Frederick skipped into the room holding a petite cedar chest that he set on the coffee table. Then he sat down next to Manuel on the edge of the sofa, his belt buckle reflecting the colored glass of the Tiffany lamp.

"So, what do we have here?" Frederick wheezed as he raised Manuel's hand and released it. Watching it fall, he clapped with glee like a toddler at the circus. He lifted the lid of the box and pulled out two long pieces of pink embroidery thread, the opposite ends of which were harnessed onto two black widow spiders. "Come on out, Cagney and Lacey, we have a visitor."

Manuel's eyes traveled from Frederick's fleshy thumb and forefinger along the length of pink to the spiders that were crawling over the edge of the box and heading straight for his thigh. Each of the eight legs doing the can-can as the pair paraded along toward him. Manuel's brain chose to focus on the minutiae of the moment. He wasn't wearing clean underwear, he hadn't been to Disneyland yet, and only yesterday he'd filled his Arby's punch card and would probably never get that Free Beef and Cheddar.

Manuel had often imagined where his thoughts would lead in the face of danger, and illusions of grandeur always took center stage during the dress rehearsal, but this was opening night and sadly, he felt full of fear. A warm trickle rolled along his leg as he ached for a safe harbor.

Frederick rested his hand on Manuel's thigh and gave it a tender pat. Leaning in, the brim of his hat grazed Manuel's face. "You said cock fighting was in your blood. I say it's a cruel and ghastly spectacle and someone should teach you a lesson," he said with a hint of Velveeta on his breath.

"We do things a mite different here in Texas. The cocks are ready, their razor's strapped on. I have them right there in my office. The only thing missing is you, the main attraction. I'm going to drag you into the ring and let those birds make mincemeat out of you. It's my attempt at retribution. What's that they say, 'payback's a bitch'? Cagney and Lacey will ride along into the ring on you since they enjoy the heat of combat. Don't you girls?" he hollered as the spiders settled into the nest of hair beneath the open collar of Manuel's shirt. "When you're at the end of your rope, begging silently for mercy, the girls will imbibe on your carotid artery and put you out of your misery. Everybody wins," Frederick said with a wink.

Manuel saw his reflection in the greasy circle of Frederick's glasses. The panic rose while his brain scrambled toward a resolution. Change was proving all too illusive, as his demons danced along the periphery in celebration. He craved a final act of contrition that might salvage his soul. The horrid truth of his fate shone from his face as the hysteria tried to crawl out from within.

✝   ✝   ✝

AMY SCHUSTER is a native of Phoenix. She loves to read, write and people watch, not necessarily in that order. She's hoping to land a literary agent for her first completed novel while hard at work on the second. She lives in Scottsdale with her husband and their four children.

A PAIR OF CALENDAR STICKS
TONI NIESEN

Arizona Territory – May 1866

This wasn't the first time Big Eagle heard his grandfather, Shining Cloud, speak of his calendar stick. Once a year, usually in winter during story-telling time, Shining Cloud would bring out his stick and relate the important events of the Pima tribe's past, reading aloud from notches, dots, and pictures he'd carved in the four foot mesquite branch.

Sometimes, they would walk together along the bank of the Gila River while Grandfather talked of Apache raids and good crop years. Since childhood, Big Eagle had reveled in these special moments. Today was different because it was summer and grandfather did not have his stick with him. The temperature hovered above a hundred degrees in the bright desert sunshine, and the fields of wheat and squash would be ready for harvesting in another month.

Shining Cloud walked with Big Eagle to his mud house on the Gila River Reservation. "Grandson," he said, "I have something to give you. It is important."

Big Eagle pulled aside the blanket covering the door for the old man and followed him into the dim interior. Shining Cloud bent down, moved his bed pallet away from the wall and pulled a long deerskin pouch from a horizontal crack in the wall. Big Eagle had seen the beaded pouch many times before and watched as his grandfather slid the treasured calendar stick from it.

"Take this and continue our Pima tradition, Grandson. I'm passing the responsibility on to you. It is a burden, but an important one. We must continue to record our people's heritage.

Big Eagle ran his hands along the knobby carved surface of the wood and lowered his head. "I'm honored, but why

Grandfather? You are still strong, your mind is sharp, and you know the ways of our people better than I do."

"The time has come to pass it on," Shining Cloud said. "Age has taught me to see these things." He moved across the room to retrieve a second stick leaning against the wall. He inserted it in the leather pouch and returned it to the cranny behind his pallet.

Big Eagle looked to his grandfather, "I don't understand. Is the stick you have hidden to be a back-up for the one you gave me?"

"No, Grandson. It is only a decoy. It can be used to deceive those who would take the waters that give life to our fields. Protect your stick. It records our rights, and will help stop those who wish to ignore our past and steal our future."

† † †

Two days later, Sheriff Osborn studied the body of Shining Cloud lying near the horse trough outside the nearby town's General Store. The old man was unarmed, and appeared to have been shot in the back, his body splayed forward, one arm dangling in the water.

"Cowardly bastard," the sheriff muttered to himself. "Who would do something like this?"

No one inside the store had seen anything, or if they had they weren't talking. No one heard a gunshot either. The owner described Shining Cloud as a peaceable fellow and couldn't suggest a reason for the murder.

Sheriff Osborn rode out to the reservation to inform Shining Cloud's family of the old man's death. He was directed to the grandson, Big Eagle.

When he heard the news, Big Eagle made a keening sound, then fell silent, took out his knife and sawed six ragged inches from his hair.

The sheriff, unsure what to do, respectfully stood and waited.

Big Eagle put his knife away and lifted his head. "I'm not surprised, Sheriff. Saddened, but not surprised."

The sheriff scratched his head. "So, you were expecting this to happen?"

"No, not exactly, but the last time I saw my grandfather, he seemed to be saying goodbye to me. I also heard the song of the owl last night, an omen of death."

"May I see his home?" the sheriff asked.

There wasn't much to see in the thatched mud house. The hard-packed dirt floor was swept clean, and it appeared all cooking was done outside. The home contained the old man's clothing, personal belongings and bedding as well as a bow with a quiver made of a shriveled wildcat skin. Two upright storage baskets decorated with geometric designs stood to the left of the east-facing door. That was all. The sheriff found nothing to suggest a motive for Shining Cloud's murder. He thanked the grandson and turned to leave.

"Wait," Big Eagle said. "I want to check something." He bent down and rummaged through his grandfather's bedding to expose the crack in the wall. "Just as I thought. It's gone. Someone has taken it."

"What's gone?"

"The second calendar stick. He told me when he gave me his original stick that he expected this one to bring trouble."

Sheriff Osborn asked the younger man if he could remember the last few years of history recorded on the stolen stick.

"I will do my best," Big Eagle said and proceeded to tell the tribe's history concluding with Shining Cloud's final prediction.

"Now, I'd like to see the genuine stick he gave you," Sheriff Osborn said.

"I keep it at my home. I will take you there and show it to you, but it cannot leave my possession."

The sheriff accompanied Big Eagle outside. They walked past several round mud houses and jumped across a shallow canal to reach a house similar to the grandfather's. After entering, Big Eagle produced the original stick, a mesquite branch, stripped clean with carved notches and symbols.

"Somehow, I expected something more," the sheriff said. "It's indecipherable to me. Will you translate what it says?"

"Not much different from the other," Big Eagle said. "Just the last entry."

"That part packs a punch all right, but I still don't understand why anyone would want to steal the stick."

† † †

Charles Timmons, the Bureau of Indian Affairs agent for the Gila River Reservation, sat in his Sacaton office, ledger books piled high on his desk.

Jackson, his assistant, entered and handed him a calendar stick. "Everything's taken care of, boss."

"Everything? The old man too?" Timmons asked.

"No one saw a thing. I made sure of it," Jackson said and pulled his chair up next to the desk.

"You can read this thing?" Timmons asked, moving the ledgers aside and holding up the carved mesquite branch.

"Yeah. The last agent stationed here interviewed several stick-keepers for his records and kept detailed notes on their methods. I have his journal here."

"So what does the stick say about the treaty? Does it mention the river or the water diversion project?"

"Nope. I don't see any mention at all," he said as he snapped his bandana against his boots to knock the dust off them. "I translated everything from the year the treaty was signed."

"You mean this stick covers more than one year?" Timmons asked.

"Some of the sticks cover over fifty years of the tribe's history. I didn't go that far back. It was hard enough for me to translate the year we needed."

"I say it's safe to go ahead with our plans then. The farmers upstream need more water. They're tired of floods wiping out their fields. A few dams and canals should solve both problems. Unless there's something in the old reports filed with Washington, it looks like the Indians won't be able to do a thing."

"Naw," Jackson said. "Even if someone checks in Washington, it will take so long the project will be completed before they realize the treaty they signed with the Pima prohibits taking their water. We had the only copy of the treaty that existed in Arizona."

A knock on the door interrupted their conversation. Sheriff Osborn entered with his deputy and said, "Boys, you're under arrest."

The Indian agent stood, stiff with indignation. "Under arrest? For what?"

"Attempted fraud. Trying to steal the Pima Reservation water by approving the Water Diversion Project. You're in violation of a signed agreement with the tribe. You must have received quite a bribe from the investors."

"I got nothing from anybody," Timmons said.

"We may not have a copy of the treaty, but we have another record available. One that the Pimas kept. We can check it against the records in Washington, but I already know what we'll find."

"You're bluffing. The Indians have no record."

"So you say, but I've seen it myself."

"Just what did you see? Shining Cloud's calendar stick didn't indicate any agreement. Here, I'll show you." Timmons held up the stick.

"You obviously stole the wrong stick. Shining Cloud wasn't born yesterday. He made this copy, and its message is clear if your know how to read it."

Jackson grabbed the calendar stick. "There's no mention of a water treaty five years ago. See?" He counted the slashes back five years.

"I think you made a small mistake in how you measured the years," Sheriff Osborn said and poked his head out the door. "Big Eagle, could you come in and help us? We need to know what this stick records five years back."

Big Eagle took the stick and traced his fingers along the carved slashes and symbols. "The Pima year doesn't start in January. It starts with the harvest of the fruit of the saguaro," he said and pointed to the slashes indicating the years. "That happens in June, and if you look back six months from your stopping point, you'll find mention of the treaty."

"Who's going to believe that?" Timmons blustered.

"I do, for one," Sheriff Olsen said. "If you read the last mark on your stick, it will tell you that this replica was designed to catch an enemy." He pulled a pair of handcuffs from his gun belt and ratcheted a cuff open. "Charles Timmons, you're under arrest for the murder of Shining Cloud. You too, Jackson."

† † †

TONI NIESEN was born in Arizona. She lived in Alaska for over two decades before returning to live in Scottsdale. She has written a weekly newspaper column, several short stories and is currently working on an aviation-themed mystery. The subject of this story was inspired by the name of the Talking Stick Resort on the Salt River Pima Maricopa Indian Reservation where she works as a health professional.

HER HAUNTING EYES
CARRIE SEARS BELL

There was no escaping her wide-open eyes. In the morning light they stared up at him from where she lay crumpled in the ferns, setting off little explosions of adrenaline inside his gut. He had not seen the eyes last night, in the drizzling dark, only her still shape on the ground, lit up by a brief flicker of lightning.

"Laurie," he had called out, squatting down to shake her arm. No reaction. He'd put his dripping index and middle fingers against the side of her neck to check for a pulse, but his own heart was pounding too hard for his fingers to detect anything. So close to her head, his nostrils had picked up the metallic scent of blood.

No, she's only stunned. No, no, no. He'd gotten up and hurried away, stumbling across the brook and through the wet, dark landscape toward the camp. A dim lantern near the make-shift john helped him find his tent, pitched away from the others along the campsite's edge. Shivering with cold and fear, he'd struggled to grasp the zipper pull and open the tent flap. Inside, he shed his wet clothes and burrowed into his sleeping bag, determined to gain control of his frantic brain and racing heart. When he finally drifted into sleep, he chased her in his dreams until he heard the crunching sound of skull against stone. His body jerked awake in the cocoon of his sweat-soaked bag.

Sleep was impossible after that. He left his tent in the dim light of the early July morning, carrying a towel, tube of biodegradable soap and water bottle. He made it to the place by the narrow stream where he thought she had been and began to hope. Just to be sure, he walked up the brook a little ways. He nearly stepped on the body before he saw it on the ground.

Now the dead eyes bored into him—a red-brown streak bleeding across the centers and a milky film muting the once-vibrant green irises—and he could no longer deny what had happened the night before. A trail of ants streamed from the corner of the partially open mouth. Larger creatures had torn flesh from an upper arm and thigh. A blackening mat of blood flowed across the damp red hair, its source a gaping dent at the back of her skull, where flies had begun to swarm. Her head rested next to a football-shaped rock, rough and bloodstained.

He swallowed hard and looked away, taking in the rushing stream. The sun would soon light up the high walls of the canyon. He had to decide what to do. Few possibilities came to mind. Leave her. Put her in the river. Hide her.

His body began to tingle all over. He bent at the knees and waist, braced both hands against his thighs, and inhaled deeply. "Think!" he hissed. If he left her, the death would seem suspicious. He thought no one had seen him follow her last night, but he couldn't be certain.

He could have put her into the river last night, in the storm. A boulder in the water could have accounted for the head wound, and she would have been well downstream by morning. But he had panicked, and now it was too late. Someone might see him carry her to the water. Rafters downriver would spot the body before it traveled very far. A medical examiner would be able to tell the woman had not drowned.

The absence of a body—and the evidence it would provide—was his best option. He checked his watch. 4:45. About forty-five minutes until the camp came to life. He ran toward the river, and then up the shoreline to the boats, where he slid the folding shovel out of the raft where it was stowed. Holding the shovel against his forearm, he draped the towel over it and hurried back to the body.

He took off his T-shirt, chose his spot and began to dig. The soft, damp earth under the low-hanging branches of a mesquite tree gave little resistance. He pictured a shallow grave about two-to-three feet deep and just wide enough to hold the body sideways. It was all he had time for. He dug quickly, but it took him twenty minutes before the hole seemed big enough. He ran to the body and again encountered the filmy eyes. A jolt of fear shot through him. He tried to push down the eyelids, but they wouldn't close. He wiped his hands on his shorts and raked his fingers through his thinning hair. *She's dead. I have to save myself.*

Sweat dripped off his chin and he breathed hard as he slid his arms under her body. The stiffness of the corpse surprised him, its limbs frozen in the position of death. He grimaced and swiveled his head away. She had been a slim woman, but it took all his strength to lift the body, carry it the ten feet to the trench and set it in on its side.

The hole was not as deep as he would have liked, but it would have to do. He pressed down hard on the partially chewed arm that stuck out of the hole and heard the tissue tear as it gave way. His stomach lurched and he tasted bile in the back of this throat. He clamped his teeth together and swallowed, turning from the grave and resting on his knees in the dirt until the nausea passed.

Using his hands and feet, he pushed and pressed the rest of the corpse as far into the space as it would go. He shoveled dirt over the body, tamped it down, and added more until the narrow grave's surface was even with its surroundings. He spread the excess dirt around the base of the tree and sprinkled it with water from his bottle so it blended with the storm-dampened ground.

Stepping back to survey the scene, he spotted a fallen branch from the tree. He broke off its brushy end to wipe away his footprints and placed the larger section over the grave. When he was finished, he thought the burial site looked undetectable.

He refilled his water bottle in the stream and used it to rinse away the blood that stained the rock and the ferns where the crushed skull had rested all night. He washed down the ferns again, adding handfuls of mud from the stream, until the blood was no longer visible. Then he tramped up and down the stream bank so that the crushed greenery appeared to be part of the primitive trail from camp to the spring. Afterward, he bathed in the spring, pulled on his shirt and headed back to the boats, the folded shovel concealed beneath his towel. He saw no one on the beach as he slipped the shovel back into the raft where it was kept.

When he reached camp, his hair wet and his towel draped around his neck, no one questioned where he had been. His stomach churned as he approached the half-dozen rafters gathering by the folding table where breakfast was underway. *Stay cool*, he told himself, certain the others would read the guilt on his face. Then he thought of the football-shaped rock and stopped in his tracks. He had rinsed away most of the blood but there was still a stain on the rough surface. What if someone noticed?

"Want some eggs, Kyle?"

"What?"

"The stove is almost ready," Tyler, one of the rafting guides said, tipping his head toward the Coleman. "I'm taking orders for eggs."

"Uh, can you save me some? I left something by the stream. Be back in ten minutes," Kyle said, hurrying away.

"Okay, no worries," the young man called after him.

At the edge of camp, Kyle threw the towel over a bush to dry and strode on. When he was sure no one was watching, he broke into a jog. At the stream, the path he had trodden had altered the bank's appearance. It took him a few minutes to find the tree. His heart pounded in his ears as he turned slowly in a circle, scanning the ground for the rock. Finally, his eyes fell upon it, and he exhaled the breath he'd been holding.

"Hey, Kyle. What're you looking for?"

Startled, he jerked his head toward the voice. Nicole, coming up the path with Elaine. "Dropped my tube of soap on the way back from the spring this morning," he improvised, careful to keep his eyes from straying toward the rock.

"Can we help you?" Elaine said.

"No," he answered quickly. "I've spent enough time looking already."

"We're a little hung over," Nicole said. "Thought a dip in the cold spring water might help. Have you seen Laurie?"

He forced a smile. "Think I'll go for some breakfast now." He saw them exchange a glance and felt his face flush. He could never find the right words with women—not with his ex-wife, with Laurie or even with these two. He turned toward the camp and they walked by.

"We'll keep an eye out for your soap," Elaine said.

When they were out of sight, Kyle strained his tired muscles to lift the rock, which was heavier than he realized. Holding it tight against his body, he staggered a few feet and set it stain-side down under a bush. Using soft earth from the stream bank, he filled the indentation where the rock had been. Then he hustled back to camp and made himself eat the food Tyler had saved for him.

"Find what you lost?" Tyler asked.

"Yeah." He pulled the tube of soap out of his pocket and held it up. "Thanks for saving me a plate."

"No problem."

Kyle leaned back in his camp chair. Too many close calls this morning, he thought, all because he'd let fear get the best of him last night. He could have gone for help, said he had heard Laurie cry out and found her unconscious on the ground. He could have put her body into the river. But no, he had simply run away, too much a coward to take control of the situation. He ran the back of his hand across his perspiring brow. In the past few hours, he had done what he could to save himself, but would it be enough?

A wave of regret broke over him. He pictured Laurie's wavy auburn hair, full breasts, slim waist, and long, toned legs. He remembered the intelligence and warmth radiating from her fiery green eyes as she told the group of rafters about Earth's ancient geologic eras and brought the canyon's silent, immutable strata to life. He wished he could have been more like her, someone who connected with people.

Kyle looked around at the campers finishing breakfast and packing up gear. When the trip ended, he wouldn't miss any of them. He had only felt close to Laurie. He sighed. She was dead now, whether he'd intended it or not. He closed his eyes and replayed what had happened the night before, wishing the events that led to her death could all be erased.

He had left the other rafters partying on the beach to use the camper's john. Just as he'd finished, he heard angry voices behind the tents.

"You lying skank!" Therese, the trip leader's wife, had slurred.

"I never meant to hurt you," Laurie responded quietly.

"Bull. You wanted him no matter what it cost me and my girls."

"Don't put this on her," Therese's husband, Alex, had cut in. "Our marriage has been in trouble for a long time."

A bright spear of lightning punctuated Alex's words. Then a thunderclap reverberated in the rock walls above, and Laurie passed through a dim arc of lantern light on her way out of the camp. While the other campers scurried for their tents, pelted by fat raindrops and unnerved by the ear-splitting thunder, Kyle used each strobe of lightning to follow Laurie.

Soaked to the bone, he'd caught up with her near the spring a quarter-mile away. In the white light of the next flash, he glimpsed Laurie's dripping face, clothes clinging to her, hair appearing waxen, unreal. She sat immobile on a small boulder, her body coming to life as she spotted him. Then it had gone dark again.

"Laurie," he'd yelled, cut off by thunder.

"I'm all right," she'd shouted when the rumbling subsided. "Go back to camp."

"You shouldn't be out here."

When the next strobe lit the night, almost directly overhead, he'd spotted her along the brook and stumbled blindly in that direction.

The rain had intensified, pounding the earth. "Laurie, wait," he'd shouted. "I heard you and Therese."

"Then you know why I want to be alone."

She was closer than he'd expected. He reached in the direction of her voice, made contact with an arm and took hold. "I can help you forget about him." He grasped her other arm.

"Kyle, no! What are you doing? Let me go!" She tried to pull away, dragging him in a circle, but he'd held fast to her wrists. "What is wrong with you?"

Rage had flared through him like a flash fire. "Nothing— is—wrong—with—me." He'd shaken her with each word.

"Stop!" she shrieked.

Before he could tell her to shut up, he felt a crushing pain on the top of his left foot. She'd tried to jerk away as she stomped him, pulling them both off balance. He tumbled to the ground on top of her writhing body and wrapped his arms around her.

"Help!"

Her upper body lunged forward and her head connected with his jaw, ramming his teeth together. Grimacing, he'd slammed her against the wet earth and clamped a hand over her mouth. His elbow struck something hard.

Lightning flashed briefly across her terrified face and a large rock at her shoulder. As thunder rumbled, he'd felt her teeth bite into his hand. The next thing he remembered was the sound of her skull cracking against stone.

Alex's concerned voice brought Kyle back to the present. "Has anyone seen Laurie?" the trip leader called out.

"No," he murmured, along with the others.

Alex went to the door of Laurie's tent and called her name.

When she didn't answer, he undid the zipper and peeked inside. "She's not here," he shouted to the campers. "Her sleeping bag is still in its sack."

"Maybe she slept in one of the boats," a male voice suggested.

"In that storm, are you kidding?" a female countered.

"Let's look anyway," Alex said. "We need to find her." He sent the fifteen rafters out in teams of two and three. They searched the boats, the tents, along the river, by the brook, beside the cliffs and in the pool beneath the spring.

As the sun rose higher, illuminating the multicolored layers of Grand Canyon's soaring walls and bringing on a wilting heat, Kyle pretended to search along the brook. He watched one person after another traipse past Laurie's grave, none of them noticing anything amiss.

After a few hours, Alex used his two-way radio to summon help. A river ranger in a motorized raft responded first.

"When is the last time any of you saw Laurie?" he asked the exhausted group.

The rafters had clustered in a tight formation on the beach, except for Kyle, who stood behind and a few feet away from them. As he peered between their shoulders toward the ranger, a few sidelong glances let him know they wished him to stay where he was, on the outside. He folded his arms across his chest. *Fine with me.*

Alex was first to speak. "Last night," he said. "She was walking away from the tents just as the storm hit. Then the sky opened up and you couldn't see anything." Others nodded in agreement, but Kyle noticed that Therese kept her eyes trained on the ground.

"Was she alone?"

Alex nodded.

"No one checked to make sure she made it back?"

Kyle watched his companions shake their heads and look away. Elaine and Nicole brushed away tears. "I wish I had," Alex finally said, his voice thick with emotion. "I think we all assumed she'd come in once the rain got bad."

Search and Rescue rangers arrived after that. They organized an expanded search along the shore and sent boats downstream to check the river and alert other rafters about a missing woman.

Later, another officer questioned each member of Alex's

group individually. "What is your relationship to Laurie Russell?" she asked Kyle.

"We're both geologists. I knew her reputation and had met her at a conference. She's an expert on Grand Canyon geology, which is why I signed up for this tour."

"Tour?"

"Yeah. We made stops along the river so Laurie could give mini-lectures about the rock layers."

"Did Laurie argue with anyone? Did anyone give her a hard time or threaten her?"

"Not that I know of," he lied, confident that he had been the only one to overhear the harsh words between Laurie, Therese and Alex.

By the next morning, when no trace of Laurie had been found, Search and Rescue believed she must have fallen into the Colorado River. "In that storm, it would have been easy for her to get turned around," the river ranger told the rafters. "If she stepped off a ledge and into the river, the strong current would have swept her away before she knew what happened. Without a life jacket and in the dark, her odds of survival would be slim.

The ranger added, "It can take days, even weeks, for a body to surface on the Colorado. Sometimes a body can make it all the way to Lake Mead, almost a hundred river miles from here."

Kyle pressed his lips into a grim line to hide his relief.

Two days later, the rafting party floated downriver to the take-out point at Diamond Creek. Kyle was almost home free, except for the filmy green eyes. Every time he drifted into sleep, they glared at him from Laurie's frozen, pale face and startled him awake.

He rubbed his own blood-shot eyes and took a last look at the river, still chocolate-milk brown from storm runoff. In time, he told himself, Laurie's dead eyes would fade in his memory, just like the lifeless images of the others that haunted him. As he climbed into the crowded van for the ride back to civilization, he almost believed it.

† † †

CARRIE SEARS BELL has written for a variety of magazines, including *Arizona Highways*, *Medical Economics*, *America West Airlines Magazine*, and *Phoenix Magazine*. She has contributed to Compass American's *Arizona* guidebook as well as the *Arizona State Park Trails Guide*. Bell is currently working on a mystery novel involving the Grand Canyon, which she has hiked from the South Rim to the North Rim and back thirteen times.

FINDERS KEEPERS
Judy Starbuck

My name is Jodi Ellis. Yesterday I returned to the old house my grandfather had built in the 1960s when he visited Arizona for his health problems. Now fifty years later, the charming place was a beaten-down wreck. The porch had sagged, windows were boarded over, the weathered wood covered with dirt, and the stone foundation hidden by shoulder-high weeds. I decided to wait until I had a contractor with me before I ventured inside.

Fortunately, besides the house, he also left me a generous trust fund. Now I needed someone to help me get my worn-out house in shape. Bobby's Big Ass Burger Café in downtown Paradise seemed a good place to ask around while I sampled their specialty. The décor was country and a huge set of steer horns hung in the weathered interior. The turquoise Naugahyde booths, cowboy art, and saddle seats at the bar completed the look. I got situated at the bar where I could see through to the kitchen. The help shouted back and forth in rapid Spanish.

A waiter appeared. "Hey cowgirl. You new in town?" He put a grease-spotted menu in my hands. "I'm Bobby Allen." He gestured with a sweep of his arm. "The namesake for this establishment." Things were looking up. He was big and tall with a sparkle in his deep blue eyes.

"Yes, I've only been here a few days. My grandfather built a house about five minutes from here, and I see it's ready to fall apart. I'm here to do some work on the place but I'm going to need some help. Any recommendations?"

"Well, let's get you fed first then we can talk about it. What will it be? Sorry I didn't catch your name." He pulled out an order book and had his pencil poised to write.

"I'm Jodi, and I'll take the Number Two."

"Okay, that's a quarter pound Bad-Ass Burger with cheese and steak fries. To drink?"

"Whatever you have on tap."

He gave me a wink and turned to go to the kitchen. His jeans fit him just right and the back of his T-shirt read, PARADISE IS FOR LOVERS.

After I finished my burger and brew, Bobby climbed on the saddle next to me. He leaned in, his face close to mine. "So what kind of help are you looking for?" I eased back to create a little space. He had the good looks and smarmy charm that would rival the best snake oil salesman.

"A contractor and carpenters. And temporary lodging within bike-riding distance of the house."

He put his hand on the back of my saddle with an uncomfortable familiarity. "So where's this house you're talking about?"

I gave him directions and his eyebrows raised. "That's not a real safe place, Jodi. You'll need a big-ass contracting firm to keep the varmints away. The place has been a free hotel for squatters, illegals, drug dealers, and every other dangerous creature in these parts. A sweet thing like you shouldn't go there alone until you get some strong doors with deadbolt locks on them. "You're not staying there now, are you?"

"No, just here and there." I wasn't about to tell him I had rented a room at the Paradise Bed & Breakfast.

"Why don't you check out my twin brother Billy's place? He has a little cabin for rent on a day-to-day basis. He's the big contractor around here and I bet he can help you out. Billy's right down the street from the Paradise B&B where you're staying." Bobby gave me a wink.

I should have known it wouldn't take more than a day for word to get out that a stranger had come to town.

A stern gray-haired woman in western gear and a no-nonsense attitude strode in as if she owned the place. "Bobby, I need to see you in the office right away." Apparently she did own the place.

Bobby stiffened and his grin evaporated. "Yes, ma'am." When she walked into the kitchen, he relaxed enough to say, "That's Martha Allen, my mother. Folks around here called her Marty."

"It looks like you've been summoned. Thanks for the recommendation and the great burger. Write down your brother's name and number." I put the money for my meal on the bar. "By the way, does this town have a bank?"

"We sure do. Right down the street. My cousin is the manager there. It's next to Allen's Trading Post." Bobby grinned. "My family can be of help with almost anything you need."

The tiny town of Paradise seemed like a picture postcard with its western motif and meticulous storefronts that surrounded a central square. It was nothing like the rundown town I had visited as a child. My grandpa had to go twenty miles for shopping. The tourist population must be booming, or something else was fueling the economy. The Allen family seemed to be the key players, and the proximity to the Mexican border certainly provided opportunities. I wanted to find out what was going on before I invested my time and money. After asking around, I learned that Billy's was the sole construction company in Paradise. If I wanted work done, he was it.

The next day I met Billy at his house and discussed the renovation. He looked and sounded so much like his brother it was eerie, but Billy lacked Bobby's confident air. He spoke softly and kept his distance, unlike his brother. When we walked toward the cabin he had for rent I noticed he had a limp. Before I could wonder what had happened to him, he told me.

"Around here we start rodeo-ing at a young age. I was knee-high when I got bucked off my horse and broke this leg. It never healed up right so I had to sit and cheer Bobby on at all his riding events. Lucky for me I took a liking to hammers and nails. It's been a fine career for me. Bobby just hangs out at the café and sweet talks the ladies. But he has to deal with Big Marty, excuse me, Mama, on a regular basis. She pretty much leaves me alone."

Billy lived on several acres in a ranch-style house he had built for himself and a multitude of pets. He showed me the cabin that was available. It was a step up from the fleabags I had stayed in before and had everything I needed and wanted. Especially privacy. And it would give me an opportunity to find out more about the Allens. I didn't get the feeling they were one big happy family but they sure seemed to own this town.

After I agreed to rent the cabin for the short term, Billy accompanied me to my grandfather's place to scope out the project. While we went around and surveyed the back, tires crunched in the pitted driveway. The engine stopped, a car door opened, and footsteps slapped on the front steps. A snarled curse followed the sound of splitting wood. When I came around to the front I saw a Sheriff's Department vehicle, so I made my presence known.

A deputy knelt on a step with one knee, the other foot wedged between the broken slats. He looked up. "I'm Deputy Watkins of the Santa Cruz County Sheriff's Department. I patrol this area and need to tell you that you're on dangerous property."

"I'm Jodi Ellis, the owner of this place. It belonged to my grandfather who left it to me."

Deputy Watkins extricated himself from the steps and shook his head. "You've inherited more than a wreck. It's been a flophouse for every kind of undesirable creature, human or animal." Once the deputy swiped the dirt off his knees he stood tall and strong with a weathered tan face and wary eyes. We heard footsteps approach from the side of the house and his hand moved ever so slightly toward his gun.

Billy limped around the corner and stopped short. "Hello, Virgil. What finds you in this part of the county?"

"Just checking up on things. What are you doing here?"

Billy looked up at Watkins. "Miss Ellis and I are discussing a renovation here. Excuse us, but we'd best go on in to see what needs to be done."

Deputy Watkins wasn't about to be excused. "I believe I'll come in with you to assure Miss Ellis's safety."

As I reached the top step, a shiny red truck pulled into the driveway. Bobby got out. "I heard you were coming and wanted to join up with you. This place has so many stories surrounding it I'd like to get a firsthand look. I brought burgers and fries as a housewarming gift." Then he turned to Watkins. "What brings you here?"

"I'm here to protect the people of the county and to have a Big Ass Burger."

Bobby laughed. "Okay, let's take a look around."

Billy whistled as he flashed his light around the corners and the ceiling, then went to the bottom step of the massive wood staircase. It groaned under his weight. "How old is this place anyway?"

"It's only fifty years old, but no one has taken care of it for half that time." I pointed in various directions. "There's a living room, dining room, and kitchen on the first floor. The rooms upstairs can be used for bedrooms and an office."

Watkins tripped over a mildewed canvas bag next to a broken-down sofa. He opened the duffel and found an old flashlight, knife, lighter and various personal care items. "Someone bunked here not too far back." He walked over to the fireplace and kicked at the ashes. "This has been used recently."

Bobby pointed his flashlight at some crumpled underwear in a corner. "Looks like he left his britches behind." Paper cups, wrappers, leaves and dirty blankets littered the floor. With no electricity this was merely a shelter, but apparently still occupied on occasion.

"Do I dare go upstairs?" I stood on the second step and it didn't cave in. Then I tried the next and soon I was surveying the second floor with my flashlight. I entered the nearest room and looked through the dirty window at the cottonwoods, willows and the distant high desert grasslands. I let out a breathless, "Wow." As I gingerly walked through the room, I tried to avoid the syringes, baggies, cans and ragged towels left behind. My imagination took hold and I envisioned waking up to the magnificent view or sitting at my desk looking out at open territory.

When I came back downstairs, Watkins shook his head. "This is a health and safety hazard. I suggest you tear the whole place down."

I looked at him in amazement. "Not on your life! This was my grandfather's and there's no way I plan to level it." I turned to Billy. "Are you interested in this project?"

He nodded and gave me a genuine smile. "It would be my pleasure."

The first order of business was to put up a chain-link fence around the house. While Billy did that, I began the tear-down in the bathroom. The cracked and crumbling plaster on the walls had to come off and the floorboards replaced. My hammering and prying skills were mediocre but I managed to do the job. I had ripped down half the bathroom walls when my hammer struck an immovable object with a clang.

"Damn, I've broken something, "I muttered.

I pulled a steel box from the wall and used a screwdriver to pry it open. The box was filled with stacks of bills in all denominations. I lifted out what must be thousands of dollars. I felt dizzy. Questions swirled around in my head. Did this belong to Grandpa? Or was it dirty money? Would someone be back for it?

I really knew nothing about the Allen family or anyone else in these parts so I didn't want to share this find yet. When the money was safely hidden I would call my attorney and get his advice.

Since I traveled by bike, I stuffed as much of the money as possible in my waistband and crammed the rest into my backpack. I slid the empty steel box back into the wall and took off, padded with bills.

Later that day I called my attorney back home and told him about my find.

"Legally the money is yours. This is called the Treasure Trove and Found Property Law," he said. "It's sometimes called the 'finders-keepers' provision. Another law, called the Hidden Treasure law stipulates that any items found in the walls belongs to the homeowners, which happens to also be you."

I paused for a moment. "So I can keep it? What if my grandfather didn't put it there? What if it belongs to someone else and they want it back?"

I suggest you turn it over to the local authorities, receive documentation from them, and wait the requisite sixty days. If no one claims the money, or it's determined not part of a criminal enterprise, you'll get it back."

"I've heard plenty about law enforcement conveniently losing track of illegal substances or monies they recover."

"Where is the money now?"

"It's safe. I'll think about what you told me and see what I can learn about the local sheriff." I didn't mention that the money was in my homemade safe deposit box. I had carefully pried a floorboard loose in the back of the bedroom closet in my rented cabin. I had wrapped the stacks of bills in oilcloth and insulation and pushed them in a crevice. After I replaced the floorboard, I laid the tool bag on top of it.

"Is there anything else I can do for you?"

"Would you contact your investigator for me? See what he can come up with about a family here in Paradise? Last name Allen. The first names are Martha, Bobby, and Billy. This town is a showplace and they seem to own most of the businesses here. I want to know where they get their money.

His answer came within hours.

I returned to grandpa's house at first light to see if the walls yielded any more money. I made a beeline to the bathroom and discovered that the plaster had been completely hacked up. Fear soured my mouth. Someone had come back for the money. Someone knew it was gone. Someone could be watching now.

As I inspected the area behind the walls with a flashlight, a hand came from behind me and covered my mouth and nose with a foul smelling rag.

I don't know how long I was out, but when I awoke, a splinter of light through my puffy eye nearly blinded me. Pain zigzagged across my head. My shoulders ached. My wrists burned from some sort of binding that tied me to the pipes behind the toilet. I glanced around and realized I was still in the first floor bathroom.

A gloved hand struck my cheek. "Where's my money?" The person spoke in a muffled whisper.

I could barely make out the image of a person in black with a ski mask covering their face. I shook my head.

The person jerked the gag out of my mouth. I felt blood running from my nose. Through my swollen tongue and a chipped tooth, I whispered. "The police have it. Get it from them."

"Don't lie to me. I am the police in this town." Even though he attempted to disguise his voice I now knew it was a man speaking.

Who was this maniac? Did I know him? His shoulders weren't wide enough to be Deputy Watkins. Was it Bobby? Or Billy? Or one of the drug dealers from the backwoods who found a handy spot to stash his haul?

He slapped my face again so hard I saw stars. Then he kicked my knee, and punched my stomach. I gagged.

"You have ten minutes to tell me where it is. The house is set to burn at the drop of a match." I smelled gasoline. "This tinderbox won't take long." He laughed and walked away. His heavy footsteps faded and I heard the front door slam shut.

Drawing on my reserves and fueled by anger and adrenaline,

I lurched forward. Using all my strength I wrenched the ties loose. I heard a crunch. The pipe shot out from the rotted wood of the wall. I lunged out the open bathroom door, shot down the hall, out the kitchen door, and tumbled down the steps of the back porch. Lying on my side wincing from the pain, I managed to wrestle the cell phone from my front pocket. I pushed 911 and wondered if that would bring someone hired by the Allens, or an actual law-abiding officer.

A voice came from behind me. My assailant. I struggled to my feet and turned to run. An arm wrapped around my neck and stopped me cold. His arm tightened around my throat. I choked.

As he squeezed the air out of me, rage replaced my fear. With a kick to his ankle, a swift twist to the right, and a mean jab of my elbow into his ribs, I caught him off guard I spun around then kneed him in the groin. He bellowed and I recognized by his voice that he was one of the Allen boys.

After he lost his footing, I saw a hammer among some discarded tools on the ground. He remained bent over. His skull was an easy target and I swung two-handed with all the force I had. I heard a bone-crunching sound. He reeled and fell.

Sirens shrieked in the distance. The other Allen twin came around the house. This one walked with a limp. So, I had Bobby on the ground but Billy headed toward me.

"What the hell?" Billy said when he saw the inert body.

I ran in the direction of the sirens but the first car that pulled up was a black Cadillac Escalade with dark tinted windows. Big Marty stepped out. Four testosterone-fueled men emerged from the back seat and stood at Marty's side.

Billy froze.

Marty railed at her boys. "What have you two bumblers gotten yourself into now? Billy, I told you to stay away from this girl. I had a feeling she was a troublemaker when she walked into our bank and asked so many questions. Your brother can't stay away from any woman. Never could." She paused and looked at the felled man. "Who the hell is that?" The black mask was pulled forward covering Bobby's face.

Bobby let out a pathetic croak. "It's me, Mama."

"What happened to you, son?"

Billy interrupted, pointing to the hulks standing next to her. "What did you bring them along for?"

"That woman needs to mind her own business." She nodded

at me. "They're here to assist her out of town."

The goons moved closer, but Billy stepped between us. "No, Mama, they're not. I'm tired of you intimidating this whole town. Don't you have enough money already? Haven't you scared off enough folks?"

Before Marty could answer, Deputy Watkins's patrol car screeched up to the house. Six other cruisers were right behind. Soon they had the Allen boys and their Mama in cuffs in the back seat of a squad car.

Watkins turned to me. "We were about to move in on them. The Allens have been terrorizing this community for ten years. No one dares turn against them because of their connections south of the border." He pointed toward their mother. "And she's the ringleader."

I nodded in understanding. "I had my attorney look into it. He found that the Allens—that is Martha and Bobby—have a dark past and are suspected to be involved in running drugs, human smuggling and selling arms. Billy kept his distance from them."

"That pretty much sums up what we discovered. "Watkins hitched his head at Bobby, slumped over in the back of one of the squad cars. "So what happened to him?"

"While I was pulling the plaster from the walls yesterday, I found a cache of money. I have it in a safe spot. You'll have to ask him when he's coherent. I'd bet Bobby was trying to hide money from Martha. He came after me when he realized it was gone. Looks like she holds the reins and controls the money to keep them under her thumb. Billy came to my rescue. Apparently they weren't the loyal sons she thought they were."

Virgil gave me an imploring look. "I hope you'll stay in spite of this mess. This town needs some new, respectable citizens.

I smiled. "I could take over the café and rename it The Hidden Treasure."

† † †

JUDY STARBUCK is a Scottsdale teacher, handwriting analyst, and mystery writer. Her publishing credits include: "The Sun Also Sets," (award-winning anthology, *Map of Murder*), "Neither Rare Nor Well Done" (*Medium of Murder*), "The Christmas Stalking" (*How NOT To Survive the Holidays*), "Liar" (*Mystery in the Wind*), and "Cowgirls Don't Cry" (*How NOT To Survive a Vacation*). She is involved in adoption search and support groups, is an Arizona-certified Confidential Inter-mediary, and an active member of Sisters in Crime.

COYOTE'S BONES
Nancy Newcomer

April 12. When Marcy brought an armful of laundry into the master bedroom, she saw a scrawny multi-colored coyote trotting up to a pile of dirt outside the open window. They both stopped abruptly and locked eyes. His were a color of gold she had never seen before. He must have decided she was not a threat—or hunger won out over fear—because he lowered his gaze and started digging in the pile of dirt with both front paws. Soon, he stopped and stuck his snout into the excavated hole.

When his head popped out, his jaws were clamped on what she recognized to be a decomposing appendage. Body parts from junior year anatomy class in her nursing program came tumbling back: a radius, carpus, some meta carpus and a few phalanges. In other words, a forearm bone with part of a wrist and a few fingers still attached.

The gold eyes looked up at her again.

"Drop it," she shouted. "Right now."

The coyote dropped his dinner, turned and trotted off through the sloping backyard and down into the large wash that bordered McDowell Mountain Park.

Deputy Matt Blake arrived at her door less than ten minutes after Marcy called 911.

"Show me what you found," he said.

Marcy led him outside and described how she had seen the coyote dig into the dirt pile and then pull out the arm fragment. It remained where the coyote had dropped it in her backyard, about six feet beyond the bedroom window.

Matt squatted down and looked at it carefully. "The remains don't look all that old," he said. "More detectives and the coroner are on the way. We'll cordon off the scene and do a thorough search of the yard and down into the wash. Hard to tell where this came from."

"We had coyotes in New Mexico," Marcy said. "From what

I've read, their hunting range is around two or three miles and they almost never attack a human."

"Most likely he scavenged this from a body in the desert and brought it back here to eat later."

"Coyote pantry in my backyard."

"Yeah, exactly," he smiled. "Well, the investigation here will probably take a few hours today and continue the next few days until we find the rest of the body."

"No problem." Marcy liked the personality and attitude of the soft-spoken deputy who looked good in his khaki and brown uniform. She guessed he was in his early thirties, like her. She decided she would like to get to know him better.

Soon the house and yard filled with law enforcement officers. Neighbors drifted down the street wondering why all these people were on their quiet cul-de-sac on a Tuesday afternoon. A few reporters were being corralled in the front yard and a TV news van was parked across the street. A sheriff's office spokesperson held them at bay.

Marcy picked up a novel and sat at the dining room table where she could see what they were doing in the backyard. The investigators put up crime scene tape around outlying saguaro cactuses, photographed everything, sketched, took notes and interviewed her in detail. A search began in the backyard and gradually moved down into the broad wash. The officers walked in grid patterns to cover every square inch of ground. The coroner had bagged the remains earlier and departed. Around sunset, the investigators called it a day.

As the sky turned deep orange and turquoise, there was nothing more to see and the neighbors went home. The preliminary search yielded no more body parts or even clues. Matt was the last to leave. When Marcy asked if he'd like a drink, he said he'd finish the bottle of water he had with him. She poured iced tea for herself and they sat at the kitchen table.

"You know," she said, "I heard coyotes really howling and yelping my first night in the house a week ago. It was chilling. They worked themselves up into quite a frenzy. Then, suddenly, nothing. It was like a police car had pulled up in front of a party at a frat house."

"That's not so unusual. But it could be related to a pack of coyotes finding the body out there."

"Horrible image. What's next?"

"Looks like this will take awhile. We're going to have to go over the whole area with a fine-toothed comb. Sorry you have to deal with this."

"I'm just sorry for whoever is out there lying in the desert and for her family. I thought I saw nail polish on the fingernails."

"Yeah, I did, too. We'll do our best to find and identify her and get her home. Maybe the DNA will point toward a known missing person."

Marcy looked at him out of the corner of her eye, "And then you'll know whether there was foul play."

"Yep," Matt said with a grin. "Just like on TV."

Marcy moved from Albuquerque to the 1960s-era ranch house in Fountain Hills, Arizona to start a nursing supervisor job at a hospital in nearby Scottsdale. The rental price was ridiculously low because the owner, Jake Turner, was in a hurry to move to San Diego to start a new job. He obviously spent a lot of time in the gym. When Marcy asked where he worked out, he said he'd been going to FountainSide Gym for five years and recommended it. His biceps were the size of Easter hams and he wore tight knit shirts to show them off. She was glad when he left for San Diego a week later and she could move in.

The search for the body went on by foot, helicopter and on horseback for four more days. On Saturday, just when they were about to call it off, a hiker in McDowell Mountain Park got off the trail to take a photo of Four Peaks and found something else instead. Something much less picturesque. A decomposing woman's body lay in a shallow grave that had been partly dug up. The local TV news stations reported that a police spokesman said the woman did not die of natural causes. They also reported that they believed the body had been there at least a month.

The next day, Marcy relaxed on the couch in front of the picture window in her living room. She wore cutoffs and a UNM sweatshirt and was reading a National Geographic, her honey-blonde hair pulled back in a ponytail and her flip-flopped feet propped on a Navajo motif throw pillow. She heard the growl of an engine and looked up to see a familiar black Hummer pull into the driveway. A surprise visit from her landlord, all the way from San Diego. She frowned, wondering why.

She opened the door to Jake. He wore a skintight black long-sleeved silk T-shirt and black jeans with creases. His belt had an ornate silver buckle with a large turquoise stone embedded in a Harley logo. He reeked of strong spicy cologne.

"Hey. I had to come back to talk to the Sheriff's deputies. Guess I'm a suspect in this murdered woman thing," he said in his gravelly voice.

"That's a drag," Marcy said. An awkward silence ensued. "Would you like to come in?"

"Sure." Jake stepped in and looked around the combination living and dining room.

"Looks nice," he said, nodding at the beige Danish sectional and glass-topped dining table set. Marcy flashed back to the man-cave she had encountered when she first came to look at the house. Massive black leather couches with silver studs, a dark carved oak dining set, paintings of large-bosomed cowgirls on the walls and a gun case in the corner.

"Thanks. Would you like some iced tea?"

"No thanks." He pulled a leather-covered flask from his back pocket and downed a slug.

Marcy gestured him to an armchair by the fireplace. She sat across from him on the couch. The room felt smaller with him in it.

"How's San Diego?"

"Great. Hot broads on the beach."

"That's nice."

"So, you found an arm in the back yard?"

"Yes, well a coyote did, in that pile of dirt under the bedroom window."

"Never got around to getting rid of that dirt after I dug a hole for the Acacia tree."

"Oh, I wondered why the dirt was there."

"What all are they saying about the body? Heard they found the rest of it."

"Yes, it was on the news all day yesterday. A Fountain Hills woman in her twenties. Shot to death and stabbed. Really brutal."

Jake nodded. "That's horrible. Do you like the house?"

"Yes. I love it here. Great mountain views. Twenty-minute commute to the hospital."

"All right then. Well, I just have some unfinished business to take care of and then I'm heading back to San Diego. Glad my place is working out. Except for the body and all." He got up and walked to the door.

"Other than that, it is."

She shut the door after him, wondering what on earth that was all about.

The following day, Matt stopped by to ask Marcy a few more questions. As they stood talking at her front door, Marcy waved at her neighbor who was turning into the driveway of the house next door.

"Who's that?" he asked.

"Suzi Faulk. She and her husband, Tim, have been really welcoming to me since I moved in here."

"And when was that?"

"Hmmm. Tuesday, April fifth," Marcy said. "Two weeks ago tomorrow."

"And before that?"

"Well, I was in Albuquerque with my parents for a week but I had just returned from six months in Cambodia."

"Wow," Matt raised his eyebrows.

"Doctors Without Borders. I was working in TB clinics over there."

"We'll need to see documentation of your time there."

"Really? Wait...I'm a suspect?"

"We have to look at everyone with any connection to the case."

Marcy's jaw dropped open. She had never been a suspect before. "Okay. I'll be right back."

The following Friday night Marcy hosted a casual barbeque dinner for her neighbors. Tim was a corporate lawyer during the day and an avid cyclist on nights and weekends. Suzi did freelance graphic design, working from her home studio. Tonight she wore one of her bright hand-painted silk scarves, which she made and sold at local arts and crafts shows. They had invited Marcy over when she moved in.

They all sat at the patio table on Marcy's back deck, Mojitos in hand, watching a killer sunset while the grill heated up. Four Peaks glowed pink-orange against a lavender sky. A couple dozen Gambel's quail made soft clucks as they fluttered up into an orange tree to roost for the night.

After some small talk about their jobs and the fine April weather, Marcy asked them if they'd heard on the six o'clock news that the body had been identified.

"No," Suzi said. "Who was she?"

"Well, in the press conference this afternoon, they said she was a twenty-nine year old Fountain Hills woman named Candy Walsh. She worked for a solar energy firm in Tempe called SunToday."

Tim jerked suddenly and spilled his drink. Suzi and Marcy grabbed paper napkins and mopped up the pool of sweet rum and mint leaves. "No problem," Marcy said. Tim's face had gone bone-white. "What is it, Tim?"

"Uh...well...that's wild. I know her...knew her. Her company is one of our clients. I've been in a few meetings with her. She was the Investor Relations Manager there. Nice person. Bright."

"I don't remember hearing you talk about her or that company, honey," Suzi said.

"No, you wouldn't have," Tim replied, looking down at his hands, locked tightly together. "They aren't normally one of my clients. I just filled in a few times over the last year when Bud Williams was out of town."

"I'm so sorry," Marcy said, pouring a new round of drinks from the frosted pitcher. "They searched her condo over by Firerock golf course and found a few personal items—her journal and a laptop. Maybe something there will lead them to the killer."

"I saw that deputy at your house the other day," Suzi said. "What was that all about?"

"I had to show proof I was out of the country until the beginning of April."

"Boy, they leave no stone unturned," Suzi said.

Marcy put the fish fillets and sliced vegetables on the hot grill while Suzi finished tossing a salad in a large Mexican bowl. Tim sat quietly and stared out at the desert.

As soon as coffee and dessert were finished, Tim excused himself, saying he had a mountain bike race, the annual "Cactus Challenge" in McDowell Mountain Park, the next day. Suzi smiled and tucked her arm in his. "He's out biking every chance he gets," Suzi said, smiling. "He came in second last year. I'm so proud of him."

Wearing a thick white Turkish robe, Bud Williams grabbed his first mug of coffee and the newspaper in the kitchen of his sprawling custom-built home in Cave Creek. He had the four-thousand-square-foot place to himself now. His wife took the kids to live with her mother in Palm Springs last September after his unfortunate lack of discretion with one of his paralegals. He sat at a brushed aluminum table by the floor-to-ceiling windows overlooking his personal patch of Sonoran desert. The headline in the *Arizona Republic* read:

BODY I.D.'D AS CANDY WALSH OF FOUNTAIN HILLS

"Dammit," he muttered. "Just my luck. I never should have gotten involved with her."

January 15. Suzi thought about how one thing led to another. Tim's nightly bike rides were getting longer and longer. And when he returned, he claimed exhaustion, immediately showered, then tumbled into bed and turned away from her, falling asleep immediately.

It wasn't difficult to follow him. She just waited until he put on his bike riding outfit and left the house.

The first two times, he actually rode up to McDowell Mountain Park. But on the third, he turned and went the opposite way to Shea Boulevard. To the Firerock apartment complex.

She followed Tim in her red and white Mini, keeping well back. She saw him turn into the parking lot and then knock on one of the doors. As the door closed, she glimpsed a young, blonde woman.

Suzi parked in a far corner of the lot and turned off the ignition. It was as good a place as any to formulate a plan.

A month after she first saw the arm in her backyard, Marcy was getting ready to leave work. She finished the last of her paperwork just after ten P.M. and gathered her purse and tote bag, glad to be ending a long, stressful Monday at work. A warm breeze greeted her as she exited the hospital and entered the sprawling, nearly empty parking lot. Lights, positioned throughout the lot, provided intermittent pools of illumination as she walked to her white Honda Accord at the edge of the lot.

She smelled it before she saw it. A dark shape on the trunk of her car. Something dripping down to the ground. She took a few more steps. A head. Golden frozen coyote eyes stared up at her. Clenched in its teeth was a white envelope.

She dug out her cell phone and, with shaking fingers, tapped a name. It rang twice before he answered. "Matt?" she heard her small voice say. Then she told him about her find.

"Go back inside the hospital, call a guard and wait in the reception area with him until we arrive," he said. "I'll be there in ten minutes."

Matt, two more detectives and a deputy arrived, documented the scene and wrapped up the coyote's head. A deputy took her car downtown to be processed. Matt drove Marcy to the Fountain Hills Sheriff's Office.

Matt and Detective Frank Bowman sat with Marcy in a small, windowless conference room. Matt passed around the plastic-enclosed white envelope and the message, printed on plain white computer paper. It stated, "Tell your deputy friend to stop investigating this case or you will end up like Wile E. Coyote." Marcy thought a smart-aleck comment was needed but she couldn't think of one.

"This is a seriously messed-up person," Matt said.

"Did you see anyone in the parking lot or any idling vehicles?" Detective Bowman asked.

"No, absolutely nothing unusual. Until I got to my car."

"Have you had any unusual phone calls, hang-ups or noticed anyone following you?"

Although wrapped in a blanket and sipping hot tea, Marcy still shivered. "Sorry, no, nothing like that."

When there were no more questions, Marcy and Matt walked out in the cool night, lit by a full moon starting to rise behind the mountains. They got into Matt's black SUV. He turned on the ignition and lights but didn't back out.

"Here's what I'd like to do," he said, looking straight into her eyes. "I'll take you to your house and wait while you pack a suitcase for the next seven days. Then I'll take you to a hotel. It will take a couple of days for them to process your car, so you'll need to rent one tomorrow. I can't assign someone to stay with you, but we'll patrol the hotel parking lot. I want you to call me if anything at all seems hinky to you."

Marcy started to shake again. "You think someone might actually hurt me?"

"To get to me, yes. It's possible. We have to take it seriously."

"Okay," she said, "Okay." She spoke in that small voice she had heard earlier.

Suzi got to know Jake one day in February when she was sunning herself in a yellow bikini on a lounge chair by the pool in her backyard. He came over to talk. Then he invited her for a cool drink. A relationship followed as night follows day. When she told him about Tim's affair with the SunToday slut, he sympathized.

"Listen, Suzi-que," he said. "I'd like to help you out here." His finger followed the tan line on her breast as they lay on his waterbed after a particularly athletic afternoon romp. "What would you like me to do to this bastard?"

"I don't want you to do anything to my husband," she said. "Just the slut. Once she's gone, everything will be fine."

"I can help you out for a price."

"How does fifty thousand dollars sound?"

Detectives interviewed Candy Walsh's parents, who lived in a small town near Flagstaff. They knew little about her life, job or friends. Interviews with co-workers were equally unproductive. Nothing seemed to move the investigation forward.

Candy's best friend, Lisa Lin, was her college roommate at Northern Arizona University in Flagstaff. Then, they shared an apartment in Tempe as they both got their MBAs at Arizona State. Lisa was a market analyst and had a condo not far away from Candy's. She also belonged to the FountainSide Gym. She couldn't think of anything at all unusual, except for one thing.

"About three months ago, I stopped by Candy's apartment one evening after work to see if she wanted to go out for a beer," Lisa told Matt and Frank. They sat in the living room of her tidy apartment. "The lights were on at her place, but Candy didn't answer the door. I definitely heard voices inside. But when I knocked again, it was quiet. When I went back to my car, I saw a red and white Mini parked in the far edge of the lot. It was funny because there were a lot of spaces closer to the building. Usually people want to park closer. As I drove out, I saw a small, dark-haired woman sitting in the Mini wearing sunglasses even though it was dark. She was wearing a pretty scarf, too."

"That's very helpful," Matt said. "Is there anything else about the woman or the car?"

"Yes, I remember the license plate because it was funny," Lisa said. "FITSME."

It didn't take the investigators long to trace the license plate to Suzi Faulk.

Suzi told her new best friend Jake to use a gun and a knife because there was a notorious unsolved murder in Tucson where the killer used both. Maybe the cops would suspect a serial killer. She made a point to ask that the body be placed near the precious bike trail where Tim went riding in the park.

She thought it would be the perfect crime. Jake did the deed, then got out of town. But that stupid deputy had to come along and had taken his responsibilities much too seriously. Suzi thought she could warn him off, so she had Jake get her a coyote's head when he came back to town. She put it in the freezer in the garage until she needed it. She even wore gloves. How did they get on to her?

Sheriff's cars pulled up to the Faulk house and deputies spread around the perimeter. Two of them came to the front door and knocked loudly, shouting, "Open up, police." No response. Suddenly, the deputies heard the crack of two gunshots a few seconds apart.

They kicked open the front door and charged inside. Tim's body, wearing his favorite biking suit, was splayed out on the white couch, a bullet hole in his forehead. When they entered the family room Suzi used for her studio, they found her slumped over her drawing table, bullet hole in her temple, revolver on the floor, blood everywhere.

On the crimson-spattered drawing table was a sketch. It showed Suzi and Tim walking off into the sunset, a happy coyote trotting alongside them.

† † †

NANCY NEWCOMER was an award-winning advertising and marketing copywriter for twenty-two years, first in Minneapolis and then in Phoenix. She has a bachelor's degree in English from the University of Iowa. After nine years as a staff member at Arizona State University, she retired last summer and has been writing fiction and nonfiction pieces since then. She lives in Fountain Hills, Arizona, with her husband and two cats, Thelma and Louise.

MURDER AT ROCKING WITCHES RANCH
MERLE MCCANN

March, 1875
Ten years after the Civil War

Behind the Immaculate Conception Church in Brownsville, Texas, Dr. Ellery Fordham and Father Julius watched three laborers load El's wagon with crates of their vineyard's growing stock.

The usually jolly priest looked worried. "Listen, Doc, you get to Arizona Territory right quick. Whitfield wants these vines this spring. No stopping at home."

"No reason to, nobody's waiting there."

"Sorry," Julius said sheepishly. "But these French vines are tender. Mustn't freeze in the mountains." He handed El an envelope. "Here're directions to the Rocking WWW, a letter to Whitfield, and a list of inns with barns to protect the vines at night."

"Anything else?"

"Watch out for Indians. They're stirred up again."

Days later, with the sun descending, El bounded into the Yavapai Trading Post near the Verde River in Arizona's central territory. Behind the counter, a gray-whiskered clerk glared at him. "Hep ya, stranger?"

"Need to find the Whitfield Ranch."

"The Three Dubya?" The fellow grimaced. "Round these parts, we call it the Three Witches 'cause o' them crazy women it's named fer. Weird stuff goes on out there."

"That so?"

"Yep." He dropped his voice. "They're real secretive. Don't cotton to strangers. Ain't nobody been there in years." He wiped his nose on his sleeve. "The widow-lady, Grandma Wilma, she never trades no more. Some say she's mighty sick but rumor is they keep her locked in a shed 'cause she's a crazy bug. The missus, Winona? Hides under a black veil whenever she comes. That girl, Wendy, she be a pretty thing but acts more like a man." He arched his brow. "She can break a horse, bulldog with the best, and shoot the heart of a quarter tossed in the air. Ain't got a lick a female in her. They say she goes to college, but I suspect she be sent away 'cause Whitfield can't control her." He squinted. "I gave ya my caution, somethin' strange 'bout that place."

El dismissed the old magpie's gossip and headed for the door. He had a job to do, and he needed the money for doing it. "I'll take your caution, mister."

"They won't like you comin' 'round. And, they's got hired guns."

" How do I get there?"

"Follow the trail north, five miles along the creek. A sign's nailed to an old oak. Their brand's burned into it—three W's ridin' a rocker." He shoved at his specs. "Listen young feller, you keep alert. Injuns been up to no good lately."

El returned to his wagon, wondering whether freighting for a living was such a good idea after all. He hadn't bargained on scuffling with Indians, and now he'd been warned twice.

Two hours later, sunset approaching, he spotted the sign. He stopped the horses, stood and stretched his limbs. Glancing down at the rock-hard, mahogany seat, he was thankful his journey was nearly done. His bench-weary ass would welcome a rest. Inhaling the cold air, he surveyed the terrain. All looked peaceful, nary an Indian in sight.

He rubbed his hands for warmth, suspecting planting weather was still a ways off. He'd left Fort McDowell this morning in shirt sleeves and now he shivered in his coat. He turned the horses onto the track leading to Whitfield's. He'd never been to these parts but thought it right pretty...cold as hell, but pretty.

The field to his left contained a herd of cattle. To his right, casting long shadows, Lodge Pole Pine seemed to climb into the mountains for miles. He wondered if he were on triple dub land. Surely, the house was nearby.

He jolted when rifle shots scuffed the dirt in front of the horses. They reared up, whinnying loudly. El jumped to his feet, heart pounding. "Whoa!" he shouted, drawing his Colt. He dove under the bench and searched for the varmints while trying to control his team. *Indians or hired guns? Coming from the pines.* Luckily, he'd not been hit. *Warning shots, maybe.* His wagon was clearly labeled, assuming the morons could read.

After ten silent minutes, he crawled out, anxious to reach the ranch house before dark. He thought of returning to the post, but traveling in Indian country after sundown was plain loco. He hoped Whitfield would house him until morning. He urged the horses into a brisker pace.

El loaded his rifle and laid it beside him, next to his government-issued pistol, the only souvenir he'd kept from the Civil War. A half mile up the track, another volley of bullets rained down, this time from behind a dilapidated shed. *The old lady's?* He grabbed his weapons and leaped for safety beside the wagon. He studied the shanty but saw no one. Rifle ready, sweat trickled down his ribs. Seconds later, a series of shots peppered the far side of the wagon. He swore loudly while steadying the horses.

Darkness increased as he moved the horses forward. For security, he walked beside the wagon. A slanted plume of chimney smoke told him he'd arrived. Just ahead a fence encircled a log house and grassless yard. He hitched the horses to the chained gate and crept away for a better view of the house.

Two junipers framing the porch offered limited cover if he survived crossing the yard. Someone moved behind the lace curtains in the lower, golden-lit, windows. He spied no outside guards. Breathing deeply, he rolled under the fence, cleared the yard, flew onto the porch, and banged the door.

Hinges groaned. Guns cocked somewhere behind him. A dark haired, scowling young woman dressed in overalls peered out, fear in her eyes. "How'd you get to my door?"

He looked but couldn't see the gunmen. Slowly, he removed his Stetson. "Evening, Miss. I'm Dr. Ellery Fordham. I've a delivery from Brownsville."

Her expression instantly changed. "I'll be jiggered!" She opened the door and shouted, "Lower your guns, boys." She smiled and her mouth pulled severely to one side. Her hand rose and covered it. "Come in, Dr. Fordham. I'm Wendy Whitfield." She turned her face, obscuring the jagged red scar running from the corner of her mouth to her jaw.

"Are you one of the three W's?"

She chuckled. "Yes. There's Winona and Wilma, too. I'm about to eat. I'd be pleased if you'd join me."

"Thank you." He stepped into the foyer, noticing the old but elegant furnishings in the adjoining rooms. He handed her Father Julius' letter. "I best put away my rig so your vines don't freeze, then hunt me up some shelter."

"Never mind." She darted past him. "You'll have to stay over—can't travel at night in these parts. You'll be comfortable in the loft." She opened the door. "Cubby, see to Dr. Fordham's horses and park the wagon in the barn."

She gestured to the dining room. "Have a seat Dr. Fordham while I dish up supper." Happiness rang in her voice as she disappeared from view. El guessed that since her father scared everybody away, she must be starved for company.

Minutes later, she served him red wine in a stemmed glass and placed a fragrant bowl of chili before him. Curious, he watched her closely. When she poured honey over the cornpone, he noticed her manicured fingernails and recalled the clerk's ignorant female comment.

They ate alone, which pleased him, but he wondered about the rest of her family. "Does anyone else live here with you?"

She nodded. "I already took a tray up to my parents' room, and Grandmother eats early. She's bedridden now but insists on feeding herself." She eyed him over her spoon. "Sorry about my men. They only meant to scare you off. We've had bad luck with strangers." She refilled his glass. "What kind of a doctor are you, a veterinarian?"

"No, a surgeon. Lately, it's been general practice."

"A real sawbones? Why're you haulin' our vines?"

"I recently lost everything to fire. I'm working to replace my equipment."

They talked easily and when it grew late, she walked him to the barn. There, she handed him the blankets she carried.

In the moonlight, El watched Wendy return to the house and then arranged his bed. He recounted seeing lantern light in a distant, sturdy cabin and figured it must be the grandmother's as opposed to the shack he'd seen earlier. The other illuminated building looked like a bunkhouse. In need of a privy, he headed outside.

On his return, he noticed a tarp-covered buckboard parked

against the barn. He stopped for a closer look. Lifting the drape, he discovered the body of a middle-aged man. His belt buckle, engraved with the Rocking WWW brand, glinted in the moonlight.

Even though homegrown justice was common in the Wild West, El was taken aback by his discovery. He nearly missed the bullet hole in the man's leather vest and the blood staining his shirt. He rolled the cadaver to its side and found the slug's exit wound. The man had died recently. The body had no odor and was still flexible. Lowering the corpse onto his back, El wondered who he might be.

Did Wendy know about him? She hadn't seemed sad— probably not old man Whitfield—unless these women are cold-blooded killers. She'd had a strange look in her eyes when she first opened the door. Who was she expecting? *The law?*

He headed for the loft, thankful he'd be gone in the morning . . . and wearing a sidearm.

The next morning, Wendy greeted him with a heart stopping smile and invited him to see the vineyard. He pondered the notion, knowing he should hightail it out of there, but if anyone meant to kill him, they'd have done it by now. As they rode, he wanted to ask about her father but never found the right moment. If he upset her, he might not get the information he wanted...or he might get worse. Ten minutes out, they crossed a ridge opening onto a glen of well-tended vines.

"I'd never guess grapes would grow here," he muttered.

"That's good. We don't want folks to know." She smiled, and the tugging of her scar disfigured her otherwise beautiful face. He felt sad for her.

Before he could ask why the secret, she continued, "Dad, the men, and I planted every vine." She smiled as she dismounted. "In the old country Dad's people were vintners."

El heard pride in her voice but no sadness. He figured the corpse wasn't Whitfield. *Then why haven't I seen him?* Her light-heartedness made him curiously happy but at some point, he had to ask her about the body.

El gestured to the view. "These vines appear to have been here a while."

"Five years. When we came to the Verde Valley and discovered its sunny climate and limestone soil, Dad said it was like the wine regions of France and Italy." She whipped off her hat and pointed with it to the mature vines. "Immediately, he planned to establish himself first with cattle and then grapes. He longed for a vineyard."

She laughed. "Soon, I was caught up. Every year we ordered more vines. I worked with him when I wasn't at the university. He'd ferment several dozen bottles each season." She turned and her eyes sparkled in the sunlight. "Last night's wine was his. He intended to sell the cattle this year and build a winery." Her voice dropped. "Unfortunately, he ran out of time."

Enchanted by the girl, El dismounted to walk beside her. "How so?"

"Mother killed him."

His breath caught and his eyes drilled hers. "How'd it happen?"

Her face remained calm. "She shot him."

El recalled the bullet wound. It didn't appear he'd been shot close up. "When?"

She drew a deep breath. "Yesterday." Her fingers darted to her scarred face.

Will she kill me to cover up the murder? Her steadiness unnerved him. "Have others been murdered out here?"

"No. The men are excellent marksmen." She stared at her boots. "Father told them to frighten strangers away, not kill them."

"You're not upset?"

"I've been expecting it." She shrugged. "They fought continually. He'd beat Mother for any reason, and she'd take it. Yesterday, he tried to strangle her." Wendy's face reddened. "I'm sorry. I shouldn't be burdening you." She dropped her voice. "You're a nice man. I find you easy to talk to."

"Did he beat you?"

"Started a few months back."

El pointed at her scar. "He did that?" She nodded.

Standing close to her, El's emotions spun. If Whitfield weren't already dead, El thought *he* might kill him. "Does the law know?"

"Not yet. I suppose we'll have to report it—unless Cubby mentioned it to his gossipy sister when he went to the village for horse feed. He'd tell his sister but never the sheriff. All the men adore Mother."

"What scarred you?"

"Belt buckle." She studied him as if looking for a hint of judgment. "I caught him working Mother over with his belt. I rushed him. He swung around, and the buckle hit me.

"Yesterday morning, I heard a shot. From my bedroom window, I saw them halfway to the barn, his hands around her throat. When I got there, she was standing over him with her old Russian pistol. Bruises on her neck from his hands were already coloring up."

But, the man I discovered wasn't killed with a pistol. El's chest tightened. "What's next?"

"We'll bury him. I'll fight to make a success of the vineyard."

"You must have hated him."

"Completely. As much as I hated keeping his secrets. We didn't dare speak about the grapes. He fretted that if word got out, folks would buy the good producing land before he could. We need more land now to expand. Then there's Mother—I couldn't bear their fights. And he couldn't let folks know he beat her. So he hired workmen, marksmen, and ordered them to scare everybody away."

"Will you have enough men to plant the new vines?"

She pointed across the valley. "Cubby, Juan and Sylvan are sinking posts for the supporting wires. We'll start planting tomorrow after we bury the old man." She shrugged dejectedly. "Somehow, we'll get it done."

"Are three men enough?"

"Normally, but I'll have only two. Sylvan leaves tomorrow with his wranglers to drive the herd to Cheyenne."

He gnawed the inside of his cheek, worried it'd be a mistake to stay, but she seemed so vulnerable. "I'll be your third man."

She toyed with her hat. "I'll think on it."

He touched her scar. "I could improve this, too, if you'd allow me."

She covered his hand with hers. "Our local sawbones said I'd waited too long."

"It was never tended?"

"Father wouldn't allow it."

"That's why it's jagged. If I remove the scar tissue and close it properly, you'd hardly notice it."

She smirked disbelievingly. "That right?"

"Doctoring in the war, I discovered techniques to lessen scarring. I had to do a lot of amputations and it was important to smooth the underlying tissues so a wooden leg could be worn with less pain. Minimizing the surface scarring was important to the process, for restoring burn patients as well."

She took a deep breath. "I'll think on that offer, too."

When El and Wendy rode through the ranch gate, Wendy's mother, Winona, bent and crippled, limped toward them, leaning heavily on her cane. The breeze billowed her dark veil that reached to the waist of her dusty black dress.

Wendy reined to a stop. "Mother?"

When Mrs. Whitfield raised her hand to shade her eyes, her sleeve slid away. Glistening, irregular scars marked her arm. "Oh, Wendy," she wailed. "Thank God, you're back. Your grandmother died this morning."

El's breath caught. *Two dead in twenty-four hours?*

Wendy gasped and bent down from the saddle to hug her. "Mama, I'm so sorry. I know how much you loved her. We all did." Slowly straightening, she glanced at El. "Dr. Fordham and I'll go there right now."

Winona nodded and stepped back from the horses.

They rode at a clip while Wendy explained that Grandma Wilma suffered with tuberculosis. "That's why we came here. The Eastern doctors wanted her institutionalized, but Mother said no. When we arrived, Grandmother insisted my father build two cabins. She wouldn't move into our house for fear of infecting us."

At the cabin, El trailed Wendy inside. It was only two rooms with a privy out back. He remained in the parlor when Wendy entered the bedroom. Removing his hat, he noticed the furnishings were similar to those in the main house, the floors and windows recently scrubbed. Wendy invaded his thoughts. She needed his help, and he wanted to give it. Is it love when you want to help a woman this much—to risk your life for her?

Wendy came from the bedroom weeping. He embraced her, relishing the warmth and feel of her body. "Will your mother be all right?"

She took a ragged breath. "Mother's strong." She blotted her tears on the bandana she wore at her neck.

Hoping to distract her, he gestured around the room. "The

cabin's well kept."

"Mother's doing. Grandma wouldn't let the rest of us near." Wendy glanced about. "As a girl, I'd sit on the porch and talk to her through the window. Even after Mother was crippled, she did the cleaning." She sighed. "Another body to bury."

He rubbed her shoulder. "I'll help." They walked outside. "We should burn the cabin and her things. Tuberculosis is nasty."

While leading their horses to the barn, El asked, "How was your mother crippled?"

"I'm not sure. I was at school. She said she slipped on the stairs, but I figure Dad pushed her during a tantrum."

"Would your mother have supper with us?"

"No, she'd have to expose her face to eat. She doesn't know you well enough for that." Wendy stared past him. "It's scarred far worse than mine."

That evening, El moved out of the barn and into the bunkhouse.

After the double burial the next day, he stayed on to plant vines. The following Sunday, he invited Wendy to go riding. Twenty minutes out, she asked him to remove her scar. "I saw Doc Malloy and he said you can use his tools and supplies."

"I'll operate whenever you say. Perhaps he'd assist."

"Doc'd like that. Mother, however, is fretted. She wants to talk to you tonight."

They were seated in the parlor when Mrs. Whitfield appeared, minus her veil, wearing a jeweled comb in her graying hair.

"Mother," Wendy said, "This is Dr. Ellery Fordham."

Winona sat at the opposite end of the small settee from El. He briefly studied her damaged face. *A man had to be pure evil to do this to his wife and daughter.*

She raised her chin defiantly. "Does my face disgust you, Dr. Fordham?"

"No, ma'am, I've seen worse." He moved closer and raised his hand. "May I?" She hesitated, looked in his eyes, then she nodded.

He held her chin. "Many of your scars can be improved."

Wendy exhaled loudly. "You should see her back. Dad was good at beating her where it wouldn't show. Of late, he became careless and hit her face. He nearly put out her left eye."

"The scars near your eye are repairable," he said to Winona. "Are they also from a belt buckle?"

"Yes." Tears flowed along the web of scars that covered the left side of her face.

Whitfield was right handed.

She rose. "Wendy trusts you. Nevertheless, try your skills on my face before you touch Wendy's."

The next morning, El and Wendy rode to Dr.Malloy's to evaluate his operating facilities. On their return to the ranch, as El opened the gate, a shot rang out. On foot, they ran for the house.

Face down in the dirt a few feet from the porch steps, Cubby moaned. A growing blood stain marked his shirt. His rifle rested two feet beyond his reach. The angry-eyed sheriff stood near Cubby, rifle in hand.

Winona Whitfield, without her veil, watched from the porch, sobbing into her handkerchief. Her facial scars glistened in the sun, and finger wide bruises on her neck were obvious.

El hurried to Cubby. Wendy went to her mother. He eased Cubby over and cradled him in his arms. Cubby had been shot through his side. El glared at the sheriff. "Was shooting him necessary?"

The sheriff ignored him. Instead, he stared at Mrs. Whitfield. El thought he saw the sheriff shudder.

Cubby whispered to El. "I thought the sheriff might arrest Miss Winona. I tried to scare him away. Said she killed the mister but she couldn't. She's too good a woman.

The sheriff shifted his focus to Wendy, as if he could no longer bear to look at her mother. "Mrs. Whitfield's been accused of killing your pa. I'm takin' her in."

"Nooo," Cubby protested softly. "She's got one of them old Smith and Wesson Russian pistols. Have a gander at it."

El looked up at Mrs. Whitfield. "Have you a handgun?" She nodded. "May I see it?"

The sheriff squared his stance. "The murder weapon? We'll need to take that along."

Winona disappeared inside and when she returned she handed the antiquated Smith and Wesson to El, who broke it open and examined it. Seeing the gun's clean interior, he believed he knew how Whitfield had died. He also knew the shooter had saved Winona's life. It was time he did something about it, even if it meant a little fudging.

He handed the weapon to the sheriff. "Take a look. That old thing hasn't been fired in months. She didn't shoot Whitfield. By the size of the hole I saw, he was killed with a rifle."

"Why didn't you report it?" The sheriff glared at El.

"I only just arrived. No reason to think you didn't know."

The sheriff scoffed. "I'll need a chin wag with the hired men."

"Suit yourself," El said. "But it was an accident. I'll testify to that. When I drove up, I encountered warning shots. Whitfield was riding in the Pines at a lower level than the guards. They'll tell you he caught a ricochet bullet off a boulder. I examined Whitfield. The angle of his wounds agreed with a ricocheted slug. Ain't that right, Cubby?"

"Yup."

After the sheriff left, El tended Cubby's wound, then joined the women in the house. Winona rested on the parlor's settee while Wendy, overwrought, paced the room.

"What does this mean?" Wendy asked.

"How's Cubby?" Winona interrupted.

"He'll be fine. I think the sheriff bought my story." El raised his brow. "He seemed uneasy with your scars—and he noticed Wendy's. He knows a jury wouldn't convict you once they saw your flesh. They'd accept self-defense. Justice in the west is still wild and raw, but it's fair. The sheriff realizes an *accident* is the best answer."

"Does Cubby know who shot my husband?" Winona asked.

"Not sure, ma'am."

"But you do, right?"

"Yes, ma'am—a sharpshooter who loves you." He glanced at Wendy. *I hope she'll love me that much one day.* "The edges and angle of the wound suggested the bullet came from a distance and high up, like a second floor window." He stared at Wendy who stood beside hm. "Only upper window on the barn's side of the house is your bedroom. Why'd you lie to me?"

Again, Winona interrupted. "I made Wendy promise to name me if anybody asked about it. She's got her whole life ahead—no sense messing it up." She sneered. "Mine doesn't matter."

She stood. "What does matter is the vineyard. Don't you two have vines to tend?"

Wendy gripped his arm and gazed into his eyes, a smile forming around her mouth.

El's heart kicked and he chuckled. "Yes, ma'am."

† † †

Award winning author, Merle McCann, is best known for her Longjohners' Mystery Series for young adults, a literacy project to which she's devoted the past seven years. Born in the Yukon, raised in Seattle, she has traveled the United States and Europe with her husband pursuing their Arabian horse business. Before settling down to write serious fiction, McCann worked as a scenic photographer. She lives with her husband in Scottsdale, Arizona.

SHADOW OF DARKNESS
Leslie Kohler

Growing up in the shadow of Folsom Prison, home to some of the most notorious criminals of all time, I knew life would prove to be daunting. The confines of that monolithic granite structure stood within shooting distance of our house—just over the ravine that cut across the front half our property. Looking at the prison's turret from my bedroom window, with its silhouetted guard, the barrel of his high powered rifle constantly trained outward, always sent prickles of fear down my spine.

Whenever I misbehaved, my mama never had to breathe a word. She simply cut her eyes to the kitchen window and nodded her head in the direction of the tower. I'd stare wide-eyed at the ever-present fortress as her subtle gesture screamed, "That's where we toss the wanton and wicked." For a ten-year-old growing up in the Northern California countryside during the early fifties, nothing seemed scarier.

I'd scurry to my room on my slender, colt-like legs, yellow ponytail bobbing frantically behind. Flopping onto the bed, I'd stare out at my prison guard, giving him my meanest scowl. Then I'd squeeze my eyes, tight, and push the image of that awful prison out of my mind.

Silently, I vowed to be a good girl—no more naughtiness. Next time Mama asked, "Who ate all the Hershey bars?" I'd tell her, "I did," instead of blaming my little brother who always got sick after a few bites of chocolate, anyway. When I spied a pile of pennies lying on my daddy's dresser, I'd leave them there, instead of spilling them into my overall's pocket. It wasn't that I was a rotten kid. I always tried to muster good intentions. But the lure of forbidden temptation always seemed to waylay my resolve.

Sometimes after one of my failings, like nibbling the frosting off one of Mama's freshly baked cakes, Daddy would plunk me down on his knee for a heart-to-heart talk. Issuing discipline not one of his strong points, he'd usually end up chuckling, "You know, Princess, I can't get too angry with you. You're a lot like your great-grandpa Gilmore. I do believe you inherited his spunk. You're growing up so fast. And pretty—I'll be out shooing the boys away with my shotgun soon."

"Oh, Daddy." I'd blush.

It was because of Granddad Gil that we lived so close to the prison. After he died, we moved into his spacious three-story ranch house he built in the late 1800s. Our home sat high on a hillside, dotted with oak trees and blanketed in grassy brush. The lands surrounding us grew lush in the winter from our plentiful mountain foothill rains, which turned dry as straw during the arid summer months. A spacious veranda, bordered by a whitewashed railing surrounded the russet wooden house. Rolling hills rose all around, providing my sisters, brother and me, plenty of room to romp and explore. The perfect setting in which to grow up—except for the dreaded watchtower perched on the knoll across the way.

Great-granddad Gil built the house here in order to live close to his dream project. One he had envisioned for many years. He planned to build a dam across the nearby American River, to harness its roaring waters, in order to create hydroelectric power. The electricity generated would be fed through miles and miles of overhead lines, all the way to the former gold rush town, now California's bustling state Capitol, Sacramento. Nowhere in our country had anything like this been accomplished before. Granddad Gil's project loomed so large, it would change the history of our river valley forever.

Once Granddad Gil began building Folsom Dam, construction costs soared sky high. Though local granite quarries provided readily available building materials, this project required thousands of hours of manpower. Paying these wages would cost a bundle of money, even for someone as wealthy as my great-granddad. Begrudgingly, he postponed work on the dam until he could figure out where to find cheap labor.

For a couple of years, Granddad Gil attempted to round up enough laborers willing to work for modest wages, but because of the dam's location, it turned out to be tougher than he thought. He decided the only way he could make his project affordable would be by using jailhouse inmates, so he made a deal with the State of California to provide him with jail labor in order to finish the dam. The only problem being, back in 1878, the only settlement near the proposed dam was nothing but a bedraggled mining camp named Stoney Bar. Its tiny population housed a few criminals, but nowhere near the number needed to build a dam.

Granddad Gil wouldn't let that stop him. He decided if the prison labor was too far away, he'd bring the inmates to him. From his vast land holdings, Granddad gave the Golden State five hundred acres overlooking the dam site on which to build a prison. Once the state completed the penitentiary and moved the inmates in, Granddad Gil put them to work constructing his dam.

Granddad's dream took thirteen years of backbreaking labor. Growing up, I heard stories about prisoners losing their lives while constructing the enormous project, and rumors passed down telling of the prison guards' harsh treatment of the chain gangs that hoisted the massive granite blocks into place. Hearing of these atrocities always made me wonder whether my granddad was a ruthless opportunist, or a victim of vicious rumors.

One day as my daddy stretched out in his easy chair to read the Sunday paper, I asked him, "Why do people tell such terrible stories about Granddad Gil? They can't be true, can they?"

"Don't listen to those tales, Princess. The truth has a way of clouding over as stories are told over and over through the years. I don't recall too much about Granddad. What I do remember, though, is that he always seemed like a fair and compassionate man."

"They aren't just things people say. I read about it in a book at the prison museum."

"It's the same for the written word. History has a way of changing, according to who's doing the telling." He smiled at me and tweaked my cheek. "Just believe in the ones you love. Have faith. I know I do."

Faith. I knew I believed in my daddy. Nobody listened to me more carefully or had a kinder heart. If my Granddad Gil was half as compassionate as my dad, then he was okay by me. I just had to have faith that I could live up to my daddy's good expectations. I vowed that the next time I faced the decision to go with the good angel or the bad, I would pick the good one. At least I hoped so. Otherwise I might find myself staring down the rifle in the tower.

Mama bustled into the parlor, a picnic basket hooked on one arm and a pile of old blankets in the other.

Daddy eased me off his knee. "Here, Mother, let me help you with those. Didn't realize it was time to leave for the river. Why don't you round up the kids while I grab my fishing gear? Princess, go check and see if your sisters have tacked up the horses."

Mama, Daddy and my brother rode in the old Ford pickup that had been around ever since anyone could remember. It had been built before the smooth paving of modern roads, and its heavy chassis could handle the ruts of the dirt road that wound through our property down to the American River. We owned newer cars, Mama's a shiny red station wagon, and Daddy had a black, high-finned Cadillac, but the truck was kept in reserve for trekking across our property.

My sisters, Linda and Trudy, trailed along with me, behind the truck on horseback, coughing on dust kicked up by the truck's tires. Riding tall upon my favorite gelding, Shiloh, I turned to my oldest sister, Linda, and said, "Race you down to the river."

Flipping back her neatly braided pigtail, she snipped, "Dad said to follow behind them."

"Yeah, but I'm sure he didn't mean *all* the way down to the river."

"Yes he did."

"Boy, for an eighth grader, you sure act like a sissy pants."

Linda glared at me. "I'm going to tell Mom you're calling me names."

"What if I tell her you've been kissing boys? I saw you smooching Kenny Stevens behind the barn."

"Liar. I didn't kiss Kenny." Looking to my middle sister, Trudy, Linda said, "You know I wouldn't kiss that yucky Kenny. Right?"

Trudy huffed," Of course not."

Looping my reins across the horn of the western saddle, I crossed my arms and grasped my shoulders like I was being hugged. Giving my lips a smack, I cooed, "Oh, Kenny, you kiss sooo good. But of course you *are* fifteen."

Linda shot me a look meaner than the ones I'd imagined glaring out from the gun toters in the prison's watchtower. Glancing to Trudy for some sibling support, my middle sister wimped out and stared straight ahead at the dirt road. Being born between two stubborn heads like Linda and me often meant keeping her nose out of our business.

Gathering the reins, I kicked Shiloh's sides with the heels of my boots, urging him into a canter. Picking up speed, I tore away from my sisters and passed the truck, racing the wind all the way to the ridge overlooking the American River. Only then did I slow down so that my horse could safely take the steep grade of the trail that led down to the river's edge.

I found the small, sandy beach that was one of the few spots along the water not covered by gray river rocks, where my family liked to picnic. Leading my horse to the water, I coaxed him to drink. Then I tethered him to a shade tree and lay down on the cool, moist sand. Closing my eyes, I listened to the babbling waters cascade over the rocks, gathering force as it tumbled downstream.

I heard the truck rumble to a stop on the hillside above me, and my family's voices as they ambled down the hill. Heavy footsteps thudded across the hardened ground to where I lay.

Uh, oh, I thought. Mama's feet stomps sounded real mad this time. Maybe I should have stayed behind the truck.

Opening my eyes, I peered into the unsmiling face not of my mama, but my daddy. The skin stretched tight across his jawbone, quivering ever so slightly. He opened his mouth to speak, then stopped. He glared down at me, squeezing his hands open and shut. When he finally addressed me, the words sounded sharp, clipped, like he would explode if he were to let it all out.

"Melissa, how dare you disobey me. I've told you never to ride out here alone."

"But you were right behind me."

"Not close enough. The road's all torn up from the spring rains. What if your horse had tripped in one of the ruts?"

"But Daddy—"

"Quiet, or I'll give you a spanking!"

"But—"

Daddy turned around and stomped down to the water.

Tears welled in my eyes and dribbled down my cheeks. I rolled away from my family, not caring how the tears mixed with sand ground into my skin. I waited that way a long, long time. Although I'd never seen my daddy so angry, I knew he couldn't stay that way for long. Any second he would return and take away the sting of his words with a kiss on my forehead, a tousle of my hair, and speak the words, "I love you, Princess."

Instead, I heard my family frolicking in the water, laughing, the buzz of Daddy's fishing line casting out and reeling in. Then Daddy calling out, "Hey, Linda, I thought you wanted to learn how to fish. Come on over here."

My temples throbbed and my head felt like it would split wide open. I had to get out of there. Somewhere quiet, where I could be alone and think. I picked myself up and crept over to Shiloh, untied the reins, and hoisted myself up into the saddle. With a gentle nudge, I turned my horse toward home—the ride back blurred by a barrage of tears.

When I returned to my house, I untacked Shiloh and put him in his corral. Shuffling up the path that led from the barn to our front porch, I wiped the sandy grit from the beach, and tears off my face. When I reached the front door, I noticed it stood wide open.

Stupid Linda must have forgotten to close it.

I padded up the stairs and headed into my bedroom. Pausing in front of the bureau mirror, I pulled the windswept hair from my ponytail and ran my fingers through the thick mane, loosening the tangles. I prodded at my puffy, red eyes, willing the aftermath of the tears to go away.

A gust of air blew through my open window, ruffling the laced curtains that had yellowed over the years. The warm breeze surrounded me like a smothering blanket, and I shut the window to block it. In the quiet of the house, I gazed at the guard in the tower.

My solitude was broken by the sound of rustling from the back of the house.

What was that? Is somebody here? Or just some pesky squirrel that snuck in through the open door?

Silently, I crept down the long hallway, ready to turn tail and run if it was a squirrel. It wouldn't be the first time a wild animal had broken into our house. Once my mom found a possum rummaging through the kitchen cabinets.

Easing my way into my parents' bedroom, I spotted a man searching through the dresser against the far wall. He stood naked, except for his underpants. He had thick, black-cropped hair, with some sprouting across his back.

Barbs of fear riddled my body. Stabbing, electric jolts.

Discarded at his feet lay a crumpled, blue cotton shirt and faded jeans. I knew what these clothes meant—I'd seen men wearing them in photographs at the prison museum.

The man turned around. He stared at me with coal-black eyes. Fire eyes, burning into mine. Face, battered with pockmarks. Rivulets of sweat trailed down his temples and chest. His breath, fast. Panting like a dog.

"Well, lookie here, a pretty young girl come to welcome me out of the slammer. What's wrong sweetheart, you never seen a man in his skivvies?"

A wave of fear seared my body. With quivering legs, I backed toward the door. My limbs could barely move. Like swimming through quicksand.

In a rush of steps that belied the man's stocky build, he rushed past me and slammed the door shut. Grabbing my hair with his fist, he twisted my head so I had to look up into his hideous face. My hair felt like it was being ripped from my scalp. I struggled back my cries of pain.

"Don't you got no manners? Tryin' to leave on me. I'll show you how to act, little girl." He pushed his face in close, bared yellow teeth clashing against mine. Smelly saliva spattered my skin. Barely releasing me from his clutch, he pulled his lips into a snarl, his hot breath covering my face.

I heaved and a wave of vomit erupted from my throat, spilling down my chin.

He shoved the back of my head, forcing me across the room. I lay sprawled on the floor.

"You're gonna' help me. I need to borrow some of your daddy's clothes, so's I don't look like no escapee. Where they at?"

"My...my daddy keeps his clothes in the closet," I said, scarcely above a whisper. Watching the man, I slowly stood up. "I'll get you some."

With trembling hands, I fumbled through the clothing rack, grabbing a white T-shirt and dark jeans. I felt my way along the back corner of the closet, nervously clutching a cold, steel weapon. I tucked it into the back of my pants. Handing the clothes to the man, I brushed past him, making a beeline for the door.

He snatched my arm with a vice grip, killing my hope of escape. Then whirled me around. Pulling me close, his stomach crushed against my chest. Hard. Muscled, like it could hurt you with its touch.

In a gravelly voice he said, "Where ya' goin, honey? Looks like your daddy didn't do his job schoolin' you how to mind. Guess I'm gonna have to be the one to teach ya'."

I tried to wrestle away, but he only held me tighter, stinging my arm with his cruel grip. The coarse hair covering his body poked into my face. His slimy sweat soaked my skin. I twisted my head to the side, trying to get a breath of freedom.

He sneered. "Got some spunk, huh? I like that."

My eyes darted around the room, searching for anything that could help me, trying to unlock my arm to grasp the weapon. Trying to gather my courage. Looking through the open window across the ravine, I spied the ever-present guard with his rifle aimed outward.

I sent a silent plea to the guard: Please, help me. Don't let this man hurt me.

Though I had felt as if the guard's eyes were always on me, I now realized this wasn't true. He stood stock-still, the rifle's barrel resting in the crook of his arm, eyes unwavering, guarding only the grounds surrounding him.

Gulping air, fighting back tears. I turned my head upward, and peered at the evil man.

He lowered his face to mine.

I scanned the blackness of his eyes. They were dark as coal. Except for the outer corner of his left eye—it held a spot of red, a drop of blood next to the pool of darkness. Like a scar from a distant accident. One that refused to go away.

With choked words, I said, "You're not gonna hurt me, mister."

His eyes grew darker. "What'd you say?"

"I said 'you're not gonna hurt me.'"

"Why you say that?"

"Because you don't want to. You're just so used to being mean, you don't hardly know how else to act."

"Why you…you don't know nothin' about me. Sittin' up here in your big fancy house. You got no idea what my life was like." He hitched his head toward the window. "Why I wound up down there."

"What do you mean?"

"I mean growin' up like an animal. Beat down all the time."

"Lots of people get beat. They don't grow up to be convicts."

He glared at me hard. "How dare you talk down to me. Looks like you need a good whippin'." With powerful arms, he pushed me away, and I fell back over my parents' bed.

Stomping to me, hovering above, sides heaving like an angry steer, he seethed, "You don't know what it was like. A drunk for a dad. Used me as his personal whippin' boy. My ma just let him at me. I couldn't do nothin' right. I learned real good. Now, you're gonna."

"I know how that feels," I mumbled.

He scanned the lavish furnishings of the room. "The heck you do."

"I'm always getting in trouble for something. Even when I try to be good. But my daddy doesn't beat me—"

The sound of the old pickup coming up the drive stopped my words. I rolled across the bed and ran to the window, yelling, "Daddy! Daddy!"

The man bolted toward me, rage bleeding in his eyes. Whatever good was ever in him was gone. I pulled the gun from my waistband and raised it—shooting straight into that bloody eye. His head snapped back and he fell to the floor. A sickly dark liquid oozed from his eye. Trembling, I let the gun slip from my hand and cried.

The next thing I remembered was my daddy's embrace. I shook so violently I couldn't get my mouth to speak. By the time I calmed down enough to tell my story, a bloody trail flowed along the bedroom floor—like a river of death.

Daddy picked up the gun and speared a second shot into the convict, in the exact spot I had fired. Then he called the prison warden.

† † †

Word came out that the escapee had been killed by my father while trying to defend me. My daddy was exonerated.

We also learned the escapee's story. He'd been in and out of prisons since he was a young man, until he landed in Folsom for life. He'd killed his father.

I think about the dead convict every time I look over at the watchtower and wonder if that evil soul had dreams when he was young. Goals he wanted to reach out and grab, work for, struggle to achieve. Like my Granddad Gil did so long ago when he dreamed of harnessing a wild river. And I wonder what that man's life would be if he'd chosen a different path. Hadn't grown so mean. Maybe if he'd known a daddy's love, like I was so fortunate to have. My daddy may have been tough sometimes, but I knew he always loved me. Unlike the prison convict who never felt love. But life deals us what we get. And we make our choices.

There is no one guarding you from a tower.

† † †

LESLIE KOHLER is the author of the murder mystery, *Sins of the Border*. She has also written fiction and nonfiction pieces for several publications including *Highlights for Children*, *The Arizona Republic, Skipping Stones, Listen, Winner* and *Positive Teens*. She is active the in the community organization, *No Mas Muertes* (No More Deaths) and is currently working on her next mystery, DISPOSABLE LIVES.

A TOMBSTONE EPITAPH
Deborah J Ledford

1879 – Tombstone, Arizona

Heat waves snaked along the expanse of Tombstone's main street. No hint of moisture relieved the air. Sane folks had abandoned the downtown for cooler interiors—except for a sheriff, one deputy marshal, and another man opposite the lawmen. They stood their ground, guns pointed, scowls on their faces, intent in their stance.

Three shots split the quiet. Loud *cracks* reverberated against the clapboard fronts of the commercial enterprises lining the streets.

"Well, Wyatt," the deputy said, holstering his revolver, "one less murderer in Tombstone."

Sheriff Earp and Virgil approached, then squatted down to the dead man, face up, his gun trailing a wisp of smoke.

Wyatt looked up and locked his eyes across the street. "Virgil," he said. "I think we killed the wrong man."

1937 – Eloy, Arizona

Annatelle Evans gasped as she crossed the threshold into the new resident's room. Everything stopped, suspended before her.

Her hold on the tray of hot tea, ginger cookies and a vase with a single daisy nearly left her grasp as she stared at the man sitting in front of the single paned window.

Annatelle could only see his profile: hawk nose, white handlebar mustache, matching shoulder length hair—thick and shiny even though his medical chart stated his age to be ninety-four.

MR. ANGELO TIMMS, the chart also indicated, had been living alone in nearby Wilcox for forty-two years. A widower for nearly that long. He had recently suffered heart problems and no longer felt safe living alone.

Now, here he sat, his first day in the Restful Tymes residential medical facility where Annatelle volunteered, generously giving her time, but never her heart.

"Dad?" she all but croaked.

Impossible, she reminded herself. Tinnley Upshaw had lain beneath six feet of dirt in Tombstone's Boot Hill Graveyard for fifty-eight years. Annatelle had been one of only three mourners at the open hole, where they had to pay a preacher five dollars to travel more than twenty miles, who then spat out Scripture as fast as he could.

Sheriff Earp and his lawmen had given their backs to thirteen-year-old Annatelle, her eight-year-old sister, Janey, and their Aunt Shelly—rifles at the ready if anyone dared take vengeance on the bereaved family. Annatelle and Janey stood across from their father's grieving sister. The older woman knelt on the ground in her dust-covered ankle-length dress, rocking back and forth, wailing above the preacher's prattle.

The girls' mother had refused to attend. Annatelle wondered if Mama had finished packing up the dishes, burning Daddy's clothes, dumping out his liquor, taken a breath to cease her unyielding sputter of curses against the husband who apparently had murdered four unarmed men.

"*Shot 'em dead*," Sheriff Earp had told them, standing at the front door, not even bothering to remove his hat in respect when he came looking for the murderer.

Annatelle blinked, erasing the memory, then continued to stare at the old man before her. Her heart fluttered in anticipation but she wasn't sure why. Hope that this actually was her father? . . . or dread that she was losing her faculties and beginning her backward spiral to the childhood so many residents of Restful Tymes chose to return to.

The man stiffened a bit, then slowly turned his head her way.

"Hello, Tillie Belle."

Unsure how, Annatelle made her way to *The Eloy Enterprise* newspaper office. Knees wobbling, she stood at the front desk and scanned through the billow of cigarette smoke that clouded the open area, in search of her grandson. Four young men and a few women tapped a constant clatter on typewriters, spoke on telephones, bustled about with focused determination. She didn't like coming here. The place made her nervous with all its chaotic energy.

She waited her turn, standing behind a man yelling at the clerk about how the boy who delivered his paper never made the toss all the way to his porch. In the far corner of the room she saw her grandson waving one hand, handset of a phone clutched in the other. Annatelle blew out a relieved breath and stepped toward him. She danced a few awkward steps with a youngster wearing wire-rimmed glasses and a scowl before he rushed past her.

Carl Evans pulled out the chair next to his desk. "Nana, what is it?"

"I just saw a ghost," his grandmother said, taking a delicate handkerchief from her purse. "Tinnley Upshaw. Your great grandfather. He's alive."

The next morning Carl climbed the steps to the wide front porch of Restful Tymes. He didn't like to go there. Refused to think the rest home could be his grandmother's eventual fate. But Nana had assigned him a duty and there would be no saying "no." Her requests had turned to pleas, which soon became demands. He tried to talk sense to his dear grandmother, looked for holes in her story, but no matter how many times he had her repeat every word his supposed grandfather had spoken to his daughter, her account of the visit never changed. All these years, she always believed her father to be innocent.

Carl entered the foyer of the twelve-bedroom former inn, and braced himself for the onslaught to his senses: gravelly voices too loud for his ears, ancient figures slumped in wheel chairs or tottering against canes, thin disheveled hair, transparent skin crossed with bulging blue veins, the smell of disinfectant. Everything...old. The facility wasn't as bad as some of the horrors his colleagues had written about, or stories he had heard from friends who had visited grandparents in other towns. Still, it took all he could muster not to flee.

He introduced himself to a nurse dressed in white from cap to shoes. She gave him a big smile and a pat on the shoulder, told him how much they all loved his grandmother, then gave him the room number for the man he had come to expose.

Carl encountered no one in the halls and wondered if everyone was napping, or worse. He stood at the door with the number 12 stenciled in blue paint and waited for more than a minute before he knocked.

"Enter if you dare," a surprisingly strong voice boomed from behind the door.

Carl reared back at the playful tone. He turned the knob and entered a room neat as a pin, bright sunlight streamed from curtains opened wide as would allow, bed made, nothing but a leather book on the bedside table.

A white haired man sitting in a rocking chair at the window turned to Carl. He nodded and hooked a finger to the chair opposite his own. It didn't take long for Carl to feel comfortable with the man who seemed so familiar. He wanted to dislike him, to discount everything he said, but the time passed easily until Carl remembered why he had sought out the old man.

"Why didn't anyone ever question why you would have killed four unarmed men?"

"From what I heard, Sheriff Earp wouldn't even allow an open casket viewing. I figured he knew he was wrong. Either didn't know how to rectify his situation, or maybe…didn't care to. Anyway, after Wyatt locked eyes with mine I got on the nearest horse and left Tombstone. Turned out, forever."

"What about your family? Didn't you worry about them?"

"My Sarah had plenty of kinfolk in Benson. Knew they'd take her and my young'uns in." His cheeks reddened and he chuckled, as if to mask embarrassment. "Her family never did take a shine to me. I knew they'd be all right. I also knew I'd face the same fate as John Osborn if I even went back to Tombstone and tried to clear my name. Figured it was best to keep everyone thinking it was me stretched out in a pine box. But I never forgot my girls."

Carl took out a notebook and a fountain pen from the inside pocket of his jacket. "Can you tell me about that day?"

"The day when my life stopped?"

Carl looked away from the sorrow in the old man's eyes. He flipped to a fresh sheet of paper and settled back in the chair.

"It was August, eighteen seventy-nine. A Wednesday, about two o'clock. Hot. Hotter than I ever remembered. Nobody was out. Just me and young Bobby Osborn, trying to finish up shoeing a bay gelding so its owner could head out of town that night. You see, I was the best blacksmith in town. Shod every horse worth riding in Tombstone. Bobby was only thirteen, but big and strong for his age and nobody could keep him away from the horses. He helped me out a lot that summer. He was also sweet on your grandma, but he'd never admit to it." He gave Carl a playful smile.

The light moment passed in an instant. The old man turned to the window. "We heard shouts, louder than the strikes of my hammer against the anvil. Bobby went to see what all the commotion was about. When the boy came back his face had gone white and he looked like he'd seen the devil come a calling. 'It's Pa' is all he said. Enough for me though—his dad seemed to always be in trouble with the law. I didn't know at the time he'd killed four men that morning."

A cough racked the old man's body. He poured water into a glass and held it to his trembling lips. Minutes later the words continued again, this time more ragged and a bit breathless.

"John Osborn and I resembled each other. Same height, build, same color hair, dark skin from working in the sun. People of Tombstone said we could've been twins till we stood side by side. Someone must have witnessed the shooting of those four men and told Wyatt and Virgil it was me. That's what I figured anyway. Maybe it was a grudge. Virgil's wife was bucked from her horse earlier that week. Her mount threw a shoe and got spooked. Virgil blamed me—said I did a piss-poor job. Had it in for me."

Carl tapped his foot against the linoleum, his mind spinning. "Do you think his kid, Bobby Osborn, is still alive?"

The old man snickered and didn't seem to take any offense. "You mean to corroborate my story?"

"Is it a story? Did you make all this up? I mean, are you the real Tinnley Upshaw?"

"Well, Bobby was your grandma's age at the time, so I suppose he's still living. As for whether I'm the 'real' Tinnley Upshaw, I guess that's up to you to believe."

Carl drummed his pen on the notepad and thought about the man's words a moment. "My grandmother's convinced. She told me you said her nickname. The one only you called her by or even knew about."

"But you're not sure."

Carl shrugged as he stuffed the notepad into his pocket and rose from the chair.

"Then you'll have to go with your gut," the old man said.

"And your heart."

"Sorry, sir. I'm a newspaper man. I'm afraid I need proof."

Carl returned to the newspaper office, his mind whirling with doubt and possibilities. He wanted to believe the old man, wanted to solve the mystery his grandmother had wondered about for decades, wanted most of all to clear a man's name of a wrong covered deeper than the graveyard dirt that concealed the coffin in Tombstone.

He took up the receiver of his phone, spun the dial and waited as the Western Electric sounded its clacking ring. Hours after darkness fell, Carl remained at his desk, the only light in the newspaper office bathed a scatter of papers marked with notations and X's. He clutched a single sheet he had circled five times in red and nodded his head as he listened to the crackled voice on the other line of the handset.

The next morning Carl sat in room twelve of Restful Tymes. He waited for the old man to talk who merely sat there, stroking the tip of his moustache, patient, waiting...for what, Carl didn't know. He decided the man would either divulge the answer to secrets hidden away for decades, or Carl would walk out the door never to return. He sighed and dug into the inside pocket of his suit jacket.

Carl handed him a tintype showing a man with longish curly hair, full handlebar moustache, hammer in one hand, the other clutched into a fist at his chest, bicep bulging.

The older man hacked into a red bandana, then held out shaking fingers. He smiled as he gazed at the photograph. "That picture was taken before I married Sarah."

"Your sister gave it to my grandmother," Carl said. "It's the only photograph that exists of you. Turns out your wife burned all the others."

"Doesn't surprise me much."

"It's you, isn't it?"

"Yep," Tinnley Upshaw said. "Do you believe me now?"

"I made some phone calls. Found Bobby Osborn. Want to see him?"

Tinnley's face whitened nearly as light as his hair. "Doubt he'd want that."

Carl rose from his chair, crossed the room and opened the

door.

A man dressed in faded jeans, a plaid shirt with mother of pearl buttons, his head topped with a wide rimmed cowboy hat entered the room.

Tinnley squinted and struggled to stand from his chair. "Well, I'll be. Is that Bobby Osborn standing there?"

"Robert, now," he said, shifting from one hand tooled cowboy boot to the other. He faced the window behind Tinnley, meeting the older man's eyes for a moment before looking away again.

"Still have a love for the horses?" Tinnley asked, sitting back down. He coughed so long that Carl and Robert exchanged a worried glance.

When Tinnley's bout ceased, Robert continued. "Yes, sir. Got my own stable. More than twenty years now. I'm involved in a breed new to the southwest. Arabians. The U. S. Army Remount Service is interested in my herd."

"That's fine. Real fine, young man."

"You taught me well. I...I always wanted to tell you that."

"Sit, sit, Robert. Tell us all about your horses."

Robert lowered himself into the chair opposite Tinnley but didn't offer any more words. He cleared his throat and glanced at Carl a few times, even opened his mouth, but then he frowned and no sound emerged.

After a long silence Carl asked him in a low voice, "Why didn't you tell?"

Robert blinked time and time again, then shrugged. "He was my dad."

"No real harm done, son," Tinnley said. "Your pa paid for the crimes with his life. Doesn't matter anymore."

"It matters to me," a voice said from the door.

The men turned to Annatelle standing there, hands clenched at her side, back straight.

Robert rose, swept off his hat and strangled its brim. "Annatelle. You're pretty as ever."

"You remember Bobby Osborn, dear. He looks the same, doesn't he? Bit taller is all."

Osborn offered a crooked smile. "And much older."

Annatelle's tense features relaxed. Her fingers went to the neck of her dress, then fiddled with a loose lock of hair that had fallen from its bun. Carl suppressed a smile when he noticed her eyes rest on Robert's left hand, devoid of a wedding ring.

Carl broke the awkward silence with a question he hadn't been able to figure out on his own. "Robert, didn't anyone wonder about your dad when he didn't come home that night?"

"Naw. He was always disappearing. No one ever gave him much thought. After a week or so no one even spoke his name. Nobody was happier than my mom." He turned to Tinnley. "She married Nigel Cutburth the next year. Remember him?"

"The druggist. Couldn't be a more different man to take to."

"I think that was the point."

The men shared a chuckle. Robert turned to Annatelle who had made her way fully into the room, never taking her eyes off the horseman.

"I owe all of you an apology," Robert said. "Most of all you, Tinnley." Robert held Osborn's gaze. "'Cause I didn't tell, you missed out on a life of your own."

Tinnley's eyes sparkled with tears as he looked from Robert, to Carl, to Annatelle before he said, "But I got it back."

Three weeks later Tinnley Upshaw lay in his bed, eyes closed, slight smile on his lips. No breath raised or lowered his chest. He clutched *The Eloy Enterprise* newspaper in one hand. The headline read:

TINNLEY UPSHAW CLEARED OF QUADRUPLE MURDER
CHARGE IN 1879 TOMBSTONE
BY CARL TINNLEY EVANS

✝   ✝   ✝

DEBORAH J LEDFORD's latest suspense thriller novel *SNARE* is The Hillerman Sky Award Finalist. Classical music-themed *STACCATO* is the first book of her Steven Hawk/Inola Walela series, both novels are presented by Second Wind Publishing. A three-time nominee for the Pushcart Prize, her award-winning stories appear in numerous print publications, as well as mystery and literary anthologies. Deborah invites you to download the first chapters of her novels and read previously published short stories from her website: www.DeborahJLedford.com.

HOG HEAVEN
NANCY MCCURRY

Sunday night, sound asleep, I lay on the couch with my little dog, Lily, curled behind my knees. When I heard a loud knock on the front door, my heart started up like a chainsaw.

"Who is it?" All I got back was another pair of knocks, more direct. Lily alternated her gaze between me and the door. "Who's there," I yelled a little louder.

"Heber police, ma'am. We're here about Doyle Bredlow."

Just last Tuesday Mae and I killed Doyle so I was a bit unnerved. Lily jumped off the couch and started barking like mad.

I yanked the quilt off my lap. "I'll be right there," I shouted, "Hang on," then turned on the light by the TV and looked in the mirror to check for boogers and fix my hair. I tucked in my shirt, adjusted my cleavage and opened the door.

Deputy Singer and Sheriff Pearl Norman stood in my doorway. I'd known Pearl since Junior High. He'd gotten to second base with me behind the gym once and both of us remembered when his gaze fell to my bosom.

"For the love o' Pete, Pearl. Grow up."

His cheeks flushed. "Listen, Willa, we're here on official business. Is Mae still staying with you?"

"Yes," I said, crossing my arms.

"We need to speak to her, and we ask that you stay present, as well."

† † †

Let me start by saying that every man can count on dying, but a man who beats a woman can count on dying sooner. Ask Doyle.

Mae, my very best friend for twenty three years is the sweetest thing alive. She's big as a hummingbird with hair like cotton candy. When I first discovered Doyle hit her on a regular basis I told her what every girlfriend says, "You should leave that man, Mae." To which she replied what every beaten woman does, "I know that. But if I leave him he'll find me. And if he finds me he'll kill me."

In the end Doyle left us no choice.

I remember one fall afternoon I'd gone to visit Mae at their place. From the road, past an acre of grass, sat the house. To its right was the barn, and to the right of that were the hog pens. A big driveway horseshoed around the back of the barn allowing room and access for stock haulers and feed trucks.

Mae and I often fed the animals up there, over two hundred hogs, a couple old quarter horses and three goats they kept to keep the grass down out front. In the barn we'd load the hay and feed into Doyle's beat up old truck. It was rusted and dented, a two-tone clunker, burnt orange and white. Everyone in town knew his truck and when they saw it, understood trouble would follow.

Mae climbed into the driver's seat and buckled up. The starter complained then the engine turned over and the truck rumbled to life, loud and sputtering, belching blue smoke. She gunned it a couple times to get the idle right and we pulled out of the barn and had just turned onto the drive that ran along side the hog pens when she looked at me, stopped the truck and said, "Put your seatbelt on, honey."

"We're only going fifty feet."

"Doesn't matter. Buckle up. I love you, Willa, and I don't want anything to happen to you. Ninety-six percent of all accidents happen close to home."

"Really?"

"Look it up."

"No, I mean do you really want me to strap in?"

She just stared at me, stone-faced, hands in her lap, so I yanked the belt over my shoulder, swore, and clicked it tight.

Once beside the big enclosures we got out and headed to the back of the truck, dropped the tailgate, pulled a bale close and tugged on the twine to unbind it. The alfalfa unfurled like a fat girl sprung from a corset. Its pretty purple blossoms crushed flat, still held their color. I pulled a sack of pig chow out of the truck bed and dropped it at my feet, yanked the threaded braid to open it and lifted the fifty-pound sack to pour it down along the trough.

Mae smiled, "You're almost a man."

"You can call me, Butch, little lady," I said, and we laughed.

The pigs that hadn't nosed up came running as the feed rattled into the sheet metal trough. They grunted and growled and snapped at each other, muscling their way to the feed. Mae turned on the water at the hose bib and slung the hose to soak the dry feed a bit. She reached into the pen and scratched a big sow on the backside. Just then, Doyle stormed up.

"What in the hell do you think you're doin'?" He yanked the hose from Mae's hand and threw it to the ground. "Don't reach in there, stupid. Those hogs will eat you sure as look at you. What, you want to die?"

Mae shrank back and moved away from the hose soaking her shoes.

Doyle grabbed her by the arm and dragged her back to the fence and pushed her against it, hard. I dropped the sack of feed and got to her fast. "You take your hands offa her," I told him.

We looked each other eye to eye. He shoved her again and said, "I'm gonna show you what a pig'll do to a person. Put your hand in there," he yelled at Mae. "Go ahead." And he pushed her hand into the trough and the pigs started snarling and fighting, the bigger ones pushing in to see the action.

I grabbed Doyle's shoulder to pull him back just as two huge sows charged up fast. Even Doyle jumped back from the fence. The pigs slammed into the trough, banged and clattered the fence, and a few smaller ones scattered and screamed. "They'll eat you, you stupid bitch." He pulled off his ball cap and slapped his leg with it. "They'll eat you till there's nothing left." Then he stomped off.

Mae looked at him and I looked at Mae. Behind her, I put my hands on her shoulders, rested my chin on her head, gave her a little squeeze and said, "You think they'd like some boiled Doyle?"

No matter the times, no matter the law, men make for a

dangerous world. Not three weeks before we killed him, Doyle beat Mae senseless. I got a knock on the door after dinner and there was Mae, fat lipped and bloody. She limped into my living room and sagged onto the couch. "Lock the door. He knows I'd come here first."

I sat down and held her while she cried and when she was done I made a couple gin and tonics and brought a wet wash cloth and some ice. "We should get another restraining order against him," I said.

"He took your door down last time."

"I know, but Pearl came when we called him."

"Yeah, but we were lucky. I just want to hide now." Lily jumped onto the couch with us and sat on Mae. "I don't know what to do anymore, Will. I'm not safe anywhere." She pet the dog and kissed her head.

"Well, you stay right here with me," I told her. "If he comes banging on my door again he better be ready to dance." I thought back to where I'd put my baseball bat and did a little weapons inventory.

Things stayed quiet for a week or so and then we heard his truck driving by the house late at night. We let the Sheriff know and he wanted us to make it official, but Mae couldn't go through with it. Having Doyle served papers promised bigger problems.

That last night, the night when everything changed, we saw his truck parked in front of the Pit Bar-B-Q. We were in my old Fleetwood with the top down. We saw the truck at the same time and Mae said, "I need to get back to the farm and get some of my things."

"You wanna go right now? You know he'll stay put, drunken bast—"

"Do you think we should?"

"I think we should run up there right now and get this thing over with once and for all."

"Okay," she said. "Let's go."

So we pointed my big car out of town and took the trip we knew so well out of Heber and north on 260.

The house was dark. I pulled up by the kitchen door where I always parked and we got out. Even though we knew he wasn't there Mae whispered, "I only want to get some clothes and my old pictures from under the bed. I don't care about the rest."

So we opened the kitchen door and turned on the light. The place was a mess, dirty dishes everywhere, cupboard doors open, shelves empty. Plates were smashed on the floor. It had only been about three weeks since Mae left and it looked like a cattle drive had been through the place. Pictures knocked off the walls, the bookcase overturned. Nothing was left in place except the TV and couch, which was apparently his bed now. The old afghan was tumbled in a heap, a stained pillow, and his dirty clothes lay around. The coffee table was buried under trash and beer cans, and a couple empty bottles of Jim Beam.

When we saw his coat on the hook by the front door we just looked at each other. "Let's hurry."

We crept up the stairs, each one creaking. My heart hummed like a June bug. We got to the bedroom, clicked on the light and found the place upturned. Mae's clothes were thrown all over. Her jewelry box was crushed, her small little treasures scattered and broken. She turned the little white box over and the ballerina lay smashed on her side, her spring sprung and crushed and Mae looked at me in the mirror and I could see she was ready to cry.

"Honey," I said. "Where should I start?"

"There's a suitcase up there in the closet."

Things crunched under my feet and I couldn't bear to look down at the shards of her life. I made my way to the closet half expecting a monster to jump out. I opened the door and saw bent hangers where her clothes had been, shoes and boots a mess. When I looked up on the top shelf it was empty. I turned and saw her by the bed, on her knees, looking into the box of pictures. "It's not here. Where else can it be?" and I looked around at the demolition of their room.

It was then we heard his truck roar up the driveway.

We froze, staring at each other. "Move," I said, and we both shot out of that room and down the stairs. As we got into the living room we heard him come through the kitchen door.

"Mae! Get your ass down here."

We could hear him crash into the kitchen chairs. More glass

broke. He cursed and yelled again for Mae. We both headed for the front door, but when we got there found it locked. Both of us twisted at the deadbolt, too many hands, when it finally clicked back he was in the room and grabbed Mae by the back of the head, a fist full of hair, yanked her around. She screamed and he slapped her. "Shut up," he roared and then slammed her onto the floor.

I looked around for something to swing and took the leg of their end table there by the couch and swung it, smashing it across his back. It blew into a hundred pieces and he stood there hunched for a second, but when he looked up at me I knew we were in for something bad.

He grabbed a dead bottle of Beam and came at me. I heard Mae cry out, but I couldn't hear what she said. He yanked me around, but I'm no little woman and he'd made me mad and I came up swinging, bottle or no bottle. I pulled back and drove my fist right into his face.

I heard bones break.

Doyle dropped like a sack of millet.

The room went quiet.

"Quick," I said. "Let's get out of here."

We hit the kitchen door running. Mae ran around to her side of the car and I jumped in mine. With my hand swelling fast I had trouble pulling my keys from my jeans front pocket, both feet now pressed against the floorboard, trying to straighten up enough to get in there.

"Sweet mother of a brother," I shouted and got out of the car, stood straight and pulled the keys out.

"By God, Willa, get in here right this second."

I jumped back in and shoved the key in the ignition and the engine came to life. While I slammed my door shut Mae pulled her seatbelt tight and I put the car in gear and floored it heading toward the near corner of the barn.

"Put your seatbelt on," she yelled.

"*Are you—*"

"Just do it!"

"Here," I said, "take the wheel."

She made the big turn around the back of the barn while I wrestled with the belt. My hand felt like clay. I had my foot on the accelerator as we went for the straightaway along the barn's long wall, probably two hundred feet, the big car lifting up, getting lighter as we gained speed. I remember turning to look at Mae. She was watching straight ahead, her hand still on the wheel. I think we were both feeling that sense of lightness too, with all the air in the car, top down, wind pushing our hair around. But when I saw her eyes go big and wide the whole world down shifted.

I turned to look forward just in time to see Doyle stagger out into the path of the car. He must have come straight from the house, past the barn to stop us. He put his hand up like he was a traffic cop and yelled something we couldn't hear just as the Fleetwood mowed him down.

We felt his body rumble and twist under the car. The back end bucked before I hit the brakes. We ground to a stop, there in the dark, Doyle surely dead behind us.

When we could speak, Mae said, "We need to go look."

"It's gonna be bad."

Mae reached for my hand. "We have to go. We have to look. We have to do something."

"I know, I know, I'm just trying to think. You don't get to do this twice. There's no rewind button here."

Mae rubbed her face hard and pushed her hair back, looked me in the eye and took a deep breath. "Holy Jeezer, Doyle's dead."

I don't know who thought of it first, me or Mae. Maybe it was because we sat there by that big huge hog pen and listened to those pigs snuffle and growl and bark. Maybe it was because sows are so horrendous. Maybe it's because it just seemed fitting.

Mae and I decided we'd throw Doyle to the hogs.

While the decision wasn't hard to make, it became a great deal worse when we looked down at Doyle in the dirt. He lay on his back, mostly. His whole body bent like a question mark. The right leg was snapped back at the knee. The other foot wore only a sock. The boot lay five feet behind us. One arm was twisted behind his back, the other badly broken lay across his chest. His flannel was covered with mud or blood. But far and away his face was the worst, shiny ground sirloin, shaped like a fist.

"I can't touch him," Mae said

I looked at her over Doyle's body. "Listen, there's only one way to get to the other side of this thing. Were just gonna take a deep breath, reach down, grab his hands and both of us are gonna drag him to the pen. It's ten feet. We can do it."

The house was a ways out from town and set back on the property, but it was on a well-worn route and someone would be coming down that old highway soon. I looked off into the dark and didn't see any lights. "Mae, just grab one hand."

"I can't do it, Will, I can't."

My poor, poor, precious Mae, she was not made for business like this. I walked over and gave him a shove, then yanked the other arm out from underneath him. Now, grabbing his wrists and pulling with both hands I put my back into it. Once we got moving Mae walked over and without saying a word took hold of one arm and we dragged and grappled and huffed that man up to the pen and then dropped him there on the ground.

The enclosures were made of standard four-rail galvanized stock fence, but wood had been affixed to the lower three feet to keep the hogs contained.

"Okay," I said, "Let's see if we can get him to sit up." We pushed and we shoved and we levered our bodies to prop that damn Doyle's carcass.

After a bit Mae leaned against the fence. "Are we gonna go to hell for this, Willa?"

"No. We certainly are not. He's going to hell and we're calling him a cab."

I grabbed dead Doyle and I pulled up as hard as I could. His long body slunk and sagged. We had to turn him around, and once I got his arms and shoulders over the board fence his head flopped in and wagged like he was saying no.

I grabbed his belt and pulled hard. The pigs were agitated now. They started to cry and scream and snuffle and bark. The noise got louder and louder and louder.

I yanked on his belt while Mae walked back and threw his loose boot in and we heard it clunk in the long feed bin. Then she came over and pulled with all her might. We picked that man up and when we got him halfway over, bent at the waist, we had to take a break. But out there in the roiling dark, back deep in the midst of that pen, we could see the movement had changed in some way. The waters had shifted. While Mae and I stood back on either side of Doyle we saw his body lurch to the right and slide quick along the top rail about a foot. Mae jumped back, and with a tug and a yank those hogs pulled Doyle Bredlow in with them. The noise got louder, crazier, and squeals from the dark prevailed.

The next day after we woke up at my house, home and safe in the sunlight, we got a good look at my car I'd parked out back the night before. For the life of me I couldn't see a new scratch or dent on that big old beast. It'd already seen some hard times, sixteen years old, over 200,000 miles, dinged and crunched with a few too many kisses in bar parking lots, I guess. Were it not for some mud that could have been blood I didn't see any real damage. Mae and I got a bucket of warm water and some suds and baptized the beautiful car. We washed it with care and love. Under my breath, as I looked at Mae safe, I said thank you twenty-three times.

Two quiet days of rain followed. We felt Doyle wash away.

† † †

Sheriff Pearl Norman and Deputy Singer stood in my living room with the little dog yipping, circling their feet. They looked to me for help. "She doesn't like hats," I told them.

As they both slid theirs from their heads, Mae came down the stairs. "What's going on?" She looked at Pearl and Singer and then looked at me and went white. "What is it?"

Singer said, "Why don't you sit down, Mrs. Bredlow."

"Mae," she corrected, then sat next to me on the couch.

"Yes, Mae, sorry, ma'am. As we told Miss Willa, we're here about your husband, Doyle."

Mae sat perfectly still. I think she stopped breathing.

"Well, it seems that he's missing. Have you seen him or had any word from him in the last week or so?"

"Not since I left a month back." She looked at me. "We

heard him drive by a few times."

"When was that, ma'am?"

Mae looked at me and I looked at Pearl, "We called you about that."

Pearl said, "It's in the file." Then he pulled out his notebook, still holding his hat under his arm. Leafing through, he said, "We can place him down at The Pit one night last week, Wednesday, Thursday, drunk again." He looked up at Mae. "Sorry."

She just shook her head.

"But Tanya, the bartender down there, can't recall exactly," Pearl said, "We're still investigating."

Then both officers took a deep breath and looked at each other. Singer nodded to Pearl, who said, "There's some indication that he might have met with, um..." he looked again at Singer, "an accident, ma'am."

Neither of us moved. Pearl looked at his notebook, "It seems that Ned from the feed store went up a few days back with a delivery and couldn't find Doyle. His truck was there and Ned looked around, knocked on the door, couldn't find him. Thought maybe he'd gone out on a ride or out working the back half, but when he walked over to the hog pen he found..." Pearl stalled here, "a boot in the feed trough."

Mae groaned out loud.

"And what looks like pieces of a flannel shirt, but maybe they're just old rags. We might need you to help identify these items." Singer moved over by Mae. "We still got a few people up there looking around."

She started to cry and I held her hand. "What now?" I asked them.

"Well, we spent most of the day looking for anything that might help us there, but the place looks like a cyclone touched down. As I said, we're still investigating. The rain hasn't helped us. Might have lost some clues in the mud. But right now it looks like he may have been drunk, feeding after leaving The Pit and made a mistake, one of the sows probably got a hold of him and..." Mae bent down, crying into her lap.

I looked up at Pearl and waved him into the kitchen. When we were alone I said, "Gad a'mighty. Imagine that," and shook my head.

Pearl said, "It must be a sight seeing a man ravaged that way."

"It's troubling," I said, "for the hogs."

†   †   †

Six years have passed since then. Pearl's investigation found nothing conclusive. Doyle slid from the town's memory like a bad flu season. After a time Mae got a nice new man and they live down the road. I warned him though, real clear, he better not hurt her. Gauging from the look he gave me, I think he takes me serious.

†   †   †

NANCY MCCURRY holds an MFA in writing, is a freelance editor, and college writing instructor. She's married and managed two kids safely from birth through high school and into college. Aside from her kids, Nancy's prize acquisition is an extensive library of stories and scholarship that spans from the microscopic to the galactic sheet and onward. She's been a published writer since the early '90s with awards granted in essay, short story, short/short story and personal narrative. www.NancyMcCurry.com.

Praise For The Desert Sleuths Anthology

How NOT to Survive a Vacation

"Yearning for a vacation? Think again. This anthology from authors who have something to say, and the style and maturity to say it well, will make sitting safely at home reading seem that much more attractive."

    -Juliet Blackwell, author of the *Witchcraft Mystery series* and the upcoming *Home Renovation series.*

"Like a macabre travel brochure, these chilling mystery stories take you on a grisly tour of choice vacation spots, except instead of Mai Tais, they serve murder. Pack your toothbrush and then pack *How NOT to Survive a Vacation*—you don't want to miss this trip!"

    -Rebecca Cantrell, award-winning author of A *Trace of Smoke* and *A Night of Long Knives.*

"A fabulous anthology of murder and mayhem from ship to shore and mountain to desert. The collection will leave you double checking with your travel agent…and begging for more! Take an excitement-packed holiday with these wonderful Desert Sleuths—all of whom prove that talent truly blossoms in the arid Southwest."

    -Kelli Stanley, award-winning author of *City of Dragons, Nox Dormienda* and *The Curse Maker.*

"Everyone will discover a favorite, and it might be based on your own favorite vacation spots, seaside, mountains, or desert. However, I can say the reader will be very glad they're not on some of these trips. If you think you've had the vacation from hell, check out these stories. It's enough to make you want to tuck in safely at home, and NOT go anywhere."

    -Lesa Holstine, Lesa's Book Critiques

Praise For The Desert Sleuths Anthology

How NOT to Survive the Holidays

"Stuff your stocking with this string of holiday sparkles, ranging from the chilling to the decidedly wacky."
    -Rhys Bowen, Agatha and Anthony award-winning author of the *Molly Murphy* and *Royal Spyness* mysteries.

"Put in a thumb and pull out a plum of a Christmas story. A holiday treat."
    -Carolyn Hart, author of *Merry, Merry Ghost*

"Good things come in small packages! Grab a mug of your favorite drink and nestle in by the fire on that long winter's night. Murder and mayhem around the holidays has never been so much fun!"
    -Robin Burcell, award-winning author *The Bone Chamber*

"The holidays will never be the same! This collection of twisted, talented authors make sure of that."
    -Sheila Lowe, author of the *Forensic Handwriting* mysteries

"There's no place like home for the holidays. That is, unless somebody in the family wants to kill you…It seems there's a lot of skullduggery going on during the Christmas season."
    -Donis Casey, author of the award-winning *Alafair Tucker* mysteries

"Are you a little tired of the sweet Christmas stories with happy endings? The Desert Sleuths Chapter of Sisters in Crime has just the collection for you. *How NOT to Survive the Holidays* has a little bit of crime for everyone."
    -Lesa Holstine, Lesa's Book Critique

www.ingramcontent.com/pod-product-compliance
Lightning Source LLC
Chambersburg PA
CBHW070116260626

47160CB00004B/1487